Trouble Comes in 3's

Trouble Comes in 3's

A Novel

Darryl E. Lawson

iUniverse, Inc.
New York Lincoln Shanghai

Trouble Comes in 3's

iUniverse books may be ordered through booksellers or by contacting:

iUniverse
2021 Pine Lake Road, Suite 100
Lincoln, NE 68512
www.iuniverse.com
1-800-Authors (1-800-288-4677)

This is a work of fiction. All of the characters, names, incidents, organizations and dialogue in this novel are either the products of the author's imagination or are used fictitiously.

ISBN-13: 978-0-595-38443-3 (pbk)
ISBN-13: 978-0-595-82821-0 (ebk)
ISBN-10: 0-595-38443-9 (pbk)
ISBN-10: 0-595-82821-3 (ebk)

Printed in the United States of America

CHAPTER 1

Genesis

The hot summer night air was enough to force many of the people of Uptown out of their apartments, and into the streets in search of that elusive cool breeze. Women sat about the stoops and benches engaged in conversation with one another while their children played freely in the streets. The men of Uptown found any place to watch "Iron" Mike Tyson demolish his next opponent. As for the young adults of Uptown, in spite of the heat and humidity, the place to be was the Rooftop Disco, the club where all the cool people wanted to be, no matter the temperature.

The Rooftop was the second home to all the Hip-Hop Stars, businessmen, and young adults in the Tri-State area. It was late and the party-goers started to exit the Rooftop. The more experienced brought towels with them to dry themselves off. Some of the people exiting the party stood in front of the Rooftop toweling off, and became captivated by the rather large moon, which sat high overhead in the early morning sky. Instead of being its usual dull white colour, the moon was an unusual dull orange colour. While some viewed the moon with vigor in its new complexion, others' eyes fell upon a group of young men who were directly in front of the entranceway.

As always, there was a group of young men outside who seemed too smooth to be seen dancing in some hot sweaty club. They parked their BMW's, Benz's and Honda Accords directly in front of the entrance and leaned against their cars; that way neither they nor their cars could be missed by anyone who exited the Rooftop. These party-poopers would have been displeased if their Trump Jewelry, fly expensive sweat suits and eighty dollar sneakers were not admired by those looking at them. In spite of the fact that each of their cars cost well over thirty thousand dollars, and each young man had several hundred dollars pocket money, these individuals still appeared to be nothing more than teenage rookie drug dealers. The most notorious of these "New Jack" drug dealers was Cassius, "Cash Money" Washington, a nineteen year old who had very little book sense, but somehow he managed to parlay his abundant street knowledge and toughness into a very lucrative business.

Cassius owned three cars, among which was a black Porsche 944. He was able to pay for the expensive toy from the proceeds from his game room, two candy stores and his coke spots. Despite his vast holdings, Cassius could not say with any certainty that he was the top New Jack Uptown. He wanted this title more than anything on earth. His violent temper along with his general distrust of the human race was the main reason why he was not "the man" uptown in Harlem. Cassius believed that the world owed him everything, and its inhabitants were nothing more than tools to be used in his quest for power and money. These deep-rooted feelings surfaced in his many dealings with his workers.

Cassius was known to have threatened to shoot an employee's children if his business was not done to his liking. Cassius' methods did not endear him in the hearts of many of his worriers, nor lower level businessmen who avoided him as if he were HIV positive; choosing only to deal with him as a last resort. Needless to say he was the last resort of many.

"If dae don't want to deal wif' me it's all good. They will hafta' deal wif' me sooner or later."

He always said.

Cassius had gone from a short snotty-nosed brown-skinned kid, to a well-off young man in a matter of years. He enjoyed his money and the power it brought to him. Cassius also sought the attention, money and power on the streets. His large amount of money brought lots of attention.

"Hi Cash!"

Said a sultry light-skinned honey that literally ran over to Cassius the instant he crossed her line of vision.

The young lady's fierce body and "all that" looks brought about a chorus of grunts, and silent wishes of trading places with him from the crew.

"Oh, hi uh…"

Cassius played, as he turned his attention from the crew to the fine young lady.

"What's the matta' Cash? Don't you remember my name?"

The young lady spoke in her best black girl voice.

"Yeah I do!"

Cassius responded. He paused for effect then blurted.

"It's Trina ain't it?"

He knew the girl's name. Cassius wanted to show everyone who stood around him how he dealt with skeezers. By calling the fine young lady out of her name Cassius put her on the spot. If she corrected him, she would look like a public fool. If she remained silent Cassius would know he could dominate her. With some hesitation the young lady chose to correct him.

"No it's Tracy!"

The young lady corrected him when she accentuated her name. As she rolled her eyes, and waited for him to respond. When this happened, the crew of men who clung around Cassius broke out in laughter.

Several minutes went by before the laughter completely stopped and Cassius said another word to Tracy, who waited patiently for him to address her. Tracy resembled the boxer Smokin' Joe Frazier, who was always willing to take punishment in order to dish out some of his own. It was only after Cash saw that no one better looking than Tracy was going to exit the Rooftop did he extend a half-hearted invitation for her to stay the night at his house.

Tracy accepted his backhanded invitation as well as his subsequent order.

"Here take this!"

Cassius said as he dug in his small change pocket and pulled out a stack of fifty dollar bills.

"Go to the stoe up da block an' buy me some rubbers, and two forty dogs; Ole Gold for me and a Colt forty five for my man Black."

Cassius paused as he watched a young girl who strolled passed. She did not look better than Tracy in any way; therefore he continued his conversation with Tracy as if he never paused.

"After you get all dat, meet me by that Burgundy Jeep up the block!"

Cassius said as he peeled one bill from the stack, and then pointed up the dark street towards both the store and the Jeep. Tracy took the money and did what she was instructed to do without question. Cassius' boy Reggie Miller heard it all because he was standing right next to Cassius. Black Reggie, as he was called was the only true friend Cassius allowed himself to have.

Black Reggie stood six feet, four inches tall, with a very dark complexion. The two became fast friends after Cassius watched Black Reggie beat the shit out of three people on 7th Avenue. When a fourth person tried to hit Reggie from behind, Cassius hit him over the head with a bottle. The two had been friends ever since. Black Reggie shook his head in amazement at his partner as he spoke.

"Cash you is one wild Mother Fucker!"

Cassius had a good answer for his friend.

"Girls like her know what time it is! I gots da' money, and they gots da' honey! She needs what I got, I want what she got! We just meet in the middle of the sheets!"

His philosophy was well received by the crew. Cassius began to tell anyone that would listen how little he cared for **bitches** like Tracy.

"Word" said one of his crew.

"**Bitches** ain't shit! All dae want is the money!"

One member of the crew announced as if it was his theme song.

"I treat every chick like shit because if you treat 'em nice they shit all over you!"

One crewmember announced. His words caused a deluge of negative comments about women. The negative comments about women continued until the soft words of one young man changed the complexion of the conversation.

"If women ain't shit why do you spend all your time chasin' em?"

His question was immediately met with calls of his being "Pussy" and "faggot" Against all odds the young man attempted to defend his comments against the angry mob who just minutes ago were his friends. Cassius stood silently as the young man was dogged unmercifully by each man who was in ear shot of his comment. He could have ended the loud one-sided exchange with one utterance however he felt the young boy step into shit and he had to deal with it on his own.

Since Cassius was no longer the focus of the conversation, he turned his attention up the block towards the store and Tracy. As he looked up the street he noticed two female coming down the street towards him. He did not recognize them because the trees, which lined the block, prevented the limited light from the few working street lamppost, from illuminating their faces. Without seeing their faces he felt that he should know who the shadowy figures were. Once the figures cleared the trees, he recognized that Cathy-Cee and Lady Bee, the two hottest female rappers of the time. Cassius' heart sunk to his knees as he watched them approach. His wish had come true. He would scoop up Cathy-Cee and make her his girl.

Cassius had met the two ladies several times in the past. He had left his pager number with the beautiful Cathy-Cee, in hopes that she would want to get with him. She never did get back to him. Now he envisioned another opportunity to show off his money and power to persuade her his way. Cassius became concerned with his appearance. He made sure his sweat suit pants fell over his sneakers just right, and that his gold rope hung outside his jacket in just the right way. Cassius even checked his breath to make sure it was not kicking. The two ladies were headed straight for the Rooftop before Cathy-Cee spotted him out of the crowd, and pulled her Lady Bee in Cassius' direction. Cassius felt confident that he would get his prize if he would just play it cool.

"What up Cassius?"

Cathy-Cee said as she walked up to him and gave him a friendly kiss on the cheek. Cassius then took his temptress by both hands and boldly said.

"How come you ain't paged me yet?"

Lady Bee, who stood next to her friend muttered under her breath loud enough to be heard, but not understood by Cassius.

"Watcha say Lady Bee?"

Cassius asked in a voice that could not hide his anger. Lady Bee received a tap on the shoulder from her girl Cathy-Cee, which succeeded in cutting her off.

"I thought about it; about you and me for a second Cash."

Cathy-Cee spoke with some hesitation as she was trying to find a diplomatic way to put the hot-headed man down. She continued on cautiously choosing her words.

"You gots a crazy rep' with…"

She was cut off by Lady Bee who wanted to tell Cassius straight out what her girl was hesitant to say what she really felt.

"My girl Cathy-Cee doesn't wanna' star in one of your homemade porno movies!"

This time Lady Bee did not mumble. She spoke loud enough for the world to hear. Cassius uncharacteristically had nothing to say about being dissed.

"Look, you two chill out! There's no need for this."

Cathy-Cee said, playing the role of peacemaker. She had heard stories of how vindictive Cassius could be and she did not want to invite trouble into her bright future. She took the dejected man by the hand and tried hard to put him down as gently as possible.

"I can't fuck with you because of your rep with the ladies."

Cathy-Cee said as she caught sight of someone who exited the Rooftop, someone she very much wanted to converse with. She took her hands from Cash, and led a gloating Lady Bee over to the entranceway to the Rooftop and the VIP section. Cassius was left feeling lower than the curb. He had everything that any woman would want. He quietly pondered why Cathy-Cee and women like her never gave him the time of day.

"I've got money, I'm fine and I gots a big Jimmi! What more could any woman want?"

He mumbled to himself. Black Reggie, who was involved in a conversation with other New Jacks, turned his attention back to his friend long enough to see him get dissed. The two men watched in disgust as the women struck up a conversation with Mike Nice.

"What do they see in that yella' bastard!"

Black Reggie said for his friend who was too angry to speak. Their attraction became apparent when J.T. exited the Rooftop into the humid night air.

"She dissed me for that Mutha' fucka' JT."

Cassius mumbled aloud as all eyes began to focus on JT.

In most people's eyes, JT was a cut above the rest of the New Jacks. Though he was three years younger than Cassius, JT had amassed almost the same amount of money as his rival Cassius. Most significantly JT had earned the respect of many in the business. JT's largest expense consisted of a house and cars he had purchased for his parents. Money was not the only reason he was in business. It was his lifestyle he lived that made JT's adrenaline flow. Having all the girls he wanted, not having to punch a clock, and the ability to control his future, kept him in the business. Being the best would be nice, but he was not going to go all out for the title of **Number One**. His cavalier attitude actually enhanced his business opportunities. People felt they could trust him much more than anyone else. To the average person on the street, JT played angel to Cassius' devil.

JT was a very unusual businessman. He spoke to almost anyone who spoke to him and it was hard to find him without a smile on his boyish face. To the people on his block JT was nothing less than a saint. During the summer months he paid for block parties for the kids. Once he sponsored a Little League Baseball Team for his block when no legitimate sponsor could be found. There was even a rumor that he once paid back rent for his old baby sitter in lieu of her late arriving Social Security Check. His benevolent ways made it easy for some to forget how he made his money. No one ever heard stories of him dissin' girls the way Cassius did. This was one reason why Cathy-Cee and Lady Bee were looking for him. The other reason was the two rappers wanted him to front them the money to start their own record label. The previous nights business dinner caused a noticeable spark between Cathy-Cee and JT. This night he was planning to start a fire.

Lady Bee greeted JT first with a kiss on the cheek and then passed him a few kind words. It was clear to her that his attention was on her friend. Lady Bee then stepped aside to let her Cathy-Cee move forward. J.T. was about to speak however Cathy-Cee, she planted a strong kiss on his juicy lips before he could say one word. She broke off their kiss and said to JT in her best bedroom voice.

"Where ya' think you're goin' honey?"

The tone of her voice surprised JT because; he did not expect her to show so much affection towards him so soon.

A broad smile came to his face when he answered her question.

"I'm goin' up da' block to get a dry shirt from my car."

After a second thought he realized what Cathy-Cee said and he had to respond.

"Are you tryin' to clock me already?"

JT said with a straight face. He was joking but Cathy-Cee had no idea JT was joking.

"No, no it's not like that JT! I just, you know, wanted to make sure you're not goin' too far. We have business to discuss."

She responded in a defensive tone. JT became serious about the mentioning of the deal that could take him to another level.

"We'll rap in a moment. Just let me get a dry shirt from my car."

JT announced. Cathy-Cee tried to keep JT from leaving.

"Let's go upstairs so that you can hear us rehearse our new record. You can even bring Mike Nice. Whatcha say?"

"Not right now, I gotta change my shirt."

Again JT insisted on going to his car.

She realized he was not going to change his mind; the two ladies turned and ascended the stairs to the Rooftop, but not before Cathy-Cee planted a kiss on JT's forehead.

"Hurry back, I'll be waiting for you."

Cathy-Cee told him. Neither Mike Nice nor JT moved as they watched the two divas climb the stairs until their beautiful bodies could no longer be seen. The instant J.T. turned around he caught Cassius locked in an envious stare.

Cassius was embarrassed, to the point that it helped to convert the stare into one of hate. The look in Cassius' eyes said, "Soon we will meet." JT knew exactly what the stare meant. In spite of their ill feelings both knew it was not the time or the place to settle their beef. JT tapped Mike Nice on the shoulder and said.

"Gimme dis' walk Mike."

The two men walked away thus ended the stare contest with Cassius. About half way up the block JT stopped to tie his sneaker. As he bent down to tie his shoe JT spoke to Mike Nice.

"You know Mike, it's almost time take care of Cash!"

Mike Nice who stood near JT nodded his head in agreement as he kept one eye on Black Reggie and Cassius.

"And if he…"

JT paused in mid-sentence as he finished tying his sneaker and started to stand erect.

Just then the sound of a car coming down the block towards him caught JT's attention. He took notice of the speeding car because it was moving like a jet. JT instinctively fixed his eyes on the fast approaching car and noticed the windows being open. He didn't have a chance to react; the moment he noticed the open windows, a hail of bullets exited from the car. The force of the bullets caused JT's body to be twisted from side to side like a washing machine agitates clothes. JT's once-white sweat suit quickly turned to a maroon colour from the blood that rapidly soaked through it.

Mike Nice tried to knock his childhood friend out of the line of fire however, his efforts were fruitless, and he failed at his task, trying to save his friend. After taking a single step in defense of JT he too was struck by several bullets, sending him to the ground. From his vantage point, Mike Nice could see the life being torn out of JT. The last bullet tore through JT's chest exiting through the left side of his neck. JT's body plummeted face first onto the edge of the curb and the gutter.

Screams echoed through the humid morning air as the car now sped away. People scattered from the gunfire like roaches when the light is turned on in a once dark room. For those handful of people who witnessed the shooting, it was a frightening experience but one that happened on the regular.

When it became clear that the shooting had stopped, party-goers emerged from behind anything they believed could provide cover at the time. It was at this moment that the fear wore off and the carnival atmosphere occurred. Just like a magnet, JT's body drew the attention of the brave people outside the Rooftop. Others who heard the shots ran from the nearby Polo Grounds Projects to see who was shot. Cassius, Reggie and the crew emerged from behind cars; some of them had their guns drawn. It took Cassius all of ten seconds for him to realize that the victim of the gunplay was JT, because a girl ran screaming at the top of her lungs "Dae Kilt JT."

The news could not have been better for Cassius. Black Reggie gave his boy a slap on the back in acknowledgement of his newfound fortune. A slight smile came over Cassius' face at the thought of moving up without getting his own hands dirty. Everyone near him began to look at him as if he had done the dirty deed. Cassius did not have much time to think about his promotion because in the distance there was a faint sound of sirens that caused all to bounce.

In a scene that resembled the Twenty Four Hours of Lemans, any and every one in the business jumped into their cars and peeled off, leaving the smell of burning rubber behind. Cassius too knew it was time to bounce, therefore, both he and Reggie moved quickly up the block towards Reggie's jeep. As Cassius came upon the place where JT came to rest, he stopped to take a quick look at his fallen enemy. He was only able to catch a glimpse of JT's body, which was positioned between two parked cars. Cassius' view was blocked from seeing JT's face because of the crowd beginning to gather around the body. Cassius did see a large amount of blood that flowed from the body. Cassius paused for a second wondering if he should get a closer look; time was of the essence. The sound of the sirens was becoming louder. Cassius thought better of being curious and moved quickly to the jeep. He was halted by the screams of Cathy Cee.

Cathy-Cee had run out of the Rooftop the moment the shooting started and without thought she ran straight to Cassius. Tears flowed down her cheeks. Her once neatly done hair looked as if she had just gotten out of bed.

"You did this to him! I know it wuz you!"

She screamed as she ran for Cassius with a box cutter in her hand. Cassius went for the thirty-two automatic he always carried, but before he could pull it from his belt, Black Reggie came from behind him to deliver a blow to Cathy-Cee's jaw worthy of Mike Tyson. Lady Bee who was on the heels of her friend only needed to see the veracity of the blow to stun her into inaction.

The blow broke Cathy-Cee's jaw, as well as a grade three concussion. She never fully recovered from the effects of the concussion, thus her music career literally ended in the streets. Cassius never saw the woman hit the street; he immediately turned and continued for the jeep. He snatched a shocked Tracy who watched Cathy Cee hit the concrete, and pulled her to his jeep. As Cassius shoved her into the back seat of the jeep, Black Reggie dragged Cathy-Cee out of the middle of the street by her ankles. Once his task was complete Black Reggie jumped into the passenger's seat allowing Cassius to speed off, nearly missing a prone Cathy-Cee and Lady Bee who felt it safe enough to assist her friend. As Cassius drove off he wondered who had the balls to pull off the hit.

As for the police they arrived to find plenty of spectators, but no willing witnesses. JT's death would remain a mystery to them as well as the people in the business. All signs pointed to Cassius but there would be nothing to link him to the murder. The one thing that was not going to be a mystery was that the level of violence in the business would be turned up another notch.

CHAPTER 2

Machiavellian

The murder of JT sent shockwaves throughout the drug business. Never before had a powerful New Jack been murdered; JT constituted the highest level of the drug trade. His murder meant that individuals who were generally untouchable were now fair game. The legend of JT quickly faded from the thoughts of many he professed would never forget him, because many other people in and out of the business succumbed to violence of the drug trade. What made the streets much more violent was the result of Richard Pryor on fire!

Richard Pryor setting his face on fire while free basing Cocaine caused some to search for a safer way to get the same high. Crack, once invented was an immediate hit for the poor drug users of America. Cocaine was essentially a white man's drug that cost an arm and a leg. Crack, processed cocaine, was just a ten-dollar bill away for anyone who could handle the intense craving.

"Crack Heads" quickly became as ubiquitous as vagrancy during the Great Depression. Many believe that the flood of cocaine into the streets was not an accident. Some feel the Reagan Administration allowed Columbian drugs lords to flood the street with their drug made the availability of crack all the more greater.

The law of Supply and Demand determined the need for street pharmacists. A young man in the ghetto could turn sneaker money into a large profit if he was willing to work hard. Hard work for a street pharmacist was usually precieved as the use of muscle rather than brain. Young people often do not think before they act. Why do you think that there is an age limit to gain a driver's license?

Crack turned the drug business on its ear by making it accessible to everyone especially the young. Throngs of disenfranchised youth flocked to the world of fast money and even faster girls. Each new wave entering the business pushed the envelope of violence as they tried to hold onto or gain more money. Anyone who wanted to be somebody the fast way jumped into the crack trade. The violence perpetrated by these New Jacks put a spotlight on a business that should be conducted in the dark. In the world of increased violence it became apparent that safety would come in numbers. As the body count began to rise four young men gathered in the backroom of a Harlem candy store to remember one of their fallen comrades. From this gathering a business empire developed.

CHAPTER 3

United We Stand

Several years after the murder of JT, four young men held the first of many meetings in the rear of Kelly's Variety Store, located at the corner of 144th and Lexington Avenue. The first meeting was nothing more that a get together after the death of a mutual friend named K-Nice. As the four young men talked, it became apparent that their survival in the business dominated each of their thoughts.

The room in the back of the store was small, yet comfortable. A fluorescent light hung from a fixture in the ceiling. The bulb was old giving off a greenish colour light, and emitting an annoying hum that some fluorescent lights can provide. The light hung directly above the center of a round table, where three of the four young men placed their sneakers under. The fourth sat on a stool away from the table; his thoughts pushed him a million miles away. The three at the table were having a heated discussion on the conspiracy theories surrounding the death of K-Nice.

"Man I don't give a fuck whatca' say Tony, I still believe that Cash had sumin' to do wit' K-Nice's death! Dat's the only thing dat makes sense to me!"

Linden "Ace" Martin said (Just about everyone in the business had a nickname, which was either a badge of distinction or an affirmation of a unique physical feature.)

Ace was a twenty-five year old high school drop out who left school because it interfered with his $5,000 a month business. Ace had followed an older brother into the business and took over for that brother after his brother was sent to prison. Ace did very well in well in his reign in the beginning, but soon his business had reached its peak. He became frustrated with his lack of economic growth in the business. He wanted more and he was not satisfied with being just a one hundred-thousandnaire.

"Bullshit! Everybody knew that Duke was jealousy of K-Nice."

Tony Dickinson, the youngest seated at the table announced. Tony was a handsome, six foot three inch tall twenty year-old who fancied himself as a lady's man. Whom ever he slept with was not as good as the next woman. Tony managed to graduate from high school and he went on to graduate from UCLA, The University on the corner on Lenox Avenue, with honors. Due to his age, Tony's words were always questioned.

"How do you know Tony? You were in Junior High school when this thing first jumped off!"

Thaddeus Philip "Bosco" Taylor Jr. quizzed Tony. Bosco was a short pudgy man of twenty-six who got into the business as a result of hanging out with the wrong crowd; his older brother Randall. He was known for his direct nature and honesty.

"If I ever go into a coma like K-Nice, my family will hafta' pull da' plug on me!"

Bosco bluntly stated. Bosco had received his nickname from his late grandmother, because in her words, "His skin was as dark and smooth like the chocolate syrup Bosco."

"How come you never believe what I say Bosco."

Tony asked Bosco.

"I just wanna' know how you came up with such information?"

Bosco said, looking right at Tony with a straight face. Tony hesitated with his answer for he knew from experience that Bosco had just baited him on an embarrassing answer. After a moment of silence Tony decided to answer Bosco in the strongest voice possible.

"Cause I wuz sexin' Duke's little cousin."

"How little was the cousin Tony?" Ace asked.

Tony was tired of the customary persecution. He delivered his answer with a sharp tongue.

"She Wuz fifteen at da' time y'all!"

Both Ace and Bosco broke out into loud laughter. Tony did not let the laughter stop him; he simply raised his voice in order to finish.

"She said more than once that Duke would like to kill K-Nice if he ever got da' chance."

Bosco laughed even harder. It was at this point that the fourth member decided to enter the conversation. He chose to sit and listen rather than talk, and it was time to get Ace and Bosco off Tony's back.

"I'm not sure who told me that they saw Duke talkin' to Black Reggie on 123rd Street two days before K-Nice got shot."

Saladin Keith said in his most serious voice.

"I heard that Duke is in Virginia selling for Bo-Bo."

Saladin continued after a brief pause.

"I heard Duke got caught in a sting in B-More. Ace added.

"No body knows were Duke is!"

Tony loudly exclaimed.

"All I give a fuck about is he ain't here and neither is our mutual friend K-Nice."

He stated as he folded his arms across his wide chest. The purpose of the conversation was lost on Bosco.

Bosco quickly became bored with the topic of the conversation. He was not one to dwell in the past and he felt that the conversation was not going to achieve anything. Bosco fidgeted with his ten thousand dollar Rolex, while his friends talked to one another. He swiveled in his chair in anticipation of the end of the conversation. The end did not come soon enough for Bosco who sought to end things with his renowned bluntness.

"What the hell does anything you said gotta' do with what's going on right now?"

Bosco said in an angry tone, which lasted the length of his tirade. The others stopped their conversation to listen to Bosco who continued on with his verbal rampage.

"Yeah, Duke might have shot K-Nice 'cause Duke wuz jealous of him. Maybe Cassius gassed his head up to do it. Who gives a fuck 'bout that shit? What you should be takin' 'bout is Cassius and Bo-Bo!"

The angry man paused to catch his breath for his next words were meant to cut to the heart.

"If Saladin would have taken care of business in the past life on the streets might be a bit different."

Remarked Bosco, looking right at Saladin.

The business Bosco referred to was the murder of his good friend JT. It was assumed that Cassius had something to do with JT's murder, but Saladin was not sure. Saladin knew any move on Cassius would be suicidal therefore he remained silent on the matter.

The lack of response by Saladin caused Bosco to continue on with a much kinder tone.

"What we needs to be talkin' 'bout is how we gonna stop them two bastards from hookin' up and runnin' all your asses out of bizness!"

Bosco pointed at each of the people in the room before he folded his hands and sat back in his chair. His boys sat quietly as the seriousness of Bosco's words hit them all equally hard. The things Bosco said were true. Everyone in the room understood that if Cash and Bo-Bo joined forces life would be more dangerous.

The rumored partnership between Cassius and Bo-Bo was a very real possibility. Cassius' violent ways and Bo-Bo's business skills would make them sweeter than the backcourt of Eric Smith and Eric "Sleepy" Floyd of Georgetown Fame. The room turned silent while each pictured what uptown would look like if the partnership came to fruition. Ace thought harder on that matter than the others. His pockets were almost empty and he understood that he would be one of the first to fall in their wake. Ace had come to the end of the road; he had no more pride left. Ace envisioned himself either dead or in jail or worse yet, broke! The scene in his mind caused Ace to come to the realization that he needed help.

"Look."

He said as he held his head low in shame.

"That Cassius and Bo-Bo thing gots me twisted."

Ace sighed heavily and continued on with his statements.

"They got da same coke supplier as me, and he has been dealing me the bottom of da barrel."

As Ace told his story each of his friends nodded their heads in quiet understanding. His poor finances were not a big secret to anyone. A blind man could see that he was very nearly broke. Ace wanted help, however pride kept his from asking his two casual friends for it straight out. He chose to be cryptic, but cryptic messages, allowed the three men to ignore the plea. Saladin and Tony looked away from Ace. Neither wanted to extend assistant to a person they met on the basketball court months earlier. Bosco gave Ace a blank stare instead. Ace looked into Bosco's eyes and could not understand the nature of the stare. Thinking that he had a booger on his nose Ace wiped his full flat nose, but Bosco continued to stare. Bosco grew tired of Ace's stupidity and decided he better answer his own stares for his friend.

"Are you asking us for help?"

Bosco's response placed Ace in a difficult position.

Bosco had asked the question that brought the prideful man to his knees. There was no place for Ace to hide, no going back into the land of self-denial.

Ace had to swallow his pride like eating Ritz crackers without a chaser and verbalized what would force him to admit that he was a failure.

"I'm in some deep shit. I need a small loan from at least one of you guys so I can get back on my feet."

Ace said as he glanced over at Saladin, the most understanding of his friends. Ace's voice resembled that of a young child confessing to his parents of a long ago wrong. Ace's admission did not bring about an immediate response from any of the intended responders. With the exception of the hum from the fluorescent light the room remained silent.

Saladin avoided eye contact with Ace. He glanced over to his left towards Bosco to see the man had very little sympathy in his eyes for Ace. Bosco shrugged his shoulders in indifference at Saladin. Saladin then spun his chair around to Tony who was busily examining the laces of his new pair of Jordans. Saladin swung side on the stool as he contemplated accepting the anointed position of spokesperson. He knew that certain things needed to be said to Ace that could take them a place no one wanted to go. Saladin took a deep breath and decided to speak to the hot headed Ace in the only many which Ace understood; bluntness!

"If you would have…"

Saladin did not have a chance to complete his sentence before an angry Ace interrupted.

"Fuck this shit, fuck all of you!"

Ace said as he pointed his finger at his helpers. "I don't need to hear "if's!"

"I want to know if any of you will help me."

Ace fired back.

"You see, that's yo' damn problem Ace, you don't damn listen!"

Bosco shot back. Bosco did raise his voice as he continued to speak to Ace.

"Wait for the answer to your question before you burn your bridges."

Bosco paused then shouted as if he were a member of the congregation.

"Preach on Saladin. You got a soul to save!"

Saladin looked over towards Ace and motioned to him in hand gestures if it was all right for him to continue. Saladin took Ace's silence as a sign to continue on with his sermon.

"First you spend your money as fast as you make it. Second you cut yo' shit so much any self respecting crack head would only buy from you out of desperation."

Saladin paused as the hum of the florescent light above caught his attention.

"Your product name is Mud on the streets. You are lucky that your supplier is even dealing you from the bottom of the barrel."

Saladin paused then pushed on with his sermon.

"If any of us lend you money it would be like puttin' it in a black hole!"

Saladin felt good that he had finally had the opportunity to get his frustration of how Ace ran his business off his chest. Saladin was not finished with Ace. There was something else that had to be addressed. Saladin caught the look on Bosco's face because each man had the same thought. Bosco knew what was coming next and he could only brace himself for the eruption. Saladin could not stop. He now understood that he had to get to the root of the problem.

"The problem is Ace…"

Saladin spoke without much emotion, however, everyone but Ace could sense the seriousness in his deep voice.

"Don't go there Saladin! We ain't that tight."

Ace said as he knew what Saladin would say next. The latter did not heed the warning for it had to be said.

"The problem is that you let your girl run *you*."

Saladin's bluntness made Tony shake his head.

"Damn Saladin you had to go there. You had to talk 'bout his girl"

Tony muttered aloud as he emerged from his silence to enter the conversation.

Ace was vexed enough that his mouth was frozen wide open, and it took some effort for him not to immediately fire back at Saladin. Ace took a deep breath then responded in kind to Saladin's comments.

"I ain't asking anyone in this room for their advice on how to handle my CHICK or how to run my bizness."

Had the comments come from anyone other than Saladin or Bosco, Ace would have pulled out his pistol.

"If you don't want to help me, then shut the hell up!"

He concluded. Ace paused to calm his heart rate then looked straight through Saladin.

"People in glass houses shouldn't throw bricks."

Ace's mix up of the old proverb brought about a correction from Bosco.

"That's stones you high school drop out!"

Bosco chuckled.

Saladin digested Ace's comment but chose not to press his luck further and returned to the topic of business. Saladin tactfully stated that he and Ace and Bosco grew up in the business together, yet he was on a firmer foundation than Ace because of financial discipline. Bosco and Saladin spent the next half hour trying to point out the glaring mistakes in judgment that Ace had taken in the past. Once Saladin and Bosco were sure that they addressed the main issues they turned back to Ace's original question.

"The bottom line is that you don't know how you got in trouble in the first place; giving you money would really be a gift not a loan."

Saladin declared. He made his way off of the stool and walked around the table to where Bosco was seated.

There was an open bag of potato chips in front of Bosco. Saladin reached over Bosco and picked up the bag of chips. He retrieved a handful of chips, dropped the bag back onto the table and strolled back to his stool. The room fell silent for several seconds for none of the three men seemingly wanted to help Ace out of his predicament. The look of despair on Ace's face caused Tony to want to do something to help.

"I thought we were 'posed to be friends? I know that we ain't known each other dat long Ace, but I feel like I…like we should help you."

Tony said in a strong voice.

The room became silent once again. Tony had extended his hand, would the other two do the same.

Saladin said nothing as he got off his stool and headed over to the chips once again, this time Bosco snatched the bag of chips from Saladin's reach.

"College Boy tell this youngster dat' dare ain't nuttin' thicker than money!"

Bosco said to Saladin as he folded the bag of chips and placed them in the chair beside him. Saladin did not have the chance to answer because now Tony was mad as hell at being picked on again and he took verbal aim at Bosco.

"I'm tired of you mutha' fuckas' dissin' me! I have as much money as anyone in this room. I damn sure got more money than Ace!"

Tony said in a half joking tone. Tony, Saladin and Bosco then got into a heated discussion about money, friendship and the lack of loyalty in the business. The conversation ironically excluded Ace much to his chagrin. Ace bulldozed his way into the conversation.

Ace did not want his request to be ignored any longer.

"I don't need to hear no speech 'bout how I spend my money, just tell me if *my friends* are gonna help me!"

Ace said. Saladin and Bosco fell silent, only Tony was moved enough to speak.

"I know I would feel more comfortable holding off Cash and Bo-Bo if I knew you guys had my back."

"Dick has a point. There is safety in numbers."

Bosco said as he nodded his head in agreement. The mention of numbers caused Tony to ponder a strange idea.

Tony was an avid fan of gangster movies. He immediately thought of the famous mob partnership.

"I think the four of us should work together, you know like Lucky Luciano, Benny Siegel, and Meyer Lansky!"

Tony's suggestion was immediately shot down with a chorus of "Shut up Dick!"

Saladin, Bosco and Ace turned back to the conversation concerning Ace's money troubles as if Tony had never spoken. Tony was not deterred. He continued to pitch his idea until Bosco began to warm to the virtues of such a partnership. It was not long before everyone had warmed to the thought of joining forces. Tony had successfully laid the groundwork for a business relationship that would not have any rival in the City. Tony had no inclination that his idea had sealed the fates of everyone in the room.

CHAPTER 4

Limbo

Saladin stood outside Kelly's Variety Store and absorbed the warm rays of the spring sun. The heat from the sun was a welcomed change from the air-conditioned back room of Kelly's. Saladin inhaled the stale, foul air of the city as he stretched the last of the chill from his tired bones. His thoughts turned to Tony's idea of joining forces to which he had a plethora of questions to sort out. Saladin began to get a headache as he remembered how the talk with Ace frustrated him. The frustration caused him to instinctively reach into his pocket for a pack of cigarettes that was not there. Saladin had to chuckle at the moment because he owned Kelly's and it was the only store on the block that did not sell cancer sticks. Saladin removed his jean jacket, slung it over his shoulder and started his four-block walk to his car and home.

From the first step Saladin took on his journey, business was erased from his mind. He was not about to allow business to creep into the relaxation of the drive upstate. Saladin had not made it half a block before his thoughts of sitting on his couch in front of his 52 inch projection television were disrupted when he spotted a group of teenaged girls seated on the stoop of a derelict building staring at him with penetrating eyes.

Saladin understood what was behind the stares of the teenaged girls. His fine dress and his walk of confidence reflected his true nature to the eagled-eyed girls. He was the epitome of the man they dreamed to catch; he was good looking and he looked as if he had tons of money! Saladin smiled at the young girls as he walked past.

"Damn, dat is one sexy ass man!"

He heard one of the young girl's say about him.

"He's too old fo' you. He'd probably rip you apart!"

A second young girl responded.

"The hospital can sew me up as long as I get a couple of diamonds for my pain!"

The first girl responded. Her remark was supposed to be funny but he found nothing humorous. Saladin had to look back at the girls one last time for he was disgusted at the bluntness of the young girl's comment about him. When he arrived at the next the corner his thoughts became more profound.

As Saladin arrived at the corner of 143rd street and Lexington Avenue, a procession of cars prevented his crossing the intersection. While he waited at the corner for the cars to pass he thought to himself how bad things in Harlem had become, and how he and people like him were being blamed for all the ills of this neighborhood and others like it throughout America.

"I am not the cause for all the abandon buildings, or the homeless people on the street."

He mumbled aloud as the last car passed and he started to cross the intersection. There was enough blame to go around for drug dealers to shoulder all the blame for urban blight, he reconciled in his mind.

On the other side of the intersection of 143rd Street were a group of young boys seated on a mailbox and a car adjacent to the mailbox. The young boys were involved in a loud argument of which the better NBA center was Patrick Ewing or Hakeem Olajawan? While the boys were in the midst of their passionate argument a man went about his daily routine of collecting empty cans and bottles from the garbage for redemption. The haggard look on the man's face made Saladin take a closer look at the man's tattered clothes and rundown boots to reveal that this unfortunate man had no hope. He had to survive from the garbage of others. The young men did not give the man a second look. Saladin shook his head in wonderment as he continued to make his way to his car.

By the time Saladin reached the corner of 142nd Street and Lexington Avenue the homeless man as well as the fresh words of the young girls became a distant memory. He had no time to worry about anyone because all he could think about was his home and the peace he craved. Saladin crossed the intersection of 142nd street; he paused at the corner because a very shapely dark skinned woman was set to cross his path. Saladin stopped to get a good look at her sexy face. The young lady understood why Saladin stopped in his tracks and she immediately put on her "Don't mess with me" face. Saladin was not deterred because he felt his game was tight enough that he could melt the frost off of any woman.

"You are a *beautiful* woman!"

Saladin said as the woman passed within inches of his body. He was not ready for the woman's response. She gave the salivating Saladin the palm of her hand for him to read. Saladin took her dis' in stride. His eyes fell from her cold stare to her luscious gluteus maximus. Her curvy rump caused two men who headed in the opposite direction from Saladin to stop and take a good long look. Both men could only smile at one another as they shook their heads.

"Her ass is God's gift to the world!"

One of the men announced before he and his friend continued on their way. Saladin took one last look at the young lady as she quickly moved down the street towards Park Avenue before he continued on his trek. Saladin turned his head and locked eyes with a young black cop who too had to take a look at the fine woman.

"Kind of makes you want to frisk her don't it?"

Saladin said with a smile. The cop did not respond to Saladin, he was a rookie; his shiny gun belt and polished nightstick gave the young man up as a rookie stuck on foot patrol alone in Harlem. The rookie looked away from Saladin and continued to make notes in his logbook. Saladin was happy to put the rookie on the spot. Saladin had two blocks to go until he reached his car. Nothing could make him any happier.

He literally breathed a heavy sigh the moment he crossed the street, which meant his car, was a stones throw away. He turned back in the direction of the Rookie police officer, and saw that the rookie was writing a parking ticket. Saladin shook his head at how different this cop would act in several months. He continued to walk forward as he looked back towards the cop, which was not a good idea. He felt something bump into his leg. Saladin quickly realized he had knocked a little boy down to the pavement.

"Are you all right?"

Saladin asked as he reached down to pick up the little boy off the ground as well as the candy that fell out the bag the boy carried. In spite of hitting the pavement the little boy did not seem to be hurt. As soon as the boy was up righted, Saladin noticed a little girl rush out of a bodega straight for the little boy. The filthy words that came out of her mouth would have made any sailor proud.

"This is what the fuck happens when you don't fuckin' listen to me!"

The little girl said as she snatched the little boy's arm and knocked out several pieces of candy he held in his hand.

"I'm gonna tell mommy you walked away as soon as she gests home from work. I hope she busts your ass!"

The young girl continued. Saladin was shocked into several seconds of silence because the words of the young girl did not match her apparent age.

"Sorry mista',"

The little girl apologized to Saladin in a more sincere voice.

"It wasn't your brother's fault I was the one to bump into him."

Saladin patted the young boy on the head to comfort the young boy who looked up at the older and wealthy man in awe. The young girl wore the latest clothes, as did the young boy but her actions projected her more as a mother than a sister.

"Take it easy little man."

Saladin said as he stuck out his hand and the young boy eagerly gave him five. Saladin then looked up at the young girl.

"Take care of your brother little sis.'

Saladin said to her.

The sister then yanked the boy from where he stood and pulled the boy down the block all the while cursing him at the top of her voice. Saladin stood silently for a moment as he and the boy kept eye contact for several seconds. Saladin's car was just down the block and around the corner, yet it seemed like a mile away.

The remainder of his walk to his car was spent thinking how fortunate his son Charles was to be raised in a loving home. Charles did not have to hang out on corners for fun, nor did he have to be raised around homelessness and poverty that gripped neighborhoods like Harlem. Saladin's illegal activities had made sure that his son would be exposed to more than the negatives life had to offer. Saladin had sold his soul to the devil in hopes of having options of how and where his family could live. Most parents claimed that they would do anything for their kid; Saladin was willing to risk his life for his child.

He turned the corner of the fourth and last block of his journey and he walked out into the street to get to the driver's side of his BMW 325I. As Saladin fumbled with his keys, from his peripheral vision he noticed a car slowly creeping towards him. The usually calm man started to wonder if he should reach for his joint, however the car that was moving towards him was a Plymouth Grand Fury. Either the car belonged to a car service or the NYPD. In the event the car belonged to the latter, Saladin decided not to open his car door as he may be inviting an illegal search. The Dodge Grand Fury quickly sped up and two plain clothed detectives leapt out of the car. Saladin immediately took the two men for Tactical Narcotics Team members or TNT, because only TNT officers wore their bullet resistant vests over their clothes. The identities of the two officers were equally easy for Saladin to determine because the two cops were African-American.

The officer who exited on the passenger's side of the Grand Fury made his way directly for Saladin who placed his car keys in his pocket.

"Nice car young man. Let me see your license and registration."

The officer demanded. Saladin was looking into the face of the speaker, and he was none other than Detective Gary Johnson, one half of the toughest officers in all of New York City. Saladin maneuvered his head so that he could get a better look at the driver of the car. Saladin was hoping that the driver was not Detective Sawyer Brown, Johnson's partner in crime. Saladin noticed when Brown jot down his license plate number in his pad then flicked the pad shut. He was boxed into a corner and there was no easy way out for Saladin. A case of nerves took over Saladin soon after, because he knew the street legend of the two Detectives. In one breath, the words tough, honest cops were used to describe Johnson and Brown, and in the next breath they were called two of the dirtiest cops in the city. Saladin was not prepared to answer any question they might pose. They had pegged him for what he was, and either the two African American lawmen were identifying him for future arrests, or they were going to extort money from him. Saladin knew that he was going to be in some real shit in a short amount of time.

"How much did ya' pay for the Bimmer?"

"I want to get my wife one sumin' like that there!"

Johnson said as he pointed to the rims on Saladin's car.

"The car belongs to my girlfriend."

Saladin said as he produced both documents from his wallet and presented them to Officer Johnson.

The officer read Saladin's information aloud then passed the document to Officer Brown who flipped his pad open and once again made notes in his pad before he flipped the pad closed. Brown handed the license back to his partner then made a comment meant to raise Saladin's blood.

"I think he is lying to us Johnson. The only way a black woman could afford a car like that if she was fucking a rich white man!"

The two men then shared a laugh at Saladin's expense. Saladin tried his best not to take the bait but their laughter made that task difficult.

For the next few minutes the men peppered Saladin with questions concerning the ownership of the car to which Saladin offered very little details. Johnson grew impatient with Saladin and made the request for Saladin to open his car door. Saladin refused by sighting the second amendment. (Illegal search and Seizure)

"I ain't behind the wheel you don't have the right to search a parked car without cause."

Saladin recited.

The two officers did not take kindly to the recalcitrant young man's attempt at being a lawyer. Brown took the toothpick he chewed out of his mouth and tossed it at Saladin.

"Don't tell me how to do my fuckin' job!"

Brown said as he closed the car door and approached Saladin. At the same time officer Johnson placed his hand on his service revolver as if he were prepared to shoot.

One man approached ready to pull his gun; the other approached as if he were intent to doing bodily harm to him. Saladin was in full panic mode. He retreated two steps until he was plastered against the door of his car. Saladin was set to fight and not take flight when he heard a voice in his head.

"The officers wanted to scare you. Relax and everything will be alright."

The voice was correct. Officer Brown moved within inches of Saladin, the officer was close enough to his target that he could smell potato chips on the young man's breath.

"You want to hit me don't you *Saladean*. Go ahead and do it pussy!"

Every word from Officer Brown was punctuated with spit flying from his mouth. Saladin had to remain still for any movement on his part would see him end up in cuffs. The seconds seemed like minutes to Saladin for he wanted to wipe the sweat from his brow. Just when he began to wonder how long it would be before he lost his temper and punch Officer Brown in the face, the voice of an angel threw water on the blue hot fire.

A woman who lived on the block had witnessed the confrontation between the officers and Saladin from the start. She was smart enough to know when someone wanted to pick a fight.

"Leave dat' boy alone. He ain't do nuttin!"

The woman said as she came to rest at the rear end of Saladin's car.

"You two black cops is trying to provoke that boy and I hope he ain't stupid enough to let you two do it to him!"

Saladin, officers Johnson and Brown were smart enough not to engage in any conversation with the older woman, which might draw more attention than they were willing to deal with at the time. Officer Brown slowly backed away and Johnson slowly removed his hands from his gun.

"That's right, why don't you two detectives mess with the white boys who come here to buy the drugs. You know the same ones your white cops let go with a slap on the wrist!"

The woman protested.

"We have your name and we will be in touch,"

Officer Brown warned.

"It's only a matter of time!"

Johnson said, as he shoved Saladin's license and registration into his chest.

The two officers then got into their car and merked off towards Lexington, and disappeared around the corner to 144th Street. Saladin had dodged a bullet thanks to the help of the angel.

The departure of his antagonists allowed Saladin the first opportunity to lay eyes on his savior. He turned around to face the woman who spoke for him. She appeared to be an older woman of 60 something. The woman wore a baseball cap on her head, which only enhanced her gray eyes.

"Thank you for everything misses."

Saladin said to the woman as he put his documents into his pants pocket.

"I'm 80 years young and I was one of your father's first customers at Kelly's. If you were to go to jail, I'd have no place to play my numbers!"

She continued. Saladin took it as a joke but the woman was dead serious.

"I know you do more than run numbers but that is something you are gonna have to take up with God."

The woman paused.

"What's "The good word?"

She asked Saladin.

"I think 098 played in Manhattan. I did not hear the Brooklyn number."

The woman muttered obesities as she made her way up the block towards Lexington Avenue. Saladin stood and waited for his nerves to calm down before he entered his car.

The fact that he was made by Officers Johnson and Brown made Saladin very nervous. The two were like blood hounds when they took matters personally and they would not give up until they had a good idea of his status in the game. Saladin once again reached for his imaginary pack of cigarettes only to be disappointed. A feeling of ambivalence came over Saladin as he took a seat in his car. He loved the money he made and the things he was able to obtain but the stakes had just been raised. He started the car, put it in drive and merked off from the curb. Saladin had much to think about concerning the business. In light of his being outted by the law, Saladin warmed to the idea of joining forces with Tony, Ace and Bosco. He was not sold on the idea, but hooking up with them would allow him to sit back in the cut. Thoughts of business were put on hold; he wanted to get home to his family and relax in order to plot out his next moves.

CHAPTER 5

Consolidation

The business arrangement between Ace, Bosco, Saladin and Tony literally got off to a flying start when the four men had their boys step to Marvin Cox. Marvin and his girlfriend Liza were tossed down the stairs of their once prosperous crack house. Marvin had moved up the ladder of success and down again with equally blinding speed because he had broken the cardinal rule of the business; never use the product you sell! Marvin's misfortune turned into the crew's gain.

As in any business, location is the key to success or failure. Marvin's spot was located near the highway, and two subway lines, which made it easy for those in the city and suburbs to frequent. Marvin's spot would be the centerpiece, a plan that would keep Cassius and Bo-Bo off their backs and at the same time make them extremely wealthy. The Crew took control of a six square block area. Tony and Ace's territory was much larger than that of Bosco's and Saladin's.

Saladin's and Bosco's territory was not as large as their counterparts; however their product was much more lucrative. The two men sold heroin and crack in a 60/40 split, while Tony and Ace would reciprocate. Each crewmember was responsible for putting money on the table for re-up. The amount of money put up dictated the amount of product each would receive. Members in turn would be responsible for their protection and to pay off the police. In spite of their bold take-over, the identities of the perpetrators of the moves were kept from the general public.

The crew managed to remain in the shadows, however two small problems cropped up that threatened to bring the four men's dirty deeds to light. The two problems would be addressed in different ways. First off a wannabe called Nigel Bent caused Tony and Ace some trouble. Nigel wanted to be a big time player; however he lacked the brains and the ability to be more than a bit player in the business. His thirst for fame and recognition caused him to act like the big shot he wanted to become. Nigel continually fought people who came onto his block. He would sometimes rob the white people from New Jersey by pretending to be a point man for drug purchases. His antics brought the police around more than Tony and Ace liked. If that were not enough Nigel would pronounce loudly that the "Block belonged to him!" That boast in itself made him a candidate for death.

On one clear summer day Tony had two of his associates pay Nigel a visit while he sat with his girlfriend in the corner eatery. Tony's boys dragged a defiant Nigel from the store, took him around the corner to a nearby playground and put two bullets into his head. Nigel's death let the rest of the people know who truly ran the block! Nigel's demise allowed the crew to take care of a more pressing issue with Bo-Bo.

CHAPTER 6

Chickens Come Home to Roost

"Baby needs new shoes!"

With a flick of a wrist three dice were flung through the humid summer air towards the base of a dilapidated building just a few feet away. The dice skidded across the dirty cracked pavement of New York City crashing against the base of the building. The dice bounced off the building, and tumbled back towards the individual who launched them. Just before the dice came to a halt on the pavement, the roller gave the ceremonial finger snap quickly followed by a sharply spoken "Ha!"

Once the dice came to rest on the concrete.

"My point is five!"

The Young man boastfully stated. His point of **five** was a very difficult one to beat. His roll put the young man a thumbnail away from winning a six thousand dollar pot and he could not contain in his own good fortune.

"My point is Five! All the fuckin' money is mine."

The man shouted in glee as he went down the line of spectators and exchanged high fives with some of its members of the gallery. He then took his place at the far end of the spectators. The young man waived several hundred dollars high in the air, as he was sure the pot would be his in a matter of time.

The next roller stepped up determined to make the pot all his, while creating a bit of magic in the process.

The next high roller was none other than Bobby "Bo-Bo" Paul. Bo-Bo was a rarity; he was a true Renaissance man. Bo-Bo stood all of six feet tall, but he was a phenomenal street basketball player, a prolific Cee-low player and most of all, a fantastic street pharmacist! When his name was mentioned, accolades quickly followed. As for his relationship with the ladies, Bo-Bo was in a class by himself. Bo-Bo was a mack that did not discriminate by race, only by social standing. On this warm summer afternoon, while most of Uptown was celebrating Harlem Week on 125th Street, Bo-Bo and thirty others were involved in a Cee-Low game larger than anyone had seen in many years. It was said that Bo-Bo could not pass up a high stakes game of Cee-low nor a phatty girl's ass. Bo-Bo stood surrounded by people silently cheering for him to prove his legend as one of the highest rollers in Harlem.

Bo-Bo walked up near the building to pluck up the dice left by the previous roller one at a time, as per his custom. The stout young man of twenty-five years of age turned around and calmly walked back to the designated spot to roll the dice. He stood in the center of the crowd that resembled the two sides of the Soul Train line and felt more like Moses than Don Cornelius. He had the strength to liberate money from its wicked owners, and in place of a staff he would use three dice to achieve the deed.

Bo-Bo stood between the two lines that had become quite noisy because of the prior roller's accomplishment. He sought to quail the excitement of the gallery by motioning for them to be silent. Once the gallery was sufficiently quiet, Bo-Bo was able to proceed with his roll. Bo-Bo blew on the dice, shook them and feverishly tossed them towards the building. He followed the toss with the ritual finger snap and the customary spoken word,

"Ha"

His heart was beating fast as he nervously waited for the dice to come to a stop. The dice revealed a combination of 4, 5 and 6, which beats all other combinations.

"Cee-Low! I win!"

Bo-Bo calmly said.

"Ooh!"

The crowd responded in chorus as they watched Bo-Bo in awe. Respect and admiration emanated from the crowd.

They began to mumble stories of the numerous big money pots he had won over the years. Bo-Bo himself was extremely happy. He believed his luck might change for the better. The money was not what excited him, Bo-Bo had more in his pockets than he had just won, and rather it was the winning that may be the start of good times. A member of the gallery shouted aloud.

"Bo-Bo is one lucky mother fucker!"

The man laughed as he exchanged high fives with the person who stood next to him. The laughter ended quickly as Bo-Bo locked eyes with the comedian.

"It ain't luck shit-head, it be skill!"

Bo-Bo shot back at the man. A hush fell over the crowd because many in Harlem thought he had a quicker temper that Cassius and the man might take two in the head from an angry Bo-Bo. Bo-Bo did not step to the nervous man because the man was right.

The little things were beginning to add up into a major streak of bad luck. The "bad luck" Bo-Bo experienced was a magnitude he never experienced. He felt that winning the Cee-Low game would somehow end his streak of bad luck. Bo-Bo would not admit to the gallery that he believed in luck therefore he told the opposite of what he knew and felt to be true to everyone in the gallery.

"I ain't rise from rages to riches by being lucky. It took hard fuckin' work."

Bo-Bo pulled down the sleeves of his velour sweat suit and dusted off his immaculately white sneakers before he spoke again.

"Cash and I are about to put all you mutha' fuckas on payroll? The cops can't pin those bodies on me and all of you lost your money."

Bo-Bo boasted as he majestically walked forward to collect his winnings. The money was held by a young boy of no more than ten years of age, he was showered with accolades heaped on him by some of the crowd. When Bo-Bo reached the young boy he snatched the money from the young boy and walked away. The older man's actions left the young boy with a stunned look on his angelic face.

The crowd continued to cheer his name, while Bo-Bo stopped to count the stack of bills that made up his winnings. He counted to make sure he had truly doubled his wealth as well as to gloat. Some of the big money losers called on Bo-Bo not to leave without giving them a chance to win back their money. Normally that is what he would have done; however there was nothing normal about his situation. Bo-Bo quickly decided that another win might somehow increase his luck. He turned around to hand his winnings back to the stunned young boy as he placed his fate in the outcome of rolling three dice.

Confidence was one of Bo-Bo's strong attributes, therefore his confidence allowed him to pass on his roll of the dice? This time, two rolls of the dice were what it took for Bo-Bo to win the money. Needless to say, Bo-Bo was elated. Once again he heard praises from the crowd of onlookers and the feeling he had was one for the ages. He walked the few feet to the young boy who was waiting nervously for the older man to take the money. This time Bo-Bo gently took the money from the boy. Bo-Bo paused for a moment, as he looked over the nappy-headed boy whose face turned a nervous shade of brown.

From his winnings Bo-Bo ripped off a fifty-dollar bill and presented it to the young boy. The nervous look on the young boy's face was replaced with one of overwhelming joy. He snatched the bill from Bo-Bo's hand and ran off towards the bodega at the corner. Bo-Bo could only smile as he watched the young boy run off towards the store, for the scene reminded him of his youth. His feeling of his good fortune turning better, forced Bo-Bo to listen once again to the crowd, forcing him to press his luck with the dice. Bo-Bo felt he was too hot to stop!

Bo-Bo plucked up the dice as per his custom and since the young boy had not returned from the bodega Bo-Bo decided to play with only one thousand, much to the chagrin of the rest of the players. Bo-Bo placed the rest of the money in the pant pocket of his Fila sweat suit. The lucky man was all set to roll when a group of sexy young ladies passed through the game in the direction of 125th Street and Harlem Week. Most of the young ladies wore very little clothing. One of the young ladies could not keep her eyes off Bo-Bo. To Bo-Bo's delightful surprise the young lady had a phatty. Bo-Bo did not attempt to roll as long as he could watch the woman with the phatty walk away. As soon as the woman's posterior turned from a close up view to a telescopic view, Bo-Bo turned back to his roll and his improved luck.

Bo-Bo made several rolls without a point being revealed. Frustration began to grow as Bo-Bo felt that maybe his luck had begun to turn bad once again. He walked over to where the dice came to rest all the while cursing the linage of the dice. As he bent over to pluck the dice up off the pavement Bo-Bo noticed from out of the corner of his eye that several of the onlookers had began to jet away from the area. The quick movement caused him to snatch the money and turn towards the street where an event seemed to be occurring. When he turned around Bo-Bo saw three men approaching from the street. He immediately recognized the men as shooters he and Cassius had used when they were on good terms. Bo-Bo knew that his luck had turned bad once again.

Two of the shooters walked around to the front and to the back of Bo-Bo's Mercedes-Benz, each of these men held 9mm's in their hands. The third man leapt on the hood, then the roof of Bo-Bo's car as to find a good angle to shoot between the metal bracing of the scaffolding. Bo-Bo was trapped with nowhere to go but Hell. In anger he threw the three dice at the man who crushed the hood under the weigh of his body. The dice missed the man who managed a half smile as he racked his weapon and squeezed off two bursts at Bo-Bo. The two other men fired on Bo-Bo and anyone else who moved too slowly out of the line of fire. The blasts from the shotgun tore countless holes into his Fila sweat suit. His body was sent flying backwards towards the building by the rapid fire of the two men with the 9mm's. When the shooting finally stopped the three men calmly got back into their car and sped away from the area.

In all, the outcome of their gunplay left five people wounded and one dying. The young boy emerged from the bodega as the last shots were being fired into Bo-Bo. He held two sodas, one in each hand. He thought it would be nice for him to share his good fortune with the person who made it possible. The young boy had to be pulled around the corner out of the line of fire by one of the older men who hung out in the store. Fear came over the young boy as he emerged from the safety of the corner as the car full of shooters sped away. He did not know what to think, however he had to see what had happened to the kind man.

The boy witnessed Bo-Bo crawl over to a chin-linked fence which extended from the bodega to the dilapidated building. His right hand gripped the fence as if Bo-Bo was trying to pull himself up from the pavement. Suddenly the young boy became extremely scared. He looked at the soda that he bought for Bo-Bo and thought that the shooters might come back for him because he knew the dead man. The young boy's heart began to race as he turned and ran towards home. He crossed from the north side to the south side of the street, as the thought of the shooters were hot on his heels. Once he had crossed the street the boy looked behind him and saw that Crack Head Jason from 144th Street was trying to pull money out of the dead man's hands. The young boy dropped both sodas to the pavement as he ran even faster to the safety of his home. As he ran, the young boy prayed to God to let him make it home safely if he promised never to hold gambling money again.

CHAPTER 7

Enough is enough

"Daddy, the phone is for you! It's Uncle Bosco!"

Charles yelled to his father Saladin who was in another room of the house. Charles called for his father like the typical eight year old that he was, when he yelled for his father, he did not take the phone away from his mouth.

"Hang up the dern phone boy!"

Saladin, like most parents shouted *over* the phone for his child to hang up. Charles met Bosco only two times and took to calling him uncle.

"Your house is crazy as hell Saladin!"

Bosco said with a chuckle. Saladin was tight from the anticipation of Bosco's call; therefore the humor of the moment was lost to him.

"Yeah, it's a real barrel of laughs!"

Saladin said in a deadpan voice.

"When are we making the move from the right coast of the Hudson in Westchester County to the left coast in Orange County?"

Bosco asked Saladin.

Saladin immediately began to bitch and moan about the long commute to the City. In the middle of his sentence he realized Charles had remained on the line.

"Get off the dern phone!"

The angry father yelled once more over the phone at his non-compliant son. Bosco got a kick out of all the comedy in Saladin's house. Somewhere in the middle of Saladin's complaint of it being too quiet in his neighborhood the conversation turned towards business.

"Bosco were your people able to take care of business yesterday?" Saladin inquired.

"My people took care of business and bounced with no problem." Bosco calmly responded.

Bosco's account of the situation did nothing to assure Saladin that all was well. If anything, Saladin was left to think of all the possibilities. Saladin Keith was not the one to make a move without first planning out the second move. His years of playing chess had taught him that valuable lesson. Bosco also knew that Saladin was one to think of all the possibilities of any move he made. Bosco did not want to spend another minute talking in code about what might happen. He was hungry and he knew what would happen if he did not feed his belly. Being as wise as he was Bosco quickly got off the phone with Saladin by abruptly announcing that he wanted to eat! Saladin was left to ponder all the "What if's" on his own.

Saladin hung up the phone and immediately delved into a trance like state of thought. He thought about the cryptic message delivered by Bosco and all that would happen because of the demise of Bo-Bo. Saladin understood that Bo-Bo had now made it easier for his new-formed alliance to hold its own against Cassius. He also knew that it would be harder for him to get out of the business. The idea of leaving the business was becoming more pronounced, especially since his encounter with Johnson and Brown. His heart said "**No**" to his leaving while his mind said, "Yes." Saladin sat on the edge of his new waterbed dwelling on the choice he would one day make, oblivious to his surroundings. Saladin was thrust out of his dream state by the yells of his long time love Sunshine Santiago.

The brown-skinned woman had been with Saladin since 9th grade Algebra class in Martin Luther King Jr. High School. Sunshine had weathered the storm of the lifestyle as well as the fear that being the girlfriend of a New York City drug dealer can bring. Through all the drama, she birthed Saladin's second son Charles, and managed to hold her five-foot eight, one hundred thirty pound frame in tact. She was proud to be the daughter of a Dominican-Puerto Rican man and a good old Georgia Peach mother. Sunshine was also proud to be Saladin's better half, but his late hours and his aloof nature drove her up the wall. Sunshine knew that he could tune the world out in the middle of a disaster, which was why Sunshine stood in the doorway yelling for her man's assistance.

"Your child called out for you and you never answered!"

Sunshine yelled from the doorway of their huge bedroom. Saladin did not look Sunshine's way and this pissed her off until no end. She seemed to be in the middle of another one-sided conversation with her man. Sunshine wanted his attention and she was more than willing to go the limit to get it by any means.

"Saladin Lee Keith, don't you freakin' ignore me!"

Sunshine yelled as she walked over to Saladin who continued to sit at the edge of the waterbed to slap him upside his clean-shaven head.

The man had warned his girl about her hand problem, and the slap awoke him from his train of thought and brought anger from deep within his soul. Saladin turned to face Sunshine, which caused the waterbed to crest and fall as if they were crashing waves. He could see that Sunshine held a bloody tissue in her hand. In spite of ample evidence of Charles being injured, Saladin continued to focus on Sunshine's response to him ignoring her.

"I tol' you, don't put your hands on me and *I won't put my hands on you!*"

Saladin spoke while he gritted his teeth. Sunshine was not the kind of person to back down easily especially when it came to Saladin. She pushed aside his statement and continued.

"Charles fell and busted his nose. We've been callin' you for five minutes!"

Sunshine reiterated.

"I have shit on my mind Sunshine. I didn't hear either of you."

Saladin said as he tired his best to be easy.

"Is Charles alright?"

He said with a straight face.

Saladin did not have the mental space to argue with Sunshine. He said what he hoped would shut her up, but there was no way to avoid the inevitable. Sunshine could have been a medieval dragon as she began to spit fire at Saladin.

"Some kind of father you are. You ain't no better than either one of your fathers!"

Her intention was to exact a measure of revenge on her man and she did a job well done. Saladin wanted to explode. She had hit a raw nerve when she claimed that he was not a good father. Saladin could feel himself slowly lose control.

"You've been naggin' me for the past month."

Saladin said in disgust. Once again he moved on the bed, which produced a stronger wave than the previous wave.

"I buy the house, you bitch about the location. I buy a new car, you bitch about the price. What da' fuck is wrong wit' you Sunshine!"

Saladin said in a voice that was just short of yelling.

"It ain't da' house or that inexpensive ass car you bought."

Sunshine responded.

"Then what the shit has made you a pain in the ass lately?"

Saladin shouted. The lack of a response from Sunshine let Saladin know the source of her anger came from a twice warmed over argument.

"I thought that conversation was put to bed when you made us move from one side of the Hudson to the other!"

Saladin was tired of the ocean ride on the bed. He stood up and walked over to the four thousand dollar dresser, leaned against the expensive piece of furniture in order to look Sunshine in the face whenever she chose to respond. Saladin watched as the tears began to well up in Sunshine's big brown eyes. As the first tears of anger rolled down Sunshine's cheeks she let her feelings be known.

"I spoke to Todd and Latesha the other day. They said life in Virginia is great. I…"

Sunshine did not get a chance to finish her sentence because an angry Saladin interrupted her.

"Every time you speak to Fat Todd and his girl you bug out on me Sunshine!"

"I wanted to move out of state Saladin."

Sunshine confessed. Saladin raised her confession with his own confession.

"I ain't Fat Todd Sunshine! I have people on three continents countin' on me to make money for them!"

"Todd got out!"

Sunshine responded. Saladin heard Sunshine and for the first time attempted to explain why it would be almost impossible for him to bail out.

"This is real life Sunshine. I can't ride off into the sunset like the end of a movie. I have to pay a heavy price to leave!"

He was angry but his self-check was still operational. He was not going to fall into a fit of anger. Sunshine still did not pay attention to anything he said. She just wanted to vent her frustrations on the one who caused them.

"I wanted you to leave the business a long time ago that is why I became a registered nurse!"

Sunshine shot back.

Sunshine's last comment struck Saladin as weird, which started to raise his pressure up another notch. Rather than continue on with an argument Saladin decided to leave the room. He was not about to be stressed by Sunshine at his most stressful time.

"I can't take this shit! You have no idea what the fuck I go through on the regular."

Saladin said as he started to walk out the room.

Sunshine grabbed him by the arm, which forced him to stop and to listen. Sunshine held tight to her man as she spoke.

"I live with the daily thought each time you walk out the door, it might be your last!"

Sunshine said as she wiped away the last of her tears.

"You knew what you were getting' into when we hooked up!"

Saladin mumbled. Saladin was always one for sarcasm especially when Sunshine was whining. Sunshine heard her man's mumbling and responded. The two lovers became involved in a back and forth argument about who knew what and when they knew it. Saladin was the one who tried to bring the argument to closure.

"You weren't worried 'bout how I made my money when I got your mother her house in Virginia or when I paid that shyster lawyer to get your brother out of jai!"

Saladin finished speaking then freed his arm from Sunshine's grip and continued to spew venom at his love.

"Who paid for your nursing school Sunshine? That money did not grow on trees. People died for most of what you have Ms. Self Righteous!"

He angrily stated. Sunshine waited for a moment before she responded.

"Yeah, that was before I had Charles and before I got weekly calls from strangers telling' me that they were gonna' kill you!"

Saladin was stunned into silence. His silence allowed Sunshine to continue.

"That is why I wanted us to move out of Harlem! The move from Westchester was for the same reason."

Sunshine said in a tone of finality. For his part Saladin put all Sunshine's concerns in a tiny neat box when he responded.

"It does not matter Sunshine, I cannot get out anytime soon, so get over it and get off my back!"

"Sunshine had enough of Saladin's foot dragging on the issue and she was woman enough to tell the man in her life how she felt.

"I don't give a damn about money if it means you gonna' get killed!"

Sunshine yelled. Her voice raised into high octaves. He had never heard her speak in that manner.

"Don't give me the bullshit speech about giving all this up."

Saladin motioned with his hands in reference to their entire house. Saladin had to laugh at the thought of Sunshine giving up riches for a middle class life. Sunshine took exception to her man's laugh. She wanted to show him how serious she was about giving up the good life. Sunshine removed each of her diamond earrings, and then tossed them onto the bed.

"Take this shit back. Take all of it back!"

Sunshine continued once the second earring hit the bed. Full of rage she walked over to the dresser where her pocketbook was located next to Saladin. Sunshine reached in the bag and retrieved Charles' tuition money. The irate woman took hold of the knot of tuition money, peeled off one bill at a time and flung them at a stunned Saladin. The sight of his hard earned money being tossed in his face was too much for the proud man to handle. The little voice in his head that had kept him calm finally turned mute.

"You're outta' yo' fuckin' mind!"

Saladin yelled as he snatched one dollar out of the air before it had the chance to strike him in the face. He could feel the veins in his head begin to tighten.

"I don't want this shit if you gonna' die to get it for me!"

Sunshine yelled as she tried ripping the bills in half. Saladin attempted to snatch the money out of Sunshine's hand and a scuffled ensued. The scuffle ended when Saladin placed Sunshine's face in his left hand and mushed her to the bed. Sunshine bounced off of the bed, back to her feet and went straight at Saladin. She took a wild swing at him and missed. Saladin countered with a pimp slap that sent Sunshine crashing back to the bed. She hit the bed with such force that it shook violently. Sunshine curled up in the fetal position and began to cry. Saladin could not believe that their relationship had returned back to the place they had worked hard to leave.

The act of violence caused a pause in their physical actions, which gave Saladin and Sunshine the opportunity to regain their composure. Saladin stood motionless. He looked down on the offending hand as if it acted without the consent of his brain. The sight of Sunshine lying on the bed and the sound of her crying struck a raw nerve with Saladin. He had broken his promise of three years to Sunshine, and that was worse than the fact that he felt the same way about everything Sunshine said.

Saladin witnessed the same things Sunshine did in his business. Many of the people his age that started with him dwindled down to a handful. It troubled him that he played with odds that were stacked against him. The longer he remained in the business, the more his odds of survival diminished. He did not want to end up like Bo-Bo or in jail like so many others. Saladin could feel his defense weakening and his heart of steel began to melt away like ice cream on a hot summer day. He had to go against the norm displayed by everyone in the business. Saladin had to let Sunshine know that they were literally on the same page but on different paragraphs.

"Sunshine, I know I can't sell drugs forever. I don't want to one day answer our son's questions."

Saladin spoke in a very apologetic tone.

Saladin sat on the edge of the bed next to Sunshine who continued to cry.

He reached out to touch Sunshine however he was met with an icy resistance from her. In spite of this he continued to speak.

"If you keep hounding me about getting' out, I'm gonna' make a mistake. I only have to make one mistake."

Saladin said in a very soft voice. He again reached out for Sunshine who rebuffed him once more. Saladin sighed as he came to the realization that he had made a big mistake already in hitting Sunshine.

"I have no excuse for putting my hands on you again. No excuse will ever do!"

He concluded. As Saladin spoke he could feel warm tears running down his face. The cry was the first he had in a great many years and it felt good for him to release his emotions. Saladin did not hold back his thoughts.

"Just trust me Sunshine."

Saladin pleaded.

"Trust me to do the right thing by you and Charles!"

Saladin found the last words difficult to speak because his emotions got in the way. He placed his hands on his head to cover his face as he cried. He soon realized that his crying made him look un-cool. Saladin tried to get off the bed but Sunshine pulled him down to the bed. Saladin buried his head deep into her bosom.

"I'm sorry Sunshine"

Saladin repeated. Sunshine continued to cry as she held her man tight for her own reasons.

Sunshine had a premonition that something bad was going to happen to Saladin if he stayed in the business much longer, which was why she pressed him on getting out. She knew she was wrong for pushing Saladin to the limit but Sunshine was not going to apologize. Sunshine was intent on doing whatever she had to do to get her man out of the business. Sunshine held her man tighter as she looked over at the door for Charles to interrupt the movie scene.

CHAPTER 8

Spare The Rod...

Bosco ended his phone call with Saladin and headed straight for the refrigerator.

"Damn I'm hungry!"

He said with a fart and rubs of his rather round stomach. Bosco held the refrigerator door wide open as he searched its entire interior for something suitable on which to nibble. In a matter of seconds Bosco twice rearranged the refrigerator's contents before he settled for a pack of chicken franks, which he found, tucked away behind his grandfather's heart medicine.

"Well, I guess this will hafta' do,"

Bosco conceded. He removed the chicken franks from the refrigerator and blindly tossed them onto the kitchen counter as he looked for the mustard. His search was thwarted by a familiar voice, which offered him some good advice.

"There is some sandwich meat at the bottom of the refrigerator."

Bosco promptly followed the direction of the voice. He put back the franks and took out the container. Bosco opened the container and began to prepare a "Taylor Special" sandwich. As he prepared to stack cold cuts between two slices of bread he thanked the owner of the voice for help.

"Thanks Pop!"

Bosco said with great joy. Bosco did his work in the dark.

"We did pay the light bill this month!"

His father joked about his son's habit of not turning on lights.

Bosco's father reached over to the light switch located on the wall to the left of the entranceway, and flicked it to the on position. The kitchen became full with light.

The dull light, however, penetrated Thaddeus Philip Taylor Senior's body, illuminating his soul to his son. Bosco only glanced over in his father's direction when the light first came on because he was too busy piling four different kinds of meats onto his sandwich. Slowly his mind processed the picture Tad presented to his eyes. A second look revealed something that Bosco had not noticed. He knew that his father, a Vietnam Veteran, widower and father of four, rock-head boys had been under a great deal of stress lately. He was not prepared to see the effect on his father's face, which started Bosco thinking about the role he played in his father's appearance.

Tad, as the elder preferred to be called, had begun to show signs that he finally buckled from the tremendous weight he carried on his shoulders, ever since he returned from the war to find his wife suffering from serious health problems. The health problems eventually ended her life, but not before she gave birth to four boys. After her death, Tad was left to raise four boys, as well as to take care of his sickly father on a conductor's salary in a neighborhood that was as unforgiving as a jilted lover. Two of his boys were sucked up by the vast lures of the street.

Randall the eldest of the four was the first to fall into the dark world of the street life. After several unsuccessful tries at being a businessman, he turned to kidnapping and extorting from those who did have the skills to make money. His line of work was lucrative but very costly. A botched job landed Randall in the joint doing a fifteen to twenty-five year bid. His family was left to deal with the angry threats of many of his victims, as well as their families. The fear of reprisals gave Tad the motivation to make sure his second son William, did not fall into life on the street. Through diligence and constant prodding by Tad, William escaped to college and then a very high level position at Boeing. As far as Tad was concerned, William's success may have come at Bosco's expense.

Tad believed that by the time William was straightened out, Bosco would adjust as he arrived at the vulnerable stage in life. Tad's gamble did not pay off, because he had no idea that the lures of the street were converting younger people every day. Guilt and frustration overwhelmed Tad because he blamed himself for Bosco becoming a businessman. Tad vowed to use every bit of his strength to keep his last son, Gregory from following in his brothers' notorious footsteps. That quest was partly the reason Tad was finally buckling from the weight upon his shoulders.

"Dang Pop, you look kind of rugged today!"

Bosco joked about his father's appearance, as was his custom. His father said nothing at first; instead he took off his MTA issued jacket. Tad draped the blue polyester jacket over his left arm and spoke to his son with deep anger in his voice.

"What the hell did you say boy?"

Bosco did not know how to respond. As he loaded his sandwich full of meat, he recalled several memories. He recalled the beating his father gave Randall after Randall pulled a knife on him. Another flash, and Bosco remembered his father holding William out of their six story window after Tad found out that William had cut school for one straight week. Bosco slowly turned his head until their eyes met. Bosco saw anger in his father's eyes. Before Bosco could wipe the sweat from his forehead, his father responded with a straight face.

"Gotcha!"

Tad then laughed as he walked past his stunned son to the refrigerator. Tad continued to laugh as he rearranged its contents in an effort to find something to drink. Bosco stood and quietly prepared his food. He did not like bearing the brunt of his father's joke; however, to see his idol laugh made the joke easier to take. Tad continued to laugh as he sipped on a bottle of Snapple, walked out of the kitchen and into the dining room. Bosco hurriedly followed his father as if he were caught in his father's wake.

Bosco sat down at the dining room table across from his father and watched as Tad lit his first cigarette in Bosco's recent memory. Bosco said nothing as his father took long deliberate pulls on the cancer stick. The sight of his father smoking the cigarette reminded him of a crack-head finding solace at the butt end of a crack pipe. Tad had pledge to his family never to smoke again after their mother's death from cancer. He had broken his promise and his son tried to find the courage to ask the question why.

"Hey Pop, what's da' matta'? Why is you smokin' again?"

Bosco tentatively asked. He sat on the edge of his chair and waited for his father's reply. Tad inhaled deeply and exhaled even slower as if the latter would aid him in his difficult answer.

"It's your brother Gregory,"

He said with great difficulty.

"I don't know what to do with him."

Tad paused to take another pull on the cigarette then spoke as he exhaled.

"I don't have the energy to stay on his ass anymore! The boy is more difficult than Randall was at his age."

Tad took a short pull and continued.

"At least Randall knew he wanted to be a crook, this boy takes turns at doing right and wrong! That really drives me crazy!"

Tad inhales one more time then speaks.

"The damn principal knows my work schedule by heart!"

Bosco sat attentively listening to his father's words. As he listened, Bosco began to feel that the cigarette was turning into some kid of drug for his father. Tad finished speaking once the cigarette had disintegrated.

"I don't know what to do wit' him Philip?" (Tad never called his junior by his nickname) I don't know what to do."

Tad's voice faded like a song in the face of a good breeze. Bosco was stunned to say the least. He had never imagined his tougher than nails father would ever act like an average man.

"Pop."

Bosco said as he moved his chair closer to the table.

"I ain't used to seein' you like dis"

Bosco said as he pushed the plate containing his sandwich aside in order to rest his folded arms on the table.

"How come you ain't busting his behind like you did wit' da rest of us?" Bosco quizzed. Tad opened his mouth to answer but another voice, an older voice answered for him.

"That's because you three hard asses wore my damn son out!"

Bosco and Tad turned to see that Tad's father; his Grandpa Douglas was who spoke. He was serious about his accusation because he was waving his cane in the air as he spoke. Grandpa Douglas slowly labored around the table until he stood directly behind his son. He stopped to collect his thoughts and the breath to finish.

"It wouldn't be a bad idea if he got out and found himself a good woman but that's another story for another day!"

Grandpa Douglas struggled for air then continued on with his thoughts.

"William is in Oregon…"

"He's in Seattle Pop,"

Tad corrected.

"Oregon, Seattle, where ever the hell he is, he can't fly back here to straighten Gregory out each time he acts a fool! That boy is too far gone for just one person to straighten out."

Grandpa Douglas paused to look a reluctant Bosco in the eyes.

"You hafta take time to take on the responsibilities of being an older brother! You hafta give yo' father a hand!"

Grandpa Douglas spoke but with much difficulty.

As his grandfather went on with his sermon Bosco became engaged in a mental debate. Bosco did not want to take on the added responsibility of helping to raise his little brother; he had enough problems of his own. He had to deal with his new partners, the two women who claimed to have had his baby, and just the general stress of being in the business, made him an unwilling volunteer. Bosco understood where his grandfather was coming from but he declined in silence. Bosco emerged from his debate long enough to hear his grandfather continue with his sermon.

"If your father would get some of dat "Ill Nay, Nay" maybe he would have enough energy to keep up with Gregory."

The trio then laughed at Grandpa Douglass' corruption of the new slang.

"Ill Na, Na,"

The laugh was long needed. It had been a long time since he got along with his fathers, laughing and telling stories about the past. Their good time ended abruptly with the sound of the apartment door being opened, and the sounds of many voices entering the apartment. The three men heard the door slammed closed. All three wondered what was causing such a ruckus. Bosco, pushed back from the table, leaned back in the chair so that the chair's two front legs where completely off the floor. From his vantage point he could see what was causing the noise.

"What's going on Bosco?

Tad asked. He was just as curious about the source of the noise.

"Looks like Greg brought some guests home."

Bosco answered as he plopped his chair onto the floor. A few seconds later Gregory and two of his friends entered the dining room in the middle of Gregory telling a dirty story. Three other of his friends did not venture past the living room.

"Yeah, and I tol' her if she didn't swallow she wuz gonna hafta' walk from Jersey!"

Gregory then led his friends in laughter at his own story.

He said nothing to his family members; he simply stared at his grandfather. The two had argued earlier that morning and there had been no resolution. He walked straight into the kitchen leaving his two friends standing in the dining room unannounced and unwanted. The dislike was evident to the two young men, but they were under the impression that Gregory ran the house. Bosco took an instant and strong dislike for them. He looked Gregory's friends over, examining their faults. Grandpa Douglas left the room rather than suffer another heart attack at the hands of Gregory.

"Oh Pop! The City Sheriff is in front of the building and they are about to tow your car."

Gregory yelled from the kitchen as he searched through the refrigerator for something to eat. Tad leapt up and immediately ran out of the apartment to check on his car. With his father's hasty departure Bosco was left alone in the room with the two young men.

Bosco looked the two young men over once more with the intent of discovering the slightest reason to throw them out on their asses. Maybe wearing their hats into his house was reason enough. Maybe it was the way each wore his jeans? Both young men knew that they were being sized up and they felt uncomfortable with the examination. Bosco sensed the tension and fed off of it. His search for a pretext to go after the two young men was interrupted by the sound of loud music echoing up the hallway from the living room. The loud music took precedence over the looks of the two young men for the moment. Bosco jumped up from out of his seat and stared at the two young men letting them know that their business was not over. He walked out of the dining room in a hurry to solve someone's problem with touching his stereo.

Bosco returned to the living room, after giving Gregory's three friends the option of turning off the stereo or going down the stairs headfirst! His blood boiled as he entered the dining room to find his brother and his two friends seated at the table. In his brief absence they had divided his beloved sandwich up between them and seemed very happy devouring his heart. Bosco stood in the doorway watching his sandwich disappear. He took notice of his little brother; dressed in clothes his money brought and acting as if their father did not instill manners in him. Gregory never wanted for anything. If he were to ask for something, Gregory knew that one of his brothers or even his father would break their necks to get him what he wanted. The more Bosco tried to figure out why his brother was acting, as he was, the madder he became at the situation. What really set him off was that one of Gregory's friends dripped mayonnaise on his father's work jacket that he draped over the back of a chair. Bosco was a fuse in search of a light.

"Nice of you to divide my sammich up Greg,"
Bosco said to his brother in a deadpan voice.
"Now what am I gonna' eat?"
He quizzed.

Gregory remembered that it was not polite to speak with one's mouth full; therefore he took the time to swallow his food before speaking. Gregory should have taken the time to think before he spoke.

"You got money. You can afford to buy yourself something to eat."

He quipped. Gregory's two friends started to laugh. One of Gregory's friends laughed loud enough that he nearly choked on the sandwich he pilfered from Bosco. Bosco had now found his light. He was going to set his little brother straight even if it meant killing him.

"Oh, shit is funny! I bet this is gonna be *hilarious*!"

Bosco said as he walked over to the two guests who sat side by side and slapped what was left of his sandwich out of their hands in succession. Both young men immediately jumped out of their seats in protest to his action, only to be knocked down like dominoes. Gregory also jumped up from his seat in defense of his pride, not his friends. Bosco saw his little brother rise up and violently pushed the dining room table with his thighs causing the table to crash into his brother to pin him against the wall for an instant. The force of hitting the wall with his head dazed Gregory. He could only watch as his older brother did demo' to his friends.

After delivering several blows, Bosco allowed one of the young men to flee. Bosco then began to beat down his brother's friend, the one who laughed until he choked. One to the eye, another to the mouth, and a swift kick to the ribs was all it took before the young man begged Bosco to stop. Bosco obliged by grabbing the beaten young man up off the floor by his torn sweatshirt and dragging him out of the apartment. The three in the living room got ghost at the first sign that an ass whipping was taking place. An angry Bosco stood in the doorway as he watched them run down the stairs. Before the last one disappeared down the steps Bosco remembered that there was one more ass kicking that must take place.

He slammed the door and stormed up the hall towards the dining room to finish reprimanding his little brother. On the way back his grandfather stuck his head out of his room door.

"What was going on in the house?"

Grandpa asked.

"I'm takin' on more responsibilities!"

Bosco replied.

By the time Bosco entered the dining room Gregory had managed to collect his thoughts and retrieve a knife from the kitchen.

"Who da' fuck you think you is?"

Gregory screamed as he clutched the knife firmly in hand.

"You gonna' die for dissin' me in front of my boys!"

He cried as he spoke. Bosco paid no attention to his brother's words, instead he cautioned his little brother on putting down the knife.

"I'm only gonna' say it one time! Put down the knife and take yo' ass kickin' like da' man you think you is!"

Bosco said as he moved closer to his brother. Gregory retreated from his older brother until he backed himself into the kitchen. He quickly realized that he had run out of real estate, therefore he charged at his brother. Bosco calmly disarmed him and sent him crashing to the floor.

"You really tried to cut me!"

Bosco exclaimed as he stood over his fallen brother.

"You wanna be a man Greg!"

Bosco yelled as he lifted his brother off of the floor. Bosco dragged his brother over to the open kitchen window and hung him out by the ankles ala his father.

"If you ever dis me, pop or grandpa again I'll be back to throw you all the way out!"

He then threw his brother down onto the floor.

"Until Pop tells me different I ain't buyin' you shit!"

Bosco then stormed out of the house. On the way out he passed his stunned, yet happy grandfather who had already begun to clean up the dining room. Neither wanted to waste words, therefore Bosco left without an explanation.

Outside the apartment Bosco, still angry, paced up and down the hallway as he waited for the elevator. He was trying to convince himself on what he would have done if Gregory drew blood. Bosco stopped pacing and pressed for the elevator once again. He leaned backwards until his back touched the wall; he could see his family's apartment door. His thoughts remained angry, but somehow his thoughts fell back upon the words of his father and his man Saladin. His father never wanted Bosco to buy Gregory things he did not deserve. Tad had warned him of what getting something for nothing might do to Reginald, however, Bosco ignored his father's warning as well as the warning from Saladin.

Saladin told him many times that their lifestyle would affect Gregory in ways that they could not easily see. The young boy saw the results of the money, free time, women, and most of all; he saw the attitude of the business. As the elevator arrived and the doors opened, Bosco understood that the way he acted around his little brother would have to change. He would not flash the dough or brag about what he had just brought. Most importantly the invincible man aura would have to be dispelled.

The new and improved Bosco stepped into the elevator and was pleasantly surprised to find Ms. Green, an ultra sexy single woman of thirty-something standing alone.

"Hey Bosco long time no see! Looks like you put on some weight since the last time I saw you."

She said as the elevator descended towards the lobby. Bosco smiled and rubbed his round stomach.

"I know your weight ain't from your father's cooking?"

She joked. Her joke reminded Bosco of his grandfather words and seized the moment.

"Speaking of long time no see, my father was just askin' 'bout you. He thought you had moved out of the building."

"No baby, I'm still here!"

She responded.

"You know Ms. Green, Pops should still be down stairs, and he is in good shape!"

CHAPTER 9

Where Does It All Go?

The murder of Bo-Bo was not blamed on Cassius for a change. To the people in the know the way the hit went down did not fit Cassius' m.o. for doing away with people. Almost immediately word hit the street that a new crew had made power moves that included the hit on Bo-Bo and Marvin Cox. Cassius should have been very pleased with one murder not being blamed on him; however the idea of an already crowded field becoming more competitive troubled him. Cassius needed to know who was behind the move and what kind of threat they represented to him. He turned to his good friend Black Reginald for information.

Black Reginald put his ear to the ground and his fist to the back of several heads and came up with the names of Tony and Ace. Black Reginald relayed the names to Cassius who failed to recognize the names of the two men. He felt that he had bigger fish to fry before he would step to the two upstarts. Cassius' choice to delay action against the crew allowed them to solidify their business position.

Business for the four men started off in a very deliberate manner at the insistence of Saladin who was very concerned with drawing attention before they could handle the fame. Once they were able to iron out the wrinkles in the plan the money came hand over fist. The four men nearly tripled their original profits at the end of their first business cycle. Money was the reason why each man got into the business. Big money also affected each man in different ways.

At the insistence of his girl Angelika, Ace went on a spending spree. Ace had to sell much of what he owned to put money on the table. Since he made huge profits Angelika persuaded him to replace what he had to sell with better more expensive versions. She convinced Ace to give up the projects for a townhouse in New Jersey. Angelika believed that Ace and she deserved to live in the lap of luxury. She held a certain lifestyle in mind as to how they would eventually live; however it would take more money. She did not have to pull Ace's arm very much. After suffering through economic hardships in the past he was eager to provide Angelika with that lifestyle. Ace became drunk with the idea of being a big timer; therefore he hastily contacted Bosco several times in hopes of getting the rest of the crew back to the table to make some money. Bosco refused all requests because he learned there was more than money to the game of life.

A woman or the need for material things did not influence Bosco. He already owned a cooperative in a quiet area in the Bronx and did not see the need to own a car in New York City. If he needed to get somewhere he would either borrow a car or call a cab. The health of his grandfather Douglass pushed making money to the back of his mind.

His grandfather suffered his second heart attack, which caused a lengthy hospital stay for the 65-year-old man. Watching his grandfather struggle for air with tubes emanating from every orifice of his body made money less important. Bosco knew that his partners needed him to come back to the table but they would have to wait until his grandfather was well enough to return home. Bosco's wish would not come forth. During a visit to the hospital he saw his beloved grandfather slip into that long sleep good night. The death of his grandfather took a huge toll on the entire Martin family, especially Bosco. All his money and prestige could not save his grandfather's life. Death taught Bosco an important lesson.

In the days leading up to the funeral of his grandfather, Bosco chose to ignore his pager, cell phone, house phone and doorbell. He did not participate in making the arrangements for his beloved grandfather instead he sat alone in his apartment in the dark and cried just as he had done when his mother passed from cancer. When Bosco finally answered his door he found his two brothers Gregory and William there to greet him with tears and hugs. Once Bosco got around to answering his communication devices he was greeted with pleas of his lieutenant Albino Charles.

Albino Charles urged Bosco to "tend to his business" before he had no business which to return. Three days after his grandfather died, Bosco contacted Saladin who wasted no time taking a dig at his friend.

"I'm glad to see you have joined the living Philip!"

Saladin quipped. Through all his sadness Bosco continued to maintain his humor.

"You know I could not leave you helpless bastards too long! Let's get down to business! I hafta' work to easy my mind."

Those last words were like music to Saladin's ears.

Saladin's reason for wanting to get back to the table was the most selfish of anyone else in his crew. Since his run-in with the law, the far-off thought of an exit from the business took a more prominent role in his mind. Each murder and arrest of a businessman made getting out much more than a novel idea. He had to stack his money like chips if it came to the point he wanted to leave. Money represented his ticket out and the crew was his best opportunity to gain enough wealth to get out. Saladin was not sure if he wanted to pass on the huge money the crew generated. He placed a call to Tony, the last member of the crew in order to make the money that would keep him in the business or allow him to leave.

Tony wasted no time to get back to the table because of pure greed. Tony learned that big money brought notoriety. He loved the attention that he received on the streets and he wanted more. In Tony's way of thinking the larger he became in the business the more famous he would become. The vain young man purchased several fancy cars for friends, as well as a Mercedes Benz 500SEC for himself. Tony also purchased enough jewelry that O'Kelly Isley (Mr. Bigs older brother) would have been proud. When Tony stepped out on the town he traveled with a rowdy entourage. They made sure to draw attention of anyone nearby.

On one particular evening Tony was approached by an old time businessman outside a bar frequented by older businessmen. The "Old Head" as they were called, wanted to take the younger Tony aside and pull his coat about the disadvantages of always drawing attention to himself. Tony took exception to the suggestions made by the older man and a vicious argument ensued between Tony and the Old Head over respect. The argument became intense enough that another old head stepped in an attempt to mediate the argument. He too began to argue with a hostile Tony. As the group of old heads grew, Tony decided to call for back up.

When Bosco arrived he immediately began to assess the situation in order to calm everyone down. By the time Ace arrived, Bosco had settled the argument, and Tony's entourage had already taken him home. Bosco was inside the bar having drinks with the very people an inebriated Tony had been arguing with.

"Yo' what's the emergency?"

Ace asked because there seemed to be no emergency. Bosco motioned for Ace to take a seat next to him in order to explain what drama Tony had caused. Ace quickly understood that the more money Tony made the more trouble he was going to make for everybody. Each time they made their way back to the table Tony would make working with him more difficult.

CHAPTER 10

From Order Comes Chaos

The approach of summer always caused individuals to reflect upon the events of the prior year and the hope of the better things to come. Summer was also the time of year when people gauge their economic and social progress. Keeping up with the Jones' is what it is called. The crowded summer streets present the material people for the world, a forum to display their wealth. It was in that atmosphere that the four men came together at the table in Kelly's. This time the sit down was more tension in the air than anytime in their first year of operation. The Hip-Hop mega star Biggie Smalls could not have said it better "More money, More problems."

The four men came back to the table just before the start of the summer rush season. The first year in business together put more cash in each man's hands than they had ever seen in a one-year period. With the expanded wallets came the ubiquitous hangers-on. Tony and Ace brought their money grubbing new friends to the table, which doubled the attendance of their first official meeting. Ace brought his long time girlfriend Angelika and her cousin Thomas while Tony brought along three "Yes Men". Bosco was tight because he left his boy Albino Charles behind, Ace and Tony should have done the same. Bosco glanced over at Saladin and it was obvious that the sight of foreigners seated at the table pissed him off too. Neither man would take long to address the disrespect they felt that

Tony and Ace had for their arrangement. Bosco was more upset than Saladin thus he voiced his opinion first.

Bosco tossed a bag of Peanut M&M's he nibbled onto the table, which caused a thud. The sound of the bag striking the table was loud enough to break Ace's chain of thought.

"Only four people in this room put money one the table. I should not hear nine opinions!"

Bosco yelled as he pointed around the table. Bosco was seated across the table from Angelika and Thomas. He stared directly into her hazel eyes as he addressed the room.

"How many of you fuckers are gonna' ante up today? Put up or sit down!"

An angry Bosco pointed to each of the new comers in the room to accent his anger. Bosco and Angelika had a feud that rivaled that of the Hatfield's and McCoy's. The origin of this feud was as esoteric as the more famous feud. The feud had not turned deadly, but it was vicious nonetheless.

Angelika grew up in the streets and she full well understood that life in the projects was not for her. Ace was the first person who shined the light of money into her dreamy eyes and she could not focus on anything else. She was street wise enough to know that her aggressive nature would strike most men as bitchy behavior but she could handle that fact. Angelika knew that men would be attracted to her dark complexion, hazel eyes and thick body. She also knew that some sort of attack would come from Bosco. Ace thought the feud ended once he and Bosco went their separate ways after high school, but he was wrong. He did not like that Bosco would come at his girl sideways and he let his partner know in no uncertain terms.

"Don't go pointing fingers at my girl, Bosco."

Ace protested.

"If your girl ain't put any money on the table, I'll point at her all I fuckin' want!"

Bosco said as he again pointed at Angelika. Bosco's anger did not subside from his initial barrage, he paused to catch his breath and to calm down before he continued.

"When we first came to the table it was just four of us. Now that the money got large there are twice as many as the original group!"

Bosco then pointed at Tony and his three newfound friends when he completed his words. He paused for a moment then continued.

"If you ain't anteing up then shut the fuck up and get out the room!"

Bosco's voice was full of anger when he spoke. Ace was about to respond to the tirade, however Angelika tapped him on the shoulder.

"I got this one Honey."

She said. The twenty-three year old woman finally had the chance to address Bosco.

"Don't hate me 'cause I stood by my man!"

Angelika pronounced in a superb angry black woman voice. She continued.

"I didn't run off wit' da' garbage man the moment things got tough!"

Her last words were a thinly veiled reference to Bosco's ex-girlfriend Stephanie who had left him for a New York City Sanitation Engineer. Immediately the two exchanged words with each other.

"Fuck you,"

Bosco said.

"No, Fuck you!"

Angelika responded in kind.

Each exchange brought more tension to the room, which could bring an abrupt end to the fragile alliance. Saladin watched the situation begin to deteriorate before his eyes. He knew something had to be said or done to keep the alliance in tact. Saladin quickly sought to bring the focus back to business.

"I'm tired of all da bitchin'!

Saladin said in a voice loud enough to cause the room to become silent.

"I'm in this room to make money! Money and bullshit don't mix, so you two (He pointed to Bosco and Angelika) need to cut the bullshit!"

Saladin said in an angry voice.

Angelika recovered from the shock of Saladin's words and simple stated.

"So what's your point?"

"My point is I agree with Bosco. Only people who put money on the table should be in this room discussing business!"

His words were met with the objections from both Ace and Tony. Ace was about to address the matter but Tony beat him to the punch.

Tony had rehearsed over and over the response he would give if the decision to bring an entourage with him came into question. He was young but Tony felt he was an equal partner in the enterprise. The eloquent words he prepared were lost to anger and primordial words replaced them.

"I don't take mutha' fuckin' orders from nobody!"

Tony announced as he made eye contact with both Saladin and Bosco.

"If my peoples gotta go, I gotta leave too!"

Tony commanded.

Tony motioned for his Three stooges to follow him out of the room. Tony then began to place the stacks of cash that he had initially placed on the table into a green Army duffle bag. To everyone in the room except his three boys, Tony that neighborhood kid who if he did not get out of his way took the thing home that would end the game. Bosco, Ace and Angelika responded to Tony's threat by pointing at the door, which they hoped would hasten his departure. Once Tony realized he was encouraged to leave he went about his task at a more rapid pace.

He placed the last stack of one hundred dollar bills in the duffle bag zipped it shut and tossed it over his mighty shoulders. Saladin sat on his stool and watched the scene unfold and knew he had to keep the alliance together in order to keep his option of exiting the business alive. Saladin put on the hat of a diplomat as he tried to soothe Tony's feelings, yet at the same time get his own point across.

"Tony, calm down a minute. Think about things before you go off the deep end!"

He spoke in the calm voice as to not upset the volatile Tony.

Saladin looked over to Angelika as he spoke. The look was meant as a cue for the boisterous antagonist to leave the room. Angelika got the hint. She tapped her cousin Thomas on the shoulder to signal for him to leave the room with her. Ace saw his support system leaving the room and started to address the matter before Angelika said in faux Queens English.

"Let's go Thomas. The air is rather stuffy in here!"

Bosco understood the comment was about him, but he had business matters on his mind. His dealing with Angelika would have to wait. Angelika then led her cousin out of the back room to Ace's brand new 85K, 500SEC Benz that was parked outside. Angelika was about money and nothing but money. She was not about to fuck up a good thing in spite of her apparent hatred for Bosco. As soon as they left the room Saladin continued on with his mission of diplomacy.

The sound of the door to the back room slamming shut was a signal for Saladin to restart his spoken words.

"You are correct Tony; you don't have to take orders from anyone."

Saladin paused then continued his sermon.

"I'm sure glad none of us were trying to give you orders Tony."

Saladin said with a smile. His words caught everyone by surprise especially Tony.

"Mutha' fucka', don't be tryin' to use that psychological shit wit' me!"

Tony protested.

Saladin did not deny he was using psychology but he used the lack of stealth to his advantage.

"There is an old saying, that 'Too many cooks spoil the broth'."
Saladin said.

Then he looked over to Bosco who looked like he was ready to explode at any moment from pent up anger. He then glanced over at Ace who had the look of a person who wanted to see if Saladin's bullshit was going to work on Tony. Saladin knew he had to put on his best performance.

"Tony you did not want to take orders from anyone, but just a minute ago I thought you were giving *us* orders."

Saladin paused as he placed a stick of gum in his mouth. He took several chews before he began to speak.

"Understand Tony we want you to be down with us, but we don't need you."

Saladin looked over towards Bosco who continued to simmer.

"If Ace could get Angelika to leave the room why can't you get your people to leave as well?"

Saladin watched Tony's facial expression change which he hoped meant that Tony may also have a change of heart. Saladin reached deep into his bag of tricks for the Coup de Grass.

"You already made it clear that you are your own man and make your own decisions. Then why do you believe you need their advice?"

Saladin made sure to look directly at the three men when he spoke. It did not take long for the men to understand how unimportant they were to the meeting.

One by one each man left his chair and walked out of the room. Tony sat down in his chair without uttering a single word. Saladin immediately checked the facial expressions. He first looked over towards Bosco who looked as if he was about to laugh. He then took a quick look at Ace who shook his head in disbelief at the lesson Saladin put on Tony. As the men settled down and got ready for business Saladin addressed the rift between Bosco and Ace.

"This ain't the time for personal shit to get in the way of money being placed on the table."

Saladin looked at both men as he spoke.

"Bosco has a problem, and that should be the first thing we will talk about, the need to change attitudes."

Bosco and Ace kept to the business at hand; however deep in Ace's mind he wondered the origin of the beef between his girl and his former best friend. Saladin's common sense talk saved the alliance but he was not sure for how long!

CHAPTER 11

All Work and No Play...

It has been said that a wise man learns from his mistakes. The next time the crew came to the table, they found themselves at Kelly's where there were only four people in the room. They were minus the extra opinions, which caused much of the drama at the prior meeting. The four men focused only on business matters.

The situation with Bosco's cocaine supplier was the first order of business that the men tackled. All decided that Bosco would locate another supplier. Tony's experience and Ace's lack of attention to detail excluded them from becoming the front man for the type of deals they needed to make. Therefore Bosco kept his job by default. The second order of business was dealing with Cassius and the police.

Five-O were busy busting one drug crew after another in response to the increased level of violence crack brought to the streets. The NYPD along with federal agencies formed a taskforce designed to put a dent in the crack trade in the city. The taskforce did an excellent job nabbing crews both new and old. Anyone who displayed their wealth in excess or shot up entire blocks became instant targets for the task force. Who ever the taskforce did not arrest Cassius made sure to take them down. Saladin, Bosco, Tony and Ace developed a strategy they felt would keep the money flowing, as well as keep them out of the minds of the law and Cassius.

One target, one bullet became the unwritten rule of the crew. Violence would be used, but broad daylight drive-by shootings would not be the preferred method of execution. Murder if needed would not play on the front pages of the New York newspapers. The four men pledged to stick by the rules, but as always, Tony remained a big concern. Bosco was the first to urge Tony to keep a low profile around town.

"We are under the radar right now; we don't need to make ourselves targets."

He said to Tony. Ace and Saladin echoed the sentiment. Towards the end of the meeting Bosco noticed how intense everyone had been during the meeting. Thoughts about how high the stakes had risen took a toll on everyone. Saladin thought a night out with the fellas would be a good way to unwind. Bosco first asked Saladin if he wanted to *chill* that night.

"Saladin, when wuz da' last time we hung out together?"

Bosco asked as the idea just popped into his head. The idea of a 'guy's night out' immediately appealed to Ace and Tony.

"Yeah, we can go out and meet some freaks!"

Tony said in an excited voice. Bosco looked at Tony as he responded to the latter comment.

"Damn, Tony don't ya' ever get tired of chasin' ass?"

Tony grabbed his beloved penis and responded.

"I'm twenty years old with a big dick and plenty of money. What else should I be doing?"

His comment brought laughter from his friends.

"I guess you got a point!"

His friends said in unison. They decided that they wanted to hang out together; the last thing to be decided was the venue.

The four shared a good laugh but as soon as the laughter died down the serious business of where to go came up. Ace was the first to chime in on where he did not want to go.

"I ain't goin' to the Disco Fever or the Rooftop, too many kids, too much gun play!"

Saladin warmed to the idea of hanging out with the fellas, and he had his own idea of where they could chill.

"I'd much rather go to a Knick game."

His suggestion was met with the approval of all. Saladin took a second as if he just remembered something important.

"First let me check in with Sunshine before I get ahead of myself."

Saladin announced. He was not the least bit ashamed of having to check in at home.

Tony produced his new smaller cell phone and offered it to Saladin.

"Here it's O.K. if you call Sunshine and ask permission on my phone."

Tony, Bosco and Ace began to chuckle at their boy being whipped.

"That's alright Tony; I'll use the pay phone on the corner."

Saladin listened to Ace laughing loud and hearty which made Saladin want to pull Ace's card on asking permission of Angelika for him to hang.

"What cha' laughin' 'bout Ace? In the end I'm gonna' do what I want. Will you?"

Saladin said with a smile.

He waited for a stunned Ace to answer back, but all Ace could muster was some stuttering.

"That's right I have to take care of home first gentlemen."

Saladin said then leapt off of his stool and walked out of the room. Bosco found Ace's getting played very amusing.

"Oh, shit Tony Dick! Tell me Saladin didn't go there!"

Bosco was laughing hysterically, so much that he began to choke.

Bosco got out of his chair to exchange 'high fives' with an equally hysterical Tony. The two men continued to laugh in spite of the angry look that slowly developed on Ace's face. In between laughing and choking Tony managed to muster his own challenge to Ace's manhood.

"Watcha gonna do Ace! Box or throw Rocks?"

Tony and Bosco waited patiently for an answer from Ace but there was only silence. The silence remained until Saladin returned to the room.

"Let's bounce!"

Saladin announced from the doorway. Tony picked up his jacket from the back of his chair to follow behind Saladin. Bosco pushed out from the table, stood up to follow Tony out of the room. Bosco stopped at the door and gave Ace one last chance to follow and motioned for Ace to join them. He turned and walked out of the room hoping that Ace would follow.

Outside Kelly's, Bosco walked up along side his two friends who were busy eyeing a group of well-built young girls that sauntered past them.

"Gotdamn, dat one in the yellow shorts got a phat ass!"

Tony said as he described the shape of the young woman's rear with his hands.

"Do you remember girls lookin' like dat' when we wuz young?"

Saladin said to Bosco in disbelief at how young girls had such grown woman's bodies.

"It's gotta be the milk!"

Bosco responded. Tony who had gone comatose looking at the young girls, did not notice Ace standing directly behind him.

"They ain't old enough for you Tony Dick. They got pubic hairs!"

Ace said. Tony and Saladin turned around in surprise that Ace was standing along side them. Neither man believed Ace would go against the strong willed Angelika. Bosco smiled; as he was glad to see the faith he held in his old friend was warranted.

Tony was not content just to look at the girls; he wanted to get with one of them.

"Yo' Honey in the yellow slow down!"

He yelled down the street at the young girl. She stopped walking and Tony darted down the street after her. Bosco was paying close attention to Tony so it took some time before he smelled cigarette smoke. He quickly realized that Saladin was the source of the smoke.

"I thought you stopped smoking a long time ago?"

Bosco quizzed.

"You know he only smokes when he is stressed Bosco!"

Ace quipped. Saladin took one long inhale of his cigarette then tossed the half smoked cigarette down to the ground.

"You two sure know how to mess a good vice!"

Saladin complained as he crushed the lit cigarette into the dirty pavement.

"Whatcha' gotta' be stressed about Saladin?"

Ace asked of his friend.

"A whole lot of drama."

Saladin stated as he headed for his car. On the way to his car a pair of female hands covering his eyes surprised Saladin.

"Guess who?"

A female voice questioned. Saladin detected a hint of Calvin Klein perfume on the female's hands. The perfume only heightened his curiosity and being the one to play guessing games Saladin moved to ascertain the identity of the female. Saladin grabbed the female by the wrists then maneuvered his body until he was face to face with Shanita, the cashier from Kelly's. Saladin took one look at the super fine young lady and instantly undressed her with his X-ray eyes.

Shanita was a 19 year old who had a body that rivaled Serena Williams and a face that would give Halle Berry a run for the money. The young girl had been putting amateurish moves on Saladin for two of the three weeks she worked at Kelly's as a cashier, however Saladin paid her no never mind. Shanita had upped her game as well as her wardrobe enough to make Saladin pay attention. She wore a black spaghetti strapped dress that barely covered her finer points. The dress clung close enough to her body that Saladin found it difficult to take his eyes off the blunt end of her mammary glands.

"You like my outfit?"

Shanita said as she twirled around in order for Saladin to get an even better look at her banging body.

The young temptress knew the answer to her question before the words entered his thoughts. Bosco and Ace watched silently as Shanita worked her mojo on Saladin. Ace and Bosco both knew that someone as fine as Shanita pushing up on Saladin could only mean trouble for their partner. Bosco had a funny way to show Saladin that he should not mess with the fine looking dark-skinned honey.

Bosco went into Saladin's pocket to retrieve a pack of cigarettes and matches. Bosco then presented them to Saladin who did not notice Bosco holding his matches and smokes in front of his face. Saladin interrupted his conversation when he saw Bosco hold a cigarette and lighted match before his face.

"What the hell is you doing Bosco?"

He then snatched his belongings from Bosco and put them in his jacket pocket.

"Thought you were stressed Saladin!"

Bosco said with a devious smile as he gave Ace a pound for a good serious joke played on Saladin. The joke was funny enough and he could not keep a straight face. Saladin decided to have Shanita walk with him towards his car instead of having more jokes played on them. Saladin's departure gave Ace and Bosco the chance to rediscover their lost friendship.

CHAPTER 12

There Were Two

Like a boomerang that returned when tossed away, Bosco's and Ace's once tight relationship had come full circle. If either man wanted to mend their tattered fences the time to act was at hand. Bosco and Ace both wondered who would be the first to introduce the reasons for their split. Neither man spoke a word of significance until they found common ground in the weather, as a strong breeze appeared from out of the night air, which caused both men to comment on the chilly wind.

"Damn, Ace it got chilly out here all of a sudden!"

Bosco stated as he shook his entire body to force the chill out of his bones.

Ace shook his head in agreement with Bosco.

"Maybe we need to find ourselves two hotties like Tony and Saladin!"

Ace had to jump up and down to warm his body.

"I keep tellin' Saladin 'bout fuckin' wit' low life bitches. Sunshine ain't the type of woman he should fuck wit'."

Bosco was about to continue when saw a police cruiser passing down the avenue, which caused him to lose his train of thought. Ace watched the same police car pass but he was able to belt out a critique of Tony.

"Tony is gonna' fuck around with the wrong chick and catch the monster!" (AIDS) Ace said as he waited for the police car to disappear from sight before he continued to speak. Ace found it hypocritical for him to speak on Tony and Saladin and not address his rift with Bosco. He turned to face Bosco to ask the question he desperately wanted answered.

"What da' fuck is goin' on between you, me and Angelika?"

The question caught Bosco by surprise.

He knew the question was coming; however it still surprised him. Bosco had often rehearsed how he would answer the question, but when the first shot is fired, the best plans fall apart. Bosco lost his practiced speech, but somehow he found the ability to speak from the heart.

"Your girl happened Ace!"

Bosco said as he watched a new Mercedes zoom down the avenue.

"What did she do Bosco?"

Ace asked as he waited for his answer. Bosco sensed the tension that was growing in Ace, therefore he had to be mindful of his words.

"You've changed, since you hooked up with Angelika."

He made sure to speak in a soft voice so as to not turn their conversation into another shouting match. Ace let out a huge sigh of relief and pressed on with the conversation.

"I am the same person I wuz when I met her Bosco!"

Ace protested. Bosco finally turned to look Ace in the eye to see that Ace did not have a clue to his metamorphosis. His father warned him against being the guiding light to a blind person. If Ace did not know Bosco was not going to tell him.

Bosco did want to bring to light the fact that Angelika drove a wedge between them in high school. He would neither inform Ace that Angelika was a controlling and manipulating person who had several skeletons in her vast closet. Bosco heard his words and knew that Ace could only take his beef with Angelika the wrong way. Bosco denied ever sleeping with Angelika.

"She turned you into some sort of Frankenstein."

He quickly added.

Bosco saw the expression on Ace's face, which meant that Ace did not understand what Bosco was trying to say. Bosco took a minute to put his words into a vernacular that Ace could understand.

"She turned you into some money hungry cat who would sell his friend out for a dollar!"

Ace continued to have the same strange look on his face as when Bosco started to explain his thoughts. Ace looked straight into Bosco's eyes and stated flatly.

"I was da one that turned Angelika onto the finer things in life, not vice versa Bosco! I thought you knew my steelo by now!"

Ace then patted a stunned Bosco on the back. The two men then began to reflect on their long history to find instances of Ace's greed. In the middle of their conversation both men saw that the same police car that passed them earlier had circled around and was headed up the avenue towards them. Ace and Bosco watched as the patrol car joined up with an unmarked car at the corner. The unmarked car had made a car stop of a jeep filled with kids at the other corner. Bosco thought the detectives in the unmarked car resembled Brown and Johnson.

"I hope those young boyz don't do nothing stupid!"

Bosco said. No sooner that the words came out of his mouth one of the young men threw a punch at one of the detectives. An all out fight between the cops and the young boys developed. Just as the incident began, Saladin pulled up with Tony in Sunshine's brand new discrete Honda Accord. Saladin motioned for the two men to quickly enter the car, before the avenue became overrun with the boys in blue. Bosco and Ace jumped into the backseat with the understanding that they had taken the first step at repairing their relationship.

CHAPTER 13

Show Me The Honey

During the late 80's and early 90's the hardest sports ticket in town to get was to a Knicks game. One had to either have hook-up money or both! Neither man had a hook-up but fortunately for them they had plenty of money to spend. Ace located a scalper who was eager to do business with the dapper street dressed young men. The unscrupulous scalper charged fifty dollars per ticket instead of the thirty-dollar face value. It was obvious they knew that they were getting jerked (Bosco protested until the very end.) but the last two Knicks versus Pacers games had been one for the ages. The decision to fork over the money for the tickets proved to be monumental.

The game was an instant classic. The two teams exchanged leads several times in the last five minutes of the game before Larry Johnson saved the day for the Knicks. Larry Johnson stole the basketball from Antonio Davis of the Pacers in the frontcourt, and finished the play with a game winning lay-up. The excitement of the game ending play did not end once the four men exited the "World's Most Famous Arena." The energy they felt was carried out into the streets.

The four friends stood outside the Garden on 33rd Street and 8th Avenue, they all felt that the evening should not conclude with the end of the game. Tony was the first to express his thoughts on what he and his friends should do with the rest of their evening.

"I'm not ready to go home. Let's go clubbin"!"

Ace objected because he did not want to chill at the Disco Fever nor The Roof Top. The two clubs was all he knew.

"Too much shooting and the bitches is wack!"

Ace protested.

"We already know Ace!"

Tony responded while he took a look at a fine light-skinned honey that happened to stroll by.

"That's why we should head to the Paradise Garage down in the Village! The music is different and the women are more sophisticated than them chicken-head broads uptown!"

"Ain't that a Gay club?"

Bosco asked.

"Gay night was last night!"

Tony said in a matter of fact voice. His friends were hesitant to head to Greenwich Village, because of the lifestyle of those who frequented the area called Greenwich Village.

The lifestyles of those who called "The Village" home were different from any other neighborhood in New York City. Gays had called the Village home since the mid 1800's and everyone who lived there led a more carefree existence. All Saladin, Ace and Bosco knew of The Village was that gays and lesbians lived there. Dancing in a place frequented by those people brought about homophobic thoughts to each of their minds. Once inside the hollowed halls of the Paradise Garage the three skeptics quickly learned why Tony secretly frequented the club.

Inside the Garage house music that boomed from he speakers took immediate hold on Saladin, however he did not want to let the others know he was enjoying himself. Tony led his boys through the crowd to an area in the back by the punch bowl (There was no alcohol sold at the Garage.) where the only seats in the place were located. All four men sat on a long couch as they watched throngs of women parade about. Tony did not sit long. He spotted a fine woman and her friend standing nearby and coerced Bosco to have his back. The conversation quickly turned into a trip to the dance floor for Bosco and Tony. Ace soon followed his friends to the dance floor leaving Saladin alone. He wanted to first soak in more of the atmosphere before he was comfortable enough to get on the dance floor.

The thump of the bass and rhythmic beats of the house music eventually forced Saladin to try to get the club dance steps just right. He took the hand of a pretty honey and led her to the dance floor near where his friends danced. Neither of the four's dancing could have had them confused with Garage regulars, each man had a hard time remembering to move to the tempo and not the beat.

Around three in the morning Saladin, Bosco, Tony and Ace each left the club with a new found female friend. They were headed for Saladin's mid-town apartment where the feeling was mutual that a real party would start.

Saladin used the apartment as a getaway from Sunshine and a place to get away from the world. Mostly he used the $1,500 per month apartment as a place to swing his episodes with his chick of the day. There were blunts of ses for all as well as Magnums of Moet to chase down the fast food they were able to find that early in the morning. By the time most of the drink and weed was finished, the mood was primed for the event to go to the next level.

Saladin had a thing for music, and he made sure that his sound system in his apartment was on the cutting edge. His living room was filled with the sounds of Hip Hop blasting from his expensive Bose Speakers. Julie, the girl that Saladin intended on sexing that night grew tired of all the Hip Hop Saladin forced them to listen to, so she decided that there should be a musical change. Julie stumbled over to the CD rack located next to the system. She sifted through the CD's until she found something more to her liking. Julie abruptly stopped the disc in the player much to the dismay of everyone in the room.

"Girl, why're you stoppin' the flow?"

Saladin said in a slurred voice.

"I tired of listening to Hip Hop! I want something that will make me move!"

Julie responded in her natural Jamaican accent.

As the young woman pushed play, the sweet sounds of Reggae music boomed out of the speakers. The men intently watched as Julie wined her body as if her life depended on making the men in the room horny! Julie did such a good job dancing that Saladin lost most of his high trying to imagine how it would be to bone Julie.

After watching Julie dance for several minutes Saladin began to foam at the mouth and at the head. He was happy when she motioned for him to join her. Saladin hesitated for a moment but when Julie "Hit the Dollar" several times he nearly tripped over Tony and his girl who were seated on the floor. The moment Saladin joined Julie they were joined by the three other couples grinding to the Reggae beat. Tony danced, but sex was deeply on his one track mine.

By the time the third song came over the stereo Tony was more than ready for action. Just as he was about to lead his girl into one of the two bedrooms Tony heard the sound of one room door slammed followed by another door. Saladin and Bosco already thought of the idea and beat Tony to the punch. Tony looked over towards the couch where Ace and his companion were in the middle of a strong kiss. The sight of Ace getting face made the thought of doing the same thing possible.

Tony settled down to the couch with his girl and found his lips on the young woman's neck. He had given up on getting any real action until the young girl reacted to his kiss on her neck.

"Don't cheat me! Give it all to me!"

She moaned. Tony looked over towards Ace who was by that time having his knob polished by his girl. Whatever inhibition Tony had about fucking in the presence of another man left him the instant the young lady held his tube stake in her hand.

"This is why I make big money!"

Tony said as he watched the young lady unzip his fly.

CHAPTER 14

Seek and Destroy

The morning festivities ended rather abruptly for Julie and Saladin. Their intense fuck session ended the moment Saladin realized that he might not make it home before sunrise. Making it home before the sunrise would serve as a type of moral victory for the player. Saladin and Julie both knew the extent of their relationship would be a one night thing, besides both of them had someone waiting for them at home, therefore getting home was a major concern.

Saladin left his apartment with Julie in tow after he rudely barged in on Bosco and his acquaintance Penelope to leave his apartment keys with Bosco. Saladin's last look into his living room left him with the sight of Tony having sex with two women on his floor, while Ace stood on the terrace looking out over Central Park smoking a joint.

Saladin wasted no time heading for the highway and his home upstate once he dropped Julie off three blocks from her apartment. All the tough man could think about were the curse words that would be directed at him by Sunshine concerning his night out without calling home. Saladin checked his watched and quickly calculated that he had to shave time off his hour drive home. The nervous man put his foot near the floor and zoomed up the Major Deagan Expressway towards home. Saladin had a feeling of fear in his gut. He knew the source was not Sunshine, but something that stood between where he was and where he was going that was dangerous. His fears would be revealed just short of home.

Saladin alternated glancing at the speedometer, (which read 95MPH), his rearview mirror, and the road in front of him as he sped down the near empty highway towards home. Saladin was extremely proud of the fact that he had not received any type of driving ticket in the last year and he wanted to make sure his streak would not end with him driving like a bat out of hell. Three miles from home Saladin eased off the gas and brought his vehicle near the speed limit. Confident that he was going to make it home before the sun would begin its journey across the horizon Saladin sat back in his seat and tried to relax, however that feeling of something being wrong did not fade away.

He checked the speedometer once again, to see that he was doing 70MPH and then peered at his rearview mirror. Through his rearview mirror Saladin noticed a set of headlights closing in on him like a rocket. Two headlights quickly turned into one as the car closed to within two car lengths. Saladin's heart nearly dropped when he noticed a blue flashing light from inside the front windshield. Saladin pulled his car over to the side of the shoulder of the road and began to wonder why he had been stopped.

Saladin shut off the ignition, reached into his glove compartment to retrieve his license and registration. The instant he opened the glove compartment a dime bag of weed fell out onto the passenger's seat. He plucked up the dime bag and popped his head up to look in his rearview mirror. There was no movement from the car that had pulled up behind him on the shoulder of the road. The lack of movement gave Saladin the opportunity to think of a way to hide the weed. Saladin found what he thought was a good place to hide the weed and looked once again into the rearview mirror to see that two Caucasian men exited the vehicle via either front door.

The two Caucasian men did not have the look of local law enforcement. Each man's style of dress was too uniformed to be NYPD. Their dark suits and white dress shirts gave the two the appearance of out of town folk.

"Fucking Feds"

Saladin said aloud as soon as he realized who approached his car.

As the two men approached Saladin noticed that two more men had exited from the back of the unmarked police car. Saladin immediately recognized the person exiting from behind the driver as Detective Brown. The second man who exited the rear had to be Johnson Saladin's heart began to pound for he was not being pulled over for a simple traffic ticket; he was being pulled over for something more sinister. Saladin wiped the sweat from his brow and tried his best to remain calm. He reacted to the tap on his car window by rolling it down slowly.

"Step out the car please!"

One of the Caucasian men demanded the second Saladin lowered his window.
"What did I do wrong?"
Saladin asked the obvious question.
His question was met by silence. It was at that point that he noticed the man speaking to him had drawn his gun and had it by his side. Saladin cautiously opened the car door and made sure both his hands were visible to all.
"Put your hands behind your head please!"
The Caucasian man said in an annoyed voice. Saladin complied with the man's requests and assumed the position.
Saladin watched as the other Caucasian man opened the passenger door and proceeded to search the interior of his car. The first Caucasian man searched Saladin and announced that Saladin was clean, just, as did the one who searched his car. Brown and Johnson stood motionless at the rear of the car, until the man who searched his car tossed them Saladin's car keys to search the trunk.
"Whenever you finish breaking the sixth amendment could you tell me what the hell this is about?"
Saladin said in a matter-of-fact voice. His question went unanswered. Then he heard:
"It's clear here too!"
Brown and Johnson declared in stereo.
Saladin then heard his trunk slammed shut. The four men had not found what they were searching for which made Saladin wonder why he was pulled over.
The Caucasian man completed his pat down of Saladin. He forcibly turned Saladin around then identified himself as Agent Powell, and his partner as Agent Fitzroy of the Drug Enforcement Agency. Saladin remained cool on the outside but he was becoming very nervous on the inside. Saladin assumed if the DEA knew his name then they must be close to pressing charges against him. Saladin thought to himself. He continued to hold his poker face as he thought of the ways the men could have found him on the Expressway on his way home alone! Agent Powell didn't identify Johnson or Brown. The two men were an after thought. Saladin did not know it at the time but Johnson and Brown had been promoted to Detectives. They were very proud of their upward move and their lack of an introduction rubbed the men the wrong way.
"Oh, so we don't rate an intro'?"
Brown said of his and Johnson's apparent diss.
"I guess what Fitzroy meant to say was that we don't *need no stinkin' introduction*!"

Johnson joked in a serious tone of voice.

Saladin picked up on the tension and filed it away for future reference.

"You were traveling at a pretty high speed Mr. Keith. Why were you in such a hurry?"

Fitzroy said as he motioned for Saladin to put down his hands.

"What the delay, yo'? This ain't 'bout no speeding ticket."

Saladin stated.

"No it is not!"

Agent Fitzroy calmly responded.

"Don't go anywhere Mr. Keith."

Fitzroy announced.

He motioned for his associates to meet him at the rear of Saladin's car. The nervous man could feel the bag a weed that he hid between his frank and his beans slip down his pant leg and to the ground. He was able to covertly kick the dime bag underneath his car without anyone noticing. Since he had avoided disaster Saladin turned his full attention to the conversation that took place just a few feet away.

Saladin strained to read the lips of the men; however they made sure to cover their mouths with their hands as each man spoke. Saladin gave up on lip reading in the dark and turned his attention to his location. He had not realized how isolated he was and that his four antagonists could claim that he did "Whatever" in order to arrest him. The fact that he was on the shoulder of Interstate 278 with the only witnesses speeding past at 80MPH left Saladin with a chill. He stood silently listening to all the sounds of a new day beginning. He was smart enough to understand that he must play the situation out by ear. The four men abruptly ended their conversation and headed towards Saladin who was ready for the worst that could happen.

"I have a problem and I think you can help me with the answer Saladin."

Fitzroy said as if he already knew Saladin's answer, but was going to ask the question anyway.

"I want to know how you live as well as you do when you have no job."

Agent Fitzroy said in a stern voice. Saladin did not hesitate with his answer.

"My father left me two candy stores and a phat insurance policy."

As he responded he looked at Brown and Johnson with malice in his heart, for he believed they put the DEA onto him. Saladin's answer forced Agent Powell to break his silence. Agent Powell decided to cut through the bullshit and get straight to the heart of the matter.

"We know you are a drug dealer, admit that fact!"

Agent Powell did not attempt to hide behind diplomacy like his partners. His hatred for drug dealers and everything they represented prevented him from pulling any punches. Saladin felt the anger and wasted very little time responding in kind.

"I'm not an ignorant nigger! I know my rights! I am not gonna' volunteer nuttin'!"

Saladin responded with enough anger to match that of Agent Powell. Detective Brown disliked the attitude of his DEA counterpart, however he hated Saladin's smug attitude more. Brown remembered their earlier run-in and he wanted a measure of revenge.

Detective Brown, always the one for smart remarks decided to push Saladin's buttons.

"You heard the young man gentlemen. He knows his right under the Constitution of these United States."

Detective Brown said in perfect Harvard ESE. He paused as a car zoomed pass their position doing close to one hundred miles an hour. When the car vanished around a bend in the road Detective Brown continued in his attempt to make Saladin angry. Detective Johnson knew what his partner was up to and he did not want to be left out of the fray therefore he jumped into the game.

"I guess you also heard that his daddy Spanish Ramon left him tons of money."

Johnson did not want to be left out of the fun of messing with Saladin, corrected his partner's intentional mistake.

"No partner, Spanish Ramon, the big time number runner, off the east side was his mother's second husband. Her first husband, his father (Johnson pointed at Saladin) was Dapper Stan Gaston."

The two detectives paused to set up their punch line, which they hoped would push Saladin to react.

"No, that is not right. I distinctly know there was an Italian man in the story somewhere."

Johnson laughed.

"Damn Saladin yo' mamma sure got around!"

Johnson and Brown said in unison.

Their game was cruel, but somewhat effective. Saladin wanted to beat the shit out of the two men for making fun of his mother however; a little voice spoke loudly in his ear to "Stay out of the trap." Saladin managed not to raise his fist but his blood pressure went through the roof. Saladin's self control lasted all but twenty seconds. He was set to answer the dis of the detectives with his usual deadpan manner when Agent's Powell and Fitzroy took control of the situation.

In tandem the two DEA agents peppered Saladin with a series of questions on his knowledge of certain individual drug dealers in New York City. It made no sense for him to deny ever hearing of the names therefore he played along with the game but he made sure not to tell the police more than they already knew. The more questions that were asked of him the more Saladin began to wonder how the law had accumulated as much information on half the people in the business. He began to wonder how much information did the law have about his role in the business, and when would they hit him in the head with it? After several minutes, the two Agents excused themselves and called another meeting with Brown and Johnson at the rear of Saladin's car. From his vantage point Saladin could tell that the four men were at odds over something. It did not take all of Saladin's brainpower to understand the topic of their disagreement. Several moments passed before the four men returned to him with some very interesting news.

Agent Fitzroy walked over to Saladin and returned his license and registration to him.

"Get the fuck outta' here!"

Agent Fitzroy said in the plainest voice possible.

Saladin was stunned that he was being allowed to leave. Saladin took possession of his license and registration and slowly opened the door to his car. He moved in slow motion as if at any moment Fitzroy would realize he had made a mistake in letting him go free. Saladin quickly entered his car and sped off before there was a change of mind. As Saladin made his way down the expressway the sky began to turn a light shade of blue. The sun was on its way and he still had a chance to achieve his moral victory and be in bed before the sun shined bright in the heavens.

He put his key into the door and the magnitude of being stopped by the law suddenly hit him like a ton of bricks. The only logical conclusion Saladin could draw was that the agents really did not know how big a player he was in the business. Saladin was happy not to be in the hands of the law but he soon found that he was batting 500, because when he opened the door his family was not home. He walked over to the nightstand by the door and found a note, which he quickly read.

"We went to visit my Aunt in Brooklyn.

I will be home late in the evening."

Love Sunshine.

Saladin placed the note back onto the nightstand. He laughed at the irony of his needless mad dash home. His laughter ceased when he once again realized he might be in the crosshairs of the law. Saladin placed his hand on his forehead as he reflected back on his narrow escape and noticed that his hands held a strong aroma of sex. He laughed cynically as he realized how lucky he was Sunshine was not at home.

The four peace officers waited until Saladin drove away before they got back into their car. Once inside the car a heated discussion took place between The DEA Agents and the Detectives over letting Saladin go free. The DEA agents had a timeline to follow that was etched in stone.

"We only have a few months to produce a solid case on a major player Johnson."

Fitzroy said from the driver's seat. He had to turn around to look straight at an angry Johnson.

"We need a big fish to keep this task force operational."

He concluded.

"We, Brown and I work the streets everyday we do not have a time limit. That kid we just let go is a big fish in a very small pond."

Johnson said as he lit a cigarette to help calm his nerves. Agent Powell disagreed and voiced his thoughts to Johnson. Powell turned around in his seat to look a disgruntled Johnson in the face while he spoke.

"We stopped ten guys in the same fashion as we did this Saladin tonight. Not one of them mentioned his name."

Powell asserted. Brown had a quick response.

"Just because you can't see it don't mean it ain't there!"

Powell continued on as if Brown had said nothing.

"All of the drug dealers I have dealt with show their wealth, they don't drive inexpensive cars and were clothes from bargain department stores."

Powell spoke as if his was the definitive word on the subject. Both Johnson and Brown shook their heads in disagreement with Powell's generalization. Fitzroy backed up his partner's comments when he said,

"We want big fish like Cassius or Fat Nat Coles! Those guys we know about. We have time to get guys like Saladin."

He said in a matter of fact voice. Brown looked at Powell and spoke in his matter of fact voice.

"Didn't your mama tell you to never judge a book by its cover?"

Brown said in disgust. He took a cigar from his jacket but in his anger he broke it in half before he was able to light the fake Cuban.

"I'm not gonna' argue wit' you Feds. You're in charge; we are just along for the ride."

Brown sat back in his seat and did not utter another word. All he could think about on the way back to the city was why did they let Saladin get away.

CHAPTER 15

In your Mother's Eyes

Tony emerged from Saladin's apartment building around 11:00am, very tired and very, very satiated! The weary man had to shield his eyes from the dust that the morning winds were kicking up. His efforts failed to prevent specs of dust from logging in his eyes. Tony had to stop walking to rub the dirt from his blood shot eyes. He completed his task and opened his eyes to find a Brunette woman walking in his direction. The young woman gave Tony a strange look as they passed each other by on the street. It was as is she wondered what he was doing on Ritzy Park Avenue early in the morning. Tony managed to give the infamous yet effective "Black Man Stare" to the young woman. The young woman tucked her Gucci purse under her arm and scurried away from Tony as quickly as humanly possible. He was tickled enough by his prank that he turned around to stare her down once again before he continued to walk towards a cab. The woman nearly broke out into a full sprint.

As he made his way down lush Park Avenue in search of a cab ride home, a buxom blonde walked passed him going in the opposite direction. He watched as two white men who walked just ahead of him nearly broke their necks trying to get a look at the long-legged blonde. The two men were enamored with things Tony never thought of as being beauty traits. He was more concerned with ass than the colour of a woman's hair or the length of her legs. The blonde was nothing like the two women he had just left sleeping on Saladin's couch. His mother had always told him "Beauty is what you make it!"

The white men had chosen something that was contrary to the choice of most black men. Tony arrived at the corner and stuck out his hand to hail a passing yellow cab. He was sure that only women of colour could be attractive to him.

Tony resembled a statue, as his arm remained extended while several cabs passed by without stopping. Just as Tony was about to give up on catching a cab, one finally pulled up in front of him. He noticed that the driver of the cab was of the Negroid persuasion. Tony opened the door to the cab to plop down on the tattered leather seat and announced his destination.

"Take me to 118th Street and Bradhurst Avenue!"

The driver sped away from the curb even before Tony had finished giving him directions.

New York City cab drivers are famous for their aggressive driving skills, their talkative nature as well as the fact that they infrequently picked up minority fares. Tony's cabbie made sure he continued the tradition of the latter. All of that did not matter to Tony because he wanted nothing more than to get to his mother's apartment. He had not seen his mother in two days, which was too long for either of them. The driver could tell that his passenger was tired but he was also tired of the absence of any real conversation therefore he talked for the sake of talking.

"You know I usually don't take people to Harlem from this part of town! You looked safe enough to have in the back of my cab!"

The man spoke in a thick Caribbean accent.

The accent made it difficult for Tony to understand what the cabbie said. The cabby's voice quickly blended into the rest of the inaudible sounds of the city.

"I love my people but they are some thievin' folk."

The man continued.

The statement was meant to get Tony involved in a conversation with the cabbie; however, Tony chose to just listen. The cabbie continued on without any input from a disinterested Tony.

"Black on Black crime is what the white man can use to keep our people down. We should not be afraid of one another."

The cabbie spoke in a very serious tone. The words and the tone of voice finally got Tony to respond.

"You sound like the father in the movie "Boyz In Da' Hood!"

Tony responded.

"Whatcha' say?"

The cabbie asked, not sure of Tony's words.

"You said boys in the nude?"

Tony had to chuckle before he filled the cabbie in on his misunderstood sentence.

The cab swerved in and out of traffic and after reaching a red light the cabbie turned around to look at Tony face-to-face as he responded as he realized what Tony said.

"If you've seen one of those movies you've seen 'em all. None of dem is close to real life!"

The light turned green and the cabbie immediately honked its horn to clear the road ahead of slow drivers. The cabbie turned to face Tony again, stepped on the accelerator, which sent Tony crashing back into his seat. The cabbie continued on with his conversation where he left off.

"I ain't seen that movie, but my youngest son Glenn Ford, like the actor, dragged me to see that movie "New Jack City." The movie made New York City look as lawless as some third world countries!"

The cabbie stopped the coversation as he dipped between a city bus and a delivery truck, once he was clear he continued.

"The worst problem that the city faces today is drugs. Get rid of the drugs and most of the problems disappear!"

The cabbie spoke as if he just gave the definitive answer to all the city's woes. The man paused again as he had to avoid another city bus that almost cut into his path.

"We are shootin' one another for the right to sell that stuff to make the white man rich!"

The cabbie reached the apex of his thoughts and returned his full concentration to the road ahead. Tony was not thinking about sleep or sex anymore. His interest had been sparked by the mentioning of his profession as the major source of trouble for the city. The cabbie made several points that Tony felt he had to address.

"The point you trying to make is that working for the minimum wage is betta' than doin' what ya' hafta' do to get enough money to get out of the ghetto?"

Tony said and he managed to sit on the edge of the rear seat as to get closer to the safety partition that separated the driver from his passenger.

He was able to read the driver's identification card that by law must be present in the cab. Tony took a long look at the driver and summarized that Radcliff Livingstone looked much older in person than he did in the picture. Tony then waited for Mr. Livingstone's response.

"That is the standard cop out young man! Ain't anybody saying a person has to work at McDonalds all their life, but there is a lesson to be had from an honest days work!"

The cabbie made eye contact with Tony through the rearview mirror, and watched as Tony shook his head vigorously in the negative.

"How many hours a day do you work?"

Tony quizzed. Mr. Livingstone waited until he arrived at the next red light before he answered the question posed by his passenger.

"I work sixteen hours per day!"

"While you are working sixteen hour days, someone is getting rich off your hard work!"

"But I don't hafta' look over my shoulder young man."

"During the day you deal with cops, crazy passengers, and dumb ass motorists."

"Stress is part of life young man. It's a matter of how you deal with the stress."

"If you had the chance to trade the stress of driving a cab for the stress of Wall Street which would you choose?"

"That's a no-brainer young man. Wall Street of course!"

"That is my point exactly. People will follow the money."

Tony said. The light turned green and the driver sped away from the intersection. Tony and the cabbie switched roles from that moment. Tony talked while the cabbie listened.

The cab screeched to a halt in front of the Bradhurst address Tony had given the cabbie just twenty minutes earlier. The cabbie announced the cost of the ride, Tony reached into his small change pocket pulled out a twenty dollar bill, presented the bill to the cabbie and exited the cab without his change.

Tony leapt out of the cab and literally landed on the already crowded stoop of his former building.

"Hey Missus Martin. How is your leg doin' Miss Mary?"

Tony asked in rapid succession of the two elderly women who from sun up to sun down made the stoop their living rooms.

Tony did not bother to wait for a response because he had heard the response many times in the past. He then pushed open the front door to the building and jumped the three stairs of the vestibule. Tony never thought of using his key to the second door, there wasn't any need to use a key. He simply pushed opened the supposedly locked door and swiftly walked into the lobby of the building. Tony passed one of the mirrors that lined the walls of the lobby. He took a look at himself in the mirror as he often did as a child. After checking out his appearance Tony made his way to the stairs, the elevator was out of order for the third straight month.

"Mutha' fucking dump!"

Tony yelled as he began to ascend the stairs.

Tony reached the fourth floor landing completely out of breath. He had to pause on the landing to catch his breath before making his way to the sixth floor. As he paused Tony began to question why he continued to return to the building. The question remained with him as he opened the door to his mother's four-bedroom apartment. The question quickly left his mind as soon as he discovered his older brother Marvin's girlfriend on the other side of the door. Deandra stood in front of the door dressed in panties, and a bathrobe that was open. Deandra looked Tony straight in the eyes as she slowly closed her robe and disappeared into the kitchen. The sight of seeing a bare chest Deandra did nothing for Tony for he did not want to go back to the future. He just shook his head and headed towards his old room.

Tony emerged from his old bedroom by early evening well rested and ready for the world. Tony could hear the sounds of singing coming from the kitchen. His nose also detected the wonderful smells of Sunday dinner being cooked. Tony followed both his ears and nose towards the source of the sweet music and sweeter smells to the kitchen. There was only one person who could captivate his nose and ears and that was his mother.

"Hey baby, I thought you were here!"

Tony's mother spoke with the giddiness of a brand new mother. She stopped preparing dinner to grab her baby boy by the back of his bald head, pulled his head down in order to plant a wet kiss on Tony's forehead. The kiss made Tony feel as if he were back in grade school again.

"Mama, stop with your wet kisses!"

Tony joked as he half-heartedly attempted to fight off his mother's kiss.

"You'll always be my baby. No matta' how old or how big you get!"

His mother said as she planted yet another kiss on her son's soggy forehead.

The light moment continued for sometime until his mother returned to the serious business of getting dinner ready. Tony stood silently while his mother worked hard preparing dinner. His thoughts turned from wet kisses and food to the question of his family's safety. He had to press the issue once more no matter how angry the subject would make her. The young man got comfortable as he zipped down his sweat suit jacket and posed the question once more to his mother. His mother shook off the question by remaining silent as she looked for a kind way to express her feelings.

"Baby, you know were I stand on the subject and you know I won't change."

His mother noticed Deandra had entered the Kitchen.

"Deandra honey, would you pass me the paprika?"

His mother asked Deandra who entered the kitchen still dressed in her bathrobe.

Tony watched his mother sprinkle Paprika on the potato salad that she was preparing for dinner. After seasoning her potato salad Tony's mother turned the conversation 360 Degrees.

"When are ya' coming to church Tony?"

She asked. Her question was met with silence, which meant that he had no adequate answer. Tony did not let his lack of a good answer stop him from getting his point of view across to her.

"Mama, I'm talkin' 'bout your safety!"

"That is the same thing I am taking about Tony."

"Mama, we've been over this topic so many times!"

"I think we have an echo in this house Tony!"

"Mama, this building ain't ever been safe!"

The conversation was at an impasse and neither side was going to back down from their argument. Just when Tony thought the silence would go on forever, his wise mother broke the silence with her prophetic.

"I feel that if I take more money than I need from you I'd only be encouraging you to keep doing what you do!"

Tony listened but he did not give up on moving his mother out of the dangerous building. He waited to find the solution to his dilemma and he found it in a word he did not often use, compromise!

"What if I gave you money to buy a Co-op here in the city, like Riverbend or Espinande Gardens? Would you still be against my helping you move?"

Tony asked.

He looked over his shoulder to see Deandra staring him right in his mouth as he spoke. He motioned for Deandra to leave the kitchen. Deandra took the hint and left Tony and his mother alone to finish their conversation.

"I know you are worried about Raymond adjusting to a new house but, this place ain't safe anymore, Mama."

Tony looked over his shoulder after he finished speaking to make sure that Deandra did leave them alone. Tony's mother stopped preparing her dinner to turn and face him. Tony saw a new look in her eyes, a look that let him know that he had finally worn her down enough that she was thinking about leaving the old neighborhood.

"If you come with me to church next Sunday then I'll think about moving son!"

"Sure I'll go wit' ya', next week!"

Tony responded.

He wanted his mother to move out of the hood badly enough that he would endure church for one afternoon. The conversation about moving and church ended when Michael, Tony's older brother entered the kitchen. As far as the world was concerned, Michael was the good son in spite of being twenty-five years old and having no thought of moving into his own place even thought he could afford to move.

"What up little brother?"

Michael said as he palmed his brother's head.

"I like the look. I can see what you are thinkin'"

Michael joked.

He pushed Tony aside to plant a quick kiss on his mother's cheek.

"I can't stay for dinner Ma. I'm going over to Vincent's house before I go to work!"

Tony then rushed out of the apartment with a great deal of haste. Tony saw the hurt in his mother's eyes. Michael had always been selfish; time did not change that fact.

"You know he did not want to pick Ray from respite that is why he ran out of here!"

Tony said as he gave his mother a big hug. His mother knew that Tony would pick his little brother from respite after dinner.

"You know I don't like to cook with people watching over my shoulder!"

In a playful jester, Tony's mother pointed him out of the kitchen. The young man laughed at his mother's jester and exited the kitchen heading for his old room.

Tony's old room was adjacent to Michael's room. In his youth being adjacent to Michael was not a good thing for Tony who had to endure his brother's inconsiderate nature. As Tony passed Michael's room he noticed the door to the room was ajar. Tony instinctively peered through to see Deandra changing her clothes. Deandra looked up to see that Tony was watching her. She paused, allowing the unintentional peeping Tom to get a better look at what he had been missing. Tony walked over to the door and gently closed the door on the young woman and then headed towards the safety of his room.

CHAPTER 16

Into Every Life...

Like the first rays of sunshine after a rainy day, Penelope came into Bosco's world and showed him a new way to view life! With his new love by his side the once blind man was able to see things just a little clearer. Bosco was able to let go of the pain of the past as he searched for the hope of the future. Penelope represented his present and future.

Their first night together at Saladin's den of sin was spent conversing rather than screwing. Bosco was amused to find a conversation with Penelope was as exciting as sex with most women he had the pleasure of knowing. In the weeks that past since their first meeting the couple spent much time talking and just a little more time sexing one another. Bosco had fallen hard for the highly intelligent and beautiful woman. He was so in love that he took Penelope home to meet Tad and Gregory, which was a major surprise. Tad even wondered silently.

"How could Bosco land such a tremendous woman?"

She was not the usual "Hood Rat" Bosco had always introduced as that moments "love of his life." His younger brother Gregory was blunter with Bosco.

"Don't mess things up with Penelope."

His brother's words stuck in his soul.

Bosco had always been a player from the Himalayas, and he was never concerned with the effects of his playing. He had made three babies with three different women. Bosco had very little contact with his children or their angry mothers. The reason he was an absentee father was the key to being a player. The moment there was any drama in the relationship he got out of Dodge! He was rich enough not to have to put up with what he saw as bullshit; therefore he just walked away from most of his responsibilities. Meeting Penelope did not infuse Bosco with an instant dose of responsibility however through conversations she showed him how wrong he lived. For that reason and more Bosco fell for Penelope.

Penelope majored in finance at one of the city colleges. She used Bosco's spending habits as a business project. Penelope received the grade of A+ and Bosco received free advice on how to make his illegal money grow legally.

"What are you looking at Bosco?"

Penelope said as she playfully gave her man a push because she realized that her man was paying more attention to her beauty than listening to her.

"You act like you're going somewhere!"

She continued.

"You don't hafta' worry baby. I ain't goin' anywhere."

Bosco responded. Penelope then continued to read her report to her man.

Deep down inside while Penelope explained her project to him, Bosco began to see that their love would not stand the test of time. They were trains, boats, and strangers; all the analogies created to say two people were not going to be together for a long time. Bosco felt strongly for Penelope but he knew he had to enjoy every moment for the next moment might be their last together as a couple. There was this underlining feeling that some skeleton would surface from his closet that would mark the end for their relationship. Bosco leaned over and kissed Penelope on the cheek as he tuned out his negative thoughts to enjoy the moment, as long as it would last.

CHAPTER 17

That Mutha' #@#%% Cash

Just when most businessmen thought it was safe to return to business, Cassius surfaced from his self imposed hiatus to serve notice that he was the number one businessman in town. Cassius and Black Reggie made sure that each move made was very silent, but very deadly.

Cassius disappeared into the shadows to avoid the glare of the spotlight being shined by both local and federal law officials on anyone of prominence. Although the police never spoke directly to him, word got back to Cassius that his name was brought to the police. Cassius went on the down low but he was a business man and money had to be made. Cassius become much more conscious of whom he did business. To make matters worse a mob war between rival New York City and New Jersey was punctuated with the gruesome murder of Cassius' drug supplier Geno Fish. A man walking his dog found the headless and handless body under the White Stone Bridge. The high profile death drew the attention of various politicians who were all in the election year. The politicians then pressed the New York City Police and the Feds to take action to stream the tide of the violence in both the mob world and drug world.

The drug initiative put in place by law enforcement officials had to be put on hold. Businessmen who had scurried out of the light like roaches in the middle of the night all breathed a sigh of relief when the Mafia replaced their face on the

Bulls-eye for law enforcement. Cassius used the lull in activity to advance his business by using the law to his advantage. Being that his name was on the so-called law enforcement hit list, Cassius decided to do a little dime dropping to gain favor. He worked with the authorities to point out anyone who may have been a threat to his economic welfare. The moment the focus of attention changed to the Mafia, Cassius was free to step out of the shadows. He had always dreamt of being the King of New York. His thoughts of royalty took Cassius back to his past.

As a child growing up in Harlem, Cassius spent most of his time dreaming about money and how having a lot of it could change his life. His childhood memories increased with Tracy's being in the hospital ready to deliver their first child. As he stood in the waiting room for his first glimpse of his new daughter, Destiny, Cassius reflected back on his own childhood experience. In spite of the years that had passed he could recall in detail his first experience of making BIG money.

Cassius remembered running home to tell his mother how much money he had made packing bags at the local supermarket. He could see himself walk past a group of young men who sat on the stairs inside his building smoking weed and drinking 40oz. of Ole English. One of the young men saw the look of happiness on the young Cassius's face and inquired about the cause for his joy. When Cassius informed the young man that he had made fifty dollars packing bags at the supermarket, the young man seemed happier than Cassius.

"That's big money for a twelve year old."

He remembered the young man said to him between sips on the 40oz.

"We gonna' call you "Cash Money!"

Another young man jokingly added.

At that moment the future toughest man in Harlem received his nickname from the most unlikely sources. Cash could remember the exchange of high fives he had with the young men. He also pictured bounding up the stairs to his apartment to tell his mother of his the good fortune.

The smile Cash had on his face thinking about how good it felt to earn money disappeared in the present as it had done in the past, when he recalled how his mother taxed him for all but ten dollars. Cash remembered returning to the steps angry with his mother for taking something that he had worked hard to get. The young men comforted Cash with his first pull of a joint, his first sip on a 40.oz as well as some advice about money and women.

"Never let a women know how much you make, cause then she will know how much to take!"

Cash stuck with the advice and the lesson learned. His philosophy worked well in his business life, but it took a toll in his personal life.

Tracy drew the wrath of Cash when he began to add up all the items she believed their child Destiny should possess that would make the infant's childhood better than both her parents. The memories of his childhood were fresh in his mind as he lashed out at Tracy as being a "Money hungry bitch!" Cash's verbal abuse of Tracy and everyone close to him became bad enough that Black Reggie had to speak to him about his rampage.

"You betta' chill out before you find yourself without a family or friends!"

Black Reggie said to Cash during a meeting at Cash's Brooklyn pool hall. Cash reluctantly took the advice of his trusted friend as if he had to swallow a spoonful of Castor Oil. Cash was close to achieving all the goals he set upon entering the business. No one not even himself would get in his way. He stormed out of the pool hall rather than get emotional in front of others.

As Cash walked the streets of Bed-Stuy, Brooklyn he noticed mothers walking with their children. Cash also saw men seated around various stores drinking beer while playing dominoes. Thoughts of his own wayward father crept back into his mind. The anger began to build in him once again; his father had made three children with his mother yet raises none of them. His father did manage to marry, move out west and raise four children. Cash did not want to be a father because he did not want to turn out like his own. A homeless man begging for money for food jostled Cash from his thoughts. He was quick to displace his anger for his mother and father onto the unfortunate man.

"How 'bout you get a fuckin' job and stop beggin'!"

Cash responded. When the man objected to Cash's tone of voice he soon found a pistol being pressed against his head. Cash thought better of killing the man because the man may have AIDS; therefore he pushed the frightened man to the pavement and stormed off towards oblivion. He arrived home to find four messages on his answering machine. The messages were from his mother who he had gladly shipped off to Alabama to live with her family.

His mother did not ask about her son or her new granddaughter. The only thought on her mind was money to add an addition to her house. Cash was not surprised that the first word he received from his mother was about his doing for her. In a fit of rage he tossed his phone across the room smashing the phone against the wall. His mother was once again getting into his pockets. Cash did not want to help her but how could he turn his mother down! As Cash made his way to his Brooklyn apartment his anger was turned towards Tony, Ace and their two unknown partners. He vowed to himself to "Destroy them" and nothing was going to get in his way.

CHAPTER 18

Payback

"Where da' fuck is she?"

Ace slammed down his phone in disgust He yelled loud enough that the neighbors across the street could have heard him. The day had just begun and he already was faced with a days worth of drama! The days events threatened to tear a hole in the fabric of his carefully woven life.

Ace had diligently created a splendid life for Angelika and himself. He had more money than he could spend and the power and respect he received gave him the feeling that he was on the top of the world, never to hit rock bottom ever again. Ace's euphoria lasted for only a brief period of time. Ace woke up one morning to find that a competitor had moved into the neighborhood. It did not take long for word to reach Ace that the competitor was Cash! The idea of Cash being next door to him sent Ace into a state of panic. All Ace could think about was the coming war with Cash!

Ace had no intentions of being plowed under by Cash as many before him had the displeasure of experiencing. His un-received call to Bosco was an attempt to confirm his worst fears of Cash moving in on his territory. Less than five minutes passed before Ace placed another call to Bosco. This time when the call was not received he slammed the phone down shattering it into many pieces. Ace held a portion of the receiver in his hand and tossed it into the fireplace, where it melted into a think white cloud.

"Why am I angry?"

Ace asked himself as he flopped down on his couch, located the television remote and began to channel surf. His agitated mood prevented him from finding anything on the tube that he could sit and watch.

"Why Am I so fuckin' vexed?"

Ace Yelled aloud. The source of anger was deep inside his soul and surfaced the moment he heard the sound of a car moving up his driveway.

Ace stood in the living room as he waited for Angelika to enter their home in order to give her a piece of his mind. He heard the loud thud of a SUV door being slammed shut. From his vantage point Ace could hear his grandfather clock chime eleven times. Ace then remembered Angelika's last words to him before she left him home alone.

"I'll be back around 8:00 pm Ace,"

Ace recalled she said to him prior to her going out the door. Thirteen hours later she arrived home without shopping bags or any other thing that could have kept her out all night. The more Ace thought about where she could have been, and the lame excuses she would give him, the angrier he became. He moved from the living room to the archway of the living room arms folded and ready for Angelika to enter the house.

Angelika entered the house, and was shocked to find Ace awake early in the morning. She quickly recovered from the initial shock and went about the task of entering the house. Angelika removed her jacket and placed it in the nearby closet, without saying a word to her man. She knew as long as he remained quiet drama was not in the cards. Angelika closed the door to the closet, and then she nonchalantly proceeded to head up the stairs towards their bedroom. Angelika acted as if Ace was not giving her the look of death, which only pushed him towards his edge. Angelika managed to make the third step before Ace grabbed by her by the arm and yanked her down to the first step. His roughhouse tactics did not go un-addressed by defiant Angelika.

"Let go, you're hurtin' me!"

Angelika loudly protested as she attempted to pull away from Ace's grip.

Her maneuver failed to free her arm from Ace's vice-like grip. Her failed attempt managed to anger an already irate man. Ace was more determined than ever to keep his strong hold and get the answer to his burning question.

"Where da' fuck wuz you all last night!"

Ace said while he tightened his grip.

"I ain't one of your hoes Ace. Get your fuckin' hands off of me!"

Angelika yelled as she tried and failed to free herself from Ace.

"I wanna' know where da' fuck you wuz and who you were wit'!"

He again shouted at Angelika.

If any word could be used to define Angelika that word would be defiant.

"You need not yell at me. I am standing right here!"

She pointed to the spot where she stood. Angelika spoke in a soft voice, as a way to calm her man down however there was no way she would mince her words. Angelika did not try to pull away because she knew Ace would only become angrier. Ace majored in street psychology and he understood the game that was trying to be played.

"Don't try to 'G' me Angelika! Answer my fuckin' question. Where wuz you?"

"Do you really want to know where I was Ace?"

"I asked the freakin' question Angelika?"

"I ain't gonna' answer you boyfriend. Ain't Payback a bitch!"

"This ain't no fuckin' game! Who the hell do you think you talking to Angelika?"

Angelika thought about Ace's question for a moment then she answered in her typical sharp-tongued manner.

"I know who I am talkin' to. I am talking to the same person who went to a basketball game with three men but came home with sperm stains in his underwear!"

Angelika finally managed to free her arm from Ace's grip. Instead of walking away, the feisty woman chose to stand her ground and give him a taste of his own medicine.

"Are you afraid I wuz doing the same thing you always do? Are you afraid that he was bigger than you?"

No sooner than the last words exited her mouth Angelika found herself looking up from the floor at the crystal chandelier as her man stood directly over her yelling at the top of his voice.

Ace was a prideful man. Angelika knew the best way to hurt her man was to talk about what he saw as his short fall.

"I tol' you not to make fun of me!"

Ace yelled.

He stood over a fallen Angelika as Cassius Clay stood over a defeated Sonny Liston. Ace had pimp slapped her to the floor, his fist was closed, ready to knock out the woman he claimed to love. Angelika slowly made her way to her feet. The shock of being knocked down yet again wore off very quickly. She checked her lip and when she did not see any blood she continued to speak her mind in spite of the possible consequences.

"Does hitting on me make you feel like a *big man*?"

Her voice was calm enough to send chills down Ace's cold heart for the last time she spoke to him in that matter after they had fought, Angelika tried to stab him.

"I've been wit ya' for ten years, and you continue to disrespect me! One day you will learn Linden Martin!"

She said in an emotionless voice.

Ace would not have any of her drama. He wanted to know her whereabouts the prior evening and continued to press his original question. Angelika never answered Ace's question. She wanted him to wonder just as she had all the times Ace stepped out for the night, however she did leave him with a question of her own.

"You have always questioned my loyalty, but let's see if your boys are loyal to you now that Cash is on your ass!"

Angelika then walked slowly up the stairs towards the bedroom.

"Sleep with one eye open mutha' fucka!"

Angelika warned as she ascended the stairs towards the bedroom.

Alone in the living room Ace began to ponder what Angelika had said about his business partners loyalty. His almost constant pages and phone calls to Bosco and Saladin going unanswered made his girl's question more possible to believe. As he sat down on his couch to take a long needed rest Ace began to believe the old saying 'There was no I in Team' he was going to look out for number one from that moment onward. He laid his head back on the couch eyeing the stairs leading to the bedroom and Angelika. He wanted to rest his head on his pillow but he thought better of that idea. He fell asleep wondering when his friends were going to contact him. Saladin was the first to answer his S.O.S.

Saladin sensed real fear in the voice of Ace as he played the first of many messages Ace left on his answering machine. He understood his friend's fears concerning Cash and the trouble that he might bring to bear. Cash was the bad dream that would never end. Saladin was sure that Cash was ready to make his move on the crew's business. The word through the grape vine was that Cash was gobbling up smaller businesses at an alarming rate, leading Saladin to believe that Cash was about to set it off on them! Neither Saladin nor the rest of his business partners were ones to wait, they would be the first to strike. The well-thought out plans were formulated at the back of Kelly's Variety Store that would see the end of Cash and Black Reginald and all the damage that they had caused all businessmen. The moment the crew found enough gunmen to go against Cash the plan would be put into motion. Throughout the planning stage Bosco warned both Ace and Tony against doing something to upset the plans before the group had the chance to finalize things. Bosco did not have to wait long before his warning went unheeded.

Two days after being warned, Tony found himself in the middle of a heated argument at a bar in the Bronx with a close relative of Black Reginald. (Tony had no idea the argument was part of Cash's plan to draw his silent partners out in the open.) The dye had been cast before there was enough muscle to comfortably deal with Cash. Harlem was about to witness the largest street battle in years, however; one small thing got in the way of the war! The hostilities were not able to ensue because of a simple phone call received by Saladin.

When problems occurred between Black businessmen, the mob called on the most infamous killer, the city did not know about The Reverend. The Reverend called Saladin on behalf of Saladin's heroin supplier Don Giovanni. He asked for Saladin and Bosco to meet with him at a location in Yonkers. Saladin did not want to attend the meeting but he had to, getting a call from The Reverend was like getting a call from the Grim Reaper. Saladin followed the instructions of The Reverend and informed Bosco that they had a meeting with the Devil Himself.

CHAPTER 19

Fear Factor

Saladin and Bosco walked into Mama's Place Restaurant, a non-descript eatery on the East Side of the City of Yonkers and were taken for a loop. The shabby exterior gave no clue to the elegance they found within the Restaurant. The two men were led by the maitre d' past tables of well-dressed black and Hispanic patrons who sipped on Moet and Cristal. The foods the two men saw on the plates of the patrons reminded both men of the food they each acquainted with white establishments. The ambiance was not going to be the only surprise the two men would experience.

The two men were led out of the dining area into the rear section of the restaurant adjacent to the busy kitchen. There were two burly men dressed in suits standing outside of a set of double doors. The maitre d' stopped some ten feet from the burly men and pointed for Saladin and Bosco to continue on towards the doors. Bosco thanked the maitre d' with a handshake as the man rushed back to the dining area as Bosco and Saladin continued on their way.

Bosco and Saladin halted in front of the burly men for the obligatory body search. The search was completed and Bosco and Saladin were ushered through the double doors, into a large room that reeked of chitterlings and hot sauce. The two men observed The Reverend slurping chitterlings and guzzling down Moet. The picture could not have been more of a contrast.

"Be seated gentlemen!"

The Reverend said as he licked his fingers clean of his tasty meal.

"I'm glad you could make it to Yonkers!"

He then motioned for his guest to have a seat. Bosco and Saladin were reluctant to take a seat being that their burly escorts stood behind each man. Bosco looked around the room and laughed aloud as he took a seat.

"What's funny Bosco?"

The Reverend asked as he sucked a small piece of food from between his teeth.

"I swear it seems like you are a cross between Michael Corleone and Nino Brown in this room!"

Bosco chuckled. Saladin weighed in with his thoughts when he said.

"I wuz thinking along the lines of Scarface and Geechie Dan Buford!"

The two men burst into laughter. The chuckles continued even after they exchanged high fives over their witticism. Needless to say the Reverend was not happy with being the brunt of their joke. The joke did not go over well with anyone in the Reverend's crew.

"No one makes fun of the Reverend!"

The man who stood directly behind Saladin said with much emotion in his voice. The Reverend motioned for the man to remain calm and the man did as he was instructed. The Reverend remained calm on the outside however he was deadly angry inside.

"Whenever you two are finished playing Abbot and Costello, we can get back on track."

The peeved man said as a way to shut up the two comedians. The Reverend wanted to make small talk about all the rumors of how much power he held to impress and strike fear, however Bosco would have none of the supposed intimidation.

Bosco looked around the dimly lit room at the men who gathered around the reverend. He took notice of the fact that all the men tried their best to emulate their boss right down to his Green Suede Converse sneakers. Bosco was not impressed and did not have time for small talk.

"Let's get past all this formal bullshit! You need to get to the point Rev, we got a long drive back to the city!"

Bosco's tone gave The Reverend the impression that the upstart needed to know the weight he carried.

"I was asked by Don Giovanni to tell you that there will never be a war between Cash and your people."

Bosco found irony in the Reverend relaying messages.

"Now on top of being a killer and extortionist, you are a high priced messenger!"

Bosco sarcastically said. He even threw up his hands in mock disgust.

"You are testing my patience. I will only take so much disrespect from you Bosco!"

The Reverend said as the sound of his voice began to fill with emotion. Bosco did not back down in the face of danger he continued to speak his mind. He adjusted the hem of his right pant then spoke directly to the Reverend's apparent power.

"I ain't gotta' take no bull from you or some Mafia cat. If Cash gets froggish with us we will set it off on him!"

Bosco plainly stated as he glanced over towards Saladin who held a blank look on his face. Saladin had remained silent during the verbal battle between Bosco and the Reverend. The directness of the comments between the two caused Saladin to become a vocal member of the conversation.

"You have our word Rev, we won't step to Cash!"

Bosco's jaw dropped to the floor. He was always told to hide his true feelings, but Saladin's words of betrayal infuriated Bosco to no end.

"I can't believe I heard that shit from you Saladin. I ain't gonna' take this shit lying down. I'm outta here!"

Bosco leapt from his chair and stormed out of the room. He made sure to slam the door behind him when he left. Saladin tried to stop Bosco from leaving, however his words fell on deaf ears. The Reverend smiled at the fact that he had drove a wedge between the two most powerful members of the crew. He took out a victory cigar, leisurely lit it and puffed in ecstasy.

"You need to check your bitch ass partner Saladin. He keeps actin' like that, I'll forget the promise I made to Don Giovanni and kill you both!"

The Reverend said as if he talked about something insignificant. He puffed on his cigar and blew the smoke high in the air that filled the room with a white cloud. Saladin watched the look on the Reverend's face and he got the impression that there was more to the conversation than meets the eye. Saladin wanted to know what The Reverend had up his sleeve.

"You did not call me down here just to deliver a message. You could have done that in Harlem. What Gives?"

Saladin questioned. The Reverend excused one of his bodyguards from the room in order to speak to Saladin in relative privacy. Saladin watched the man smoke his cigar as if some sort of icing on the proverbial cake. The Reverend did not speak until he was satiated from smoking.

"Let's get right to it. The only reason I have not stepped to you Saladin is because The Don Giovanni wants it that way."

The Reverend said as he tapped a long ash from his cigar, took another puff then continued.

"His son Handsome Paul is gradually taking over the bizness. Paul ain't got no loyalty to your long dead Stepfather! He is all about money, which should always be the case!"

The Reverend paused then continued.

"Handsome Paul favors Cash over your crew."

The Reverend said as he placed the remainder of his cigar into a crystal ashtray. Saladin understood the business and there were no free lunches. The Reverend wanted something from him and the only way Saladin would find that answer was to ask.

"Why tell me all this?"

"I want to help you Saladin. You know, one brother to another Saladin."

"This is where the extortion comes in ain't it Rev'?"

"When the time comes I want a forty percent stake in everything your crew makes."

"I have to talk it over with my partners. A five way split means less money for all."

Saladin stated as he watched the look on the Reverend's face display a sense of over confidence. The Reverend picked up up the cigar once again and began to smoke on it as if he was Red Auerback and it was a victory cigar.

"Time is of the essence Saladin and the offer is only extended to Bosco and to you. Stay away from Cash and get the fuck out!"

The Reverend then motioned for Saladin to leave the room as he puffed on the stogy once again. Saladin stood up and started out of the room but he had to ask one more question of his adversary.

"Why do they call you the Reverend?"

"Because Jesus was already taken!"

The Reverend responded. Saladin took offense to the response and left the room without shaking hands with the blasphemer.

Once outside the restaurant Saladin immediately got into an argument with Bosco who had been waiting outside for him. Two of the Reverend's men stood outside the restaurant and witnessed the shouting match between the two. One of the men immediately reported the news to his boss. The heated argument took a twist the moment the two friends entered Bosco's car.

"What happened after I left the room Saladin?"

Bosco said in a calm voice.

"He thought he had got between us and relaxed."

"What did he say Saladin?"

"He wants a piece of our business minus Tony, Ace and maybe you!"

"Is that all he wants Saladin?"

"No, he warned me that the old man might be leaving the business soon and with him goes my, our protection."

Saladin responded as he looked out the window at the dark sky above. He started the ignition to the car then turned to Bosco who had trouble adjusting the automatic seatbelt. Saladin found humor in his friend's struggle.

"What the fuck is so funny Saladin?"

Bosco said, as he finally felt comfortable in the seat.

"I hope you have better luck dealing with The Reverend than that seatbelt."

Saladin jokingly said.

"I hope the Reverend is ready to get as well as he gives?"

Bosco shot back.

CHAPTER 20

To Give Thanks

"Good afternoon Philip!"

Penelope said in her bedroom voice the instant he opened his eyes from his restful night's sleep. The couple had spent Thanksgiving eve at her parent's house on Long Island and they arrived back in the Bronx late in the morning. Bosco did most of the driving, which made his eyes very weak first thing in the morning. His eyes slowly put Penelope's lovely face into focus to reveal beauty that had been taken for granted for far too long. He realized again why he was attracted to her.

"Damn Penny you are fine as hell!"

Bosco said as his looked up at the beauty as he lay on his back as she straddled his body. Bosco looked at her perfectly white teeth and million-dollar smile and had to mentally pinch himself to see if he was truly awake. The sight of his woman straddled over him started his hormones racing.

"You sure know how to wake a brother up in the midday!"

Bosco said in an excited voice. He then reached up and opened Penelope's bathrobe and exposed her naked body to the horny man. Penelope did not try to close her robe because each time she did Bosco opened it once more.

"You betta' stop Philip, or we won't make your father's house for Thanksgiv-ing!"

Penelope laughed as she half-heartedly attempted to break free from her man's grip. Her words did not make the horny man let go, Bosco held on tighter. When

Bosco's hold became too firm, Penelope struggled to break free and let him know how she felt.

"Bosco, I ain't a freakin' sex machine! Three days in a row would be too much!"

She whined at the thought of another sex session. Penelope managed to pull away from Bosco and sat on the edge of their brand new bed. The distance apart did not curb his yearning for satisfaction.

"Please baby just one mo' time!"

Bosco pleaded with Penelope. She flashed her bright smile, which melted the horny man's heart. Bosco watched as his temptress creep towards him until their lips became interlocked in a passionate kiss. As soon as Bosco's nature started to rise Penelope abruptly broke off their kiss.

"Psych!"

She exclaimed as she made a mad dash for the bathroom. Needless to say her actions left Bosco high, bone dry and pissed.

It did not take him very long to react to Penelope's leaving him in his excited state. He jumped off the bed, stormed over to the locked bathroom door and promptly banged on the door.

"Penny, stop playing! Open the door."

The only sound Bosco heard was the sound of running water in the shower. He had already reached the height of anger when the lyrics to an old song his father used to recite to him echoed through his mind.

Tad knew of his son's temper and tried everything to calm his son down when he became angry. Bosco though, always felt that the entire "Calming down" thing by reciting song lyrics was a bit over the top. He never understood the meaning of "If It Don't Fit Don't Force It.", until he found himself standing before the door ready to cause a huge argument over sex. Bosco was able to check himself, allowing his impulse to gradually diminish until he was able to allow his common sense to win out over his libido.

He came to an understanding that the law of the street did not work well in relationships. The sound of running water in the bathroom caused Bosco to think about the long discussions his father and grandfather had with him concerning how to meet and keep women. The number one on both his father's list was patience. Patience was something that had always eluded him, but at that moment he was more than willing to try to find it. Bosco surfaced from his daydream the instant Penelope exited the bathroom.

"What cha thinking' 'bout, baby?"

Penelope asked her man as he scrambled from his thoughts. Bosco kept his true thoughts to himself, however, he opened his heart to the woman he cared for deeply.

Bosco looked up at his love and calmly said.

"I'm thankful for you and I'm also thankful that your father did not ask me too many questions."

Penelope did not expect this from a usually emotionless Bosco. She had to take the time to see if her man was being real or was he playing one of his infamous jokes.

"No Bosco, I am the lucky one. You are the best thing to have come into my life!"

Penelope said as she stood over her man. She took his head in her caring arms pressing it against her breasts.

"Penny, you have shown me a new way to look at life, and I cannot begin to thank you!"

Bosco found it hard to speak because he had a mouth full of Penelope's wet towel. Penelope was moved by her man's first real show of affection during their three-month relationship. She wanted to reward him for his honesty, but she did not know how she would be able to. Penelope dropped her towel down to the floor exposing her naked body to her once horny man.

"You can have some if you want."

Penelope reluctantly said. Bosco thought about swinging another episode, however, he remembered Penelope had earlier complained of soreness.

"It sounds tempting, but I not in the mood now."

He gently pulled Penelope down to the bed, on her back in order for him to lay his head on her chest. She knew he had lied about not being in "The Mood" and for once a lie was a good thing for Bosco to tell. As she stroked her man's head, Penelope spoke to Bosco.

"I am glad we are together. I hope we never argue"

Penelope reached down and began to remove Bosco's boxer shorts.

"We have three hours before we have to be at your father's house. You got another three minutes in ya'"

All Bosco could do was laugh as he was being molested. Bosco was happy to have Penelope in his life.

*   *   *   *

"Ifin' you two don't get yo' lazy butts' outta' bed you will be eatin' Christmas dinner instead of Thanksgiving dinner."

The voice of Saladin's loud Aunt, Mary Lou, was enough to wake Sunshine up out of her deep sleep. Aunt Mary Lou was in her mid-sixties, and had been an outspoken woman who turned into a more direct older woman.

"Did you two bums hear me?'

Aunt Mary Lou said, as she knocked on the door very hard.

"Yes, Auntie, we hear you,"

Sunshine responded.

"Well Goddammit I ain't no dern 'larm clock. Get up on your own!"

The cranky lady yelled back through the door. In spite of the closed door, Sunshine could hear Aunt Mary Lou muttering obscenities as she walked down the hall.

"If you ain't an alarm clock you do a good impersonation!"

Sunshine yelled towards the door at long gone Auntie.

Sunshine could not go back to sleep after Saladin's aunt's yelling. She rolled over in the bed to find Saladin was not in bed. Sunshine took several seconds to locate her man who was standing by one of the two large bay windows he had installed in his mother's house. His eyes peering out at the wilderness of rural Tennessee, however his mind remained in the room. Sunshine knew her man was still upset over the argument they had on the plane, which carried over into the car ride to his mother's house. The argument began over silliness, but eventually graduated into the all too familiar topic of Saladin's flirting with women. The intensity of the argument took away most of the joy of their family vacation. Sunshine sat up in the bed. Her eyes were still puffy from the lack of sleep. Saladin heard Sunshine moving about the bed behind him and it took time for him to gain enough courage to speak his mind.

"Are you finished accusing me of doing dumb shit, Sunshine?"

Saladin said without taking his eyes off a small rabbit hopping across the huge backyard. Saladin took a deep breath and continued to speak his mind.

"I made big money for my friends and they thanked me. I build this house for my mother and she thanked me."

He paused because he did not know if he wanted to continue with his chain of thought. A heavy sigh from Sunshine convinced him to continue.

"No matter what I do for you I always seem to fuck things up!"

Saladin turned towards Sunshine to see a blank expression on her face.

"Cut the bullshit Saladin. It's me you are talking to, not one of your friends."

Sunshine said in a dull voice as she rubbed the last bit of sleep out of her eyes.

"I'm definitely not a bimbo who will believe every word that comes out your mouth."

Sunshine pulled the covers back in order to sit on the edge of the bed.

Saladin felt his heart move into his throat because his Achilles Heel was his need to conquer women. The mere mention of the topic by Sunshine always caused the same reaction. There was no hiding his addiction. There was only avoidance. His only hope was that another heated argument was not on the near horizon. Sunshine's unusually calm demeanor lasted for the remainder of the conversation and sent chills down Saladin's spine.

Sunshine rubbed the plush carpet between her toes as she laid down the law to her man.

"I love you Saladin, but I ain't gonna' put up wit' your shit much longer,"

Sunshine announced. Her words caused Saladin to move from his position by the window to take a seat next to Sunshine on the bed. He buried his head in Sunshine's lap much the same way a child would do when they wanted to fall asleep. Sunshine stroked her man's head as they spoke. Saladin got caught up in the moment and tried to smooth things out with his girl.

"I'm not perfect Sunshine, but I always respect…"

Sunshine, giving him the hand interrupted Saladin's plea.

"Save that shit for your underlings. I know you all too well Saladin." Sunshine tapped her man on the shoulders as a signal for him to sit upright.

"You betta' be thankful for me. You betta' respect me before…."

Sunshine was interrupted by three hard knocks on the room door.

"Ifin you two don't get the hell outta' dat room and feed your child, I'm gonna' kick down the dern door!"

Aunt Mary Lou had returned to the door with a vengeance.

"You two ain't in there makin' more children are ya'"

Aunt Mary Lou asked, since they took too long to exit the room. Saladin always teased his favorite Aunt; it was something they did to one another.

""Ifin you stop interrupting us Auntie, we could make twins!"

Saladin responded.

"It shouldn't take you that long. I hope you keep your socks on. We need sum' girls in this here family!"

She yelled as he walked away from the door.

"Thank God you only have one Auntie Mary Lou!"

Sunshine chuckled. The chuckling stopped after a few moments when Sunshine brought the conversation back to the matter at hand.

"I love you, but if I find out you did some vile shit like mess wit' one of my girls I'll cut your little dick off!"

Saladin remained silent as he wondered which of the two friends of Sunshine he screwed would be the first to tell. Saladin was very thankful for Sunshine and his son, and he hoped his past did not come back to bite him in the ass. He was not about to screw things up with Sunshine, but screwing up was what he did best.

*   *   *   *

Tony walked through the door of his mother's brand new Co-op late for Thanksgiving dinner by himself! Tony chose not to travel with his mother and two brothers to meet the rest of their family in Virginia for the holiday. He had grown tired of the "meet your relative" thing a long time ago, besides, he was not willing to trust his business with any of his flunkies. He dropped his keys down on the coffee table and headed straight for the terrace. There was something about standing twenty-eight floors above the city that relaxed him. After spending the better part of an hour on the terrace Tony headed for the comfort of his Brother Michael's room to rest upon his fancy waterbed. Tony had been up all night counting money, smoking blunts and shooting the breeze with his flunkies, he did not feel up to taking Ace up on his invitation for dinner at his house in Jersey. Tony wanted to be alone for a change. He was tired of people, and the bull shit people put him through. Being alone was the best way for him to collect his thoughts about what he was going to do with all the money he was making.

By the time he reached his brother's room, Tony had stripped down to his boxers. He dove on the bed and was thrilled by the wave action he had created. Tony placed his gun on the floor next to his bed as sleep began to take hold of him. Tony turned on the television knowing full well that it would be watching him in a few moments. He lit a phat blunt and smoked himself to sleep.

Tony was awoken from a deep sleep when he felt and heard the door to the apartment slammed shut. He immediately reached down on the floor to grab his gun and ran from the room. In a millisecond Tony was in the living room oscillating his weapon in search of a target. He was surprised when he set his sights on his brother's girlfriend. Deandra was nervous enough that she dropped all the bags she had carried into the apartment.

"Don't shoot Tony! I ain't do nuttin'!"

The woman frantically yelled. Tony did not immediately put the gun down; his adrenaline was pumping, and he had some questions to ask Deandra.

"What the fuck are you doing with keys to my mother's house? Are you tryin' to rob my mother?"

Tony said as he slowly approached Deandra. She never took her eyes off the barrel of Tony's gun as she responded.

"She wanted me to check on da' house while she was gone."

Deandra thought that Tony would put the gun down once she had explained herself. The sight of the gun still pointed at her head made Deandra hysterical.

"Put the gun down, this shit ain't funny. What do I hafta' do to make you put the gun down Tony?"

She begged. Deandra begging for Tony to put the gun away started Tony's little member to begin to rise.

"In order for me to put the gun down you hafta take off your clothes!"

Tony said as he waved the gun to accent his request.

"Are you gonna' rape me Tony?"

She asked.

"You need to stop frontin' girl. You know you want me to tap that ass! There ain't nothing but space and opportunity!"

Tony said as he walked towards her and unzipped her coat. He used his hands to first rip her shirt apart then yank her skirt down below her knees. Deandra stood silently praying for Tony to take her where she stood. Tony had a trick for her. He placed his gun on the table and walked back towards his brother's room. A lustful Deandra quickly followed Tony to Michael's room. She finally got what she had been waiting a long time to get. She hoped money and fame would soon follow. She thanked the lord for making her dream of sleeping with Tony come true.

CHAPTER 21

Shit Happens

Shakespeare said it best, "Parting is such sweet sorrow." Those words could not touch the emotions felt by Saladin upon leaving his family in Tennessee. Grief tore at the soul of the man. He very much wanted to be close to his mother and siblings, however he knew that being close to them was not going to happen in the near future. The closer Saladin got to New York City, the more he could feel the kind, friendly pace of the south disappear and replaced by the here and now of the business world. As the plane touched down at LaGuardia Airport a familiar feeling of dread consumed the memories of his vacation.

Saladin dropped his bags at the door to his house and headed straight for the kitchen where he mistakenly left behind his pager and new fangled cellular phone. The instant he turned on his pager it started to vibrate.

"Daddy, yo' pager is goin' crazy!"

Charles said of the heavy vibration of the pager.

"I know Charles you don't hafta' say it loud!"

Saladin said quite annoyed because his son had spoken loud enough for Sunshine to hear.

He quickly checked his pager and found several 911 codes. Saladin looked up from checking his pager to find that Sunshine stood directly in front of him. He braced himself for yet another "Family before business" argument, however no argument was to be forthcoming. Sunshine recognized the concerned look on her man's face, and decided to stick to her pledge of not stressing Saladin about business. She was more concerned with helping her man.

"I knew you should have carried your cellular phone on the trip!"

Sunshine said as she handed her man his car keys.

"Don't be too late Saladin."

She then turned to her son and ordered him to take all their dirty clothes down to the basement. Sunshine then placed a kiss on Saladin's forehead before she disappeared down the stairs to the laundry room in the basement. Father and son could not believe what had just occurred. Charles was the first to address the actions of his mother.

"Daddy, how come mommy ain't yellin' at ya'?'"

He whispered as if his question would set his mother off if she heard. The only answer Saladin had for his son was a blank stare. Saladin then checked his pager once more and placed it on his belt. Charles watching his father's actions very closely became curious at why his father was always receiving pages.

"Who is always pagin' you Dad?'

Charles asked in his boyish voice.

Saladin had been waiting for the questions by his son to begin and his well-crafted answer had been prepared the moment his son was born.

"Stop being so fucking nosey! Take the clothes down to your mother like she said!"

Saladin yelled. The father hoped to end all future questions about business from his son. The sight of his son walking away as if he had missed the last shot in a championship game was too much for Saladin to bear. He had to right the wrong he had just committed.

"Come back here little man!"

Saladin said as he extended his loving arms to his son. Saladin picked Charles up that was well received by the young boy. Saladin tried his best to explain his feelings to his son.

"You know you are my little man. Don't you Charles?"

"I'm your *biiig* man Daddy!"

"That's right Charles; however I don't want you to do everything I do. I sometimes do things that are wrong. I don't want you to do everything I do Charles."

"Yeah, I think I do. Like smoking cigarettes!"

"Yes, Charles"

"Like, yelling at mommy!"

"Right, again!"

"Like when you drink milk out of the carton then put it back in da frig?"

This time Saladin shut his son up in a more polite way.

"Boy, you're over doing it. Go take the clothes to your mother like she asked."

Saladin then sent his son on his task. On the way to the shower, Saladin wondered how far Charles would have gone had he allowed him to continue.

After his shower Saladin returned to the kitchen for his pager and cellular phone, where he found Sunshine searching the refrigerator for expired food. Saladin wanted to ask Sunshine if her new attitude was an aberration. Saladin looked her right in the eye opened his mouth, but Sunshine beat him to the punch.

"You have to take care of Charles and me. Whatever you do, however late you come home because of business, you won't have any more problems from me. All I ask is that you respect me and respect the house!"

Sunshine stopped cleaning the refrigerator walked over to her man and placed a kiss on his lips.

"Hurry up and take care of business. The sooner you get back, the sooner we can make up for two weeks of lost time!"

Sunshine then shoo Saladin out of the house, leaving him with the impression that Sunshine had just 'Geed' him.

Saladin arrived at a nearby Seven-Eleven and placed several business related calls. He called his second in command, Bones, to check on how business had gone while he was on vacation. Once satisfied with Bones' response, Saladin paged Tony and Bosco in response to the 911 pages they had made. Saladin's pages went unreturned until he remembered Tony's cellular phone number was saved on his own cell phone. Saladin dialed the number on the pay phone in case Tony was in the hands of the law. Tony's cell phone rang repeatedly before it was answered.

"Yo Dick, this is Saladin what's the big emergency?"

Saladin said the moment the phone was answered. Saladin should have waited because he was caught off guard.

"This is not Tony! He is busy doin' me lovely right now! Call back—oh, yeah that's the spot, Tony—call him back later Salideen."

An unknown female voice on the other end announced. Saladin was about to hang up when he heard Tony snatched the phone from Deandra.

"Yo! who dis?" Tony angrily questioned.

"It's Saladin Dick! Who is the chicken head?"

"Neva' mind dat shit! I gots some bad news 'bout Ace, he's in the hospital!"

"What the fuck happened to him Tony? Did he get shot?"

Saladin developed a bad feeling in his gut concerning Ace's welfare as he waited for Tony's response. When Tony did respond Saladin did not know what to make of the answer.

"Nah, man he crashed riding his new motorcycle."

Tony said.

"Is it bad Tony?"

Saladin asked. His voice was full of concern.

"It could be better she keeps catching me with teeth!"

Tony exclaimed between grunts and groans. Tony had mistaken the subject of the conversation, but Saladin put the conversation back on track.

"No! Not the blow job Dick, Ace's condition."

A frustrated Saladin repeated himself twice because he wanted to make sure Tony understood him.

Tony could not give Saladin the information he wanted because his mind was on getting a blowjob. Saladin was glad when Bosco returned his page, which made it possible for him to get off the phone with a preoccupied Tony. Just before Saladin hung up the phone with Tony he recognized the voice of Deandra, Tony's brother's girlfriend. Saladin did not know what was more disturbing, Tony having sex with his brother's girlfriend, or the fact that Ace had hurt himself riding a motorcycle in the dead of winter!

The information Bosco provided about Ace was not more than Tony was able to give, however Saladin did not have to hear the sounds of Tony having sex over the phone. Bosco was able to tell the circumstances surrounding Ace's accident. Angelika threw away Ace's car keys after they had another fight about Ace hanging out in the City. Ace took his motorcycle instead of his car. On his way back to New Jersey, Ace lost control and crashed into a tree, breaking both his legs, some ribs as well as fracturing his pelvis and skull. The injuries were extremely serious, and both men believed they were ready for any bad news; however Saladin and Bosco were not prepared to see Ace in the hospital bed.

The sight of tubes protruding from Ace's mouth and nose, and his swollen face brought immediate tears to Bosco's eyes. Saladin took one look at Ace, and he had to leave the room in order to keep his composure. Saladin returned to the room just as Ace's doctor entered the room. Angelika had also entered Ace's hospital room after getting something from the cafeteria with her cousin Jason. Bosco and Angelika did not look at each other. The doctor sensed the tension in the room and believed it was caused by the uncertainty of Ace's prognosis. The doctor did not waste any time explaining that Ace would live, however he would need many months of rehabilitation to regain the ability to walk. No sooner than the doctor left the room Angelika asked the important question.

"Is the group ready to have a woman?"

Bosco walked out of the room. He could not believe that she would bring up business over Ace's hospital bed. As for Saladin, he remained in the room, because he did not know how any new business arrangements would affect his future plans.

CHAPTER 22

Back to the Grind

Angelika was ready, willing and more than able to take over for Ace. Angelika did well enough that the three business partners began to believe that she was somehow responsible for Ace's accident. In a very short time she went from a silent partner, and morphed into a very vocal and outspoken member of the team. Angelika's presence did not hurt the business; however, her presence increased the tensions between her and Bosco. Saladin tried subtle ways to keep the peace between his feuding partners, for he knew that all it would take is a small spark to cause an inferno! Saladin did not have to wait long for the spark to ignite.

Saladin was smart enough to understand that any beef in the fragile business arrangement would put an end to any attempt to leave the drug world. He passed out compliments to Angelika and made sure Tony was swimming in money. As for Bosco, Saladin kept him as entertained and far away from Angelika as possible. Saladin coerced Bosco into accompanying him to a Basketball game at the World Famous Rucker Park in Harlem. Saladin hoped that the game would relax the tight Bosco, and allow him to run the idea of leaving the business by Bosco. It turned out that attending the game proved to be an enlightening experience.

Rucker Park was located under the 155th Street Viaduct, which is the same viaduct that bridged Manhattan to the Bronx and nearby Yankee Stadium. Irony also placed the park across the avenue from the Polo Ground Projects, the former home to Willie Mays, and the New York Baseball and Football Giants. In spite of the historical locations surrounding it, "The Rucker" managed some history of its' own.

Many of Pro Basketball's superstars graced The Rucker with their presence. Everyone from Doug Collins, The Answer; to Kareem; right on down to Air Jordan were just a few NBA stars who awed Harlem with their ball skills on the tiny hovel of street basketball lore. On the day Saladin dragged Bosco to The Rucker, the star attraction was a sixteen-year-old kid from Queens nicknamed "Skip to My Lou." The young man was said to possess better dribbling skills than Isaiah, and he was a better passer than Magic. Bosco and Saladin joked that they hoped the young man could live up to the hype.

Saladin and Bosco were able to squeeze their way on the bleacher which faced the Viaduct, and sat between two loud groups of young girls who screamed at every player they felt looked good. Both Saladin and Bosco donned their matching Ray-Ban sunglasses to protect their eyes from the setting sun that was directly in their eyes. Neither man liked to wear sunglasses, but wearing them along with a baseball cap turned out to be a blessing in disguise.

"Skip to My Lou" did not disappoint the two men or anyone else who managed to squeeze into the Rucker that hot summer evening. His dazzling feats for dribbling brought the crowd to its feet numerous times. It was after "Skip to My Lou" dribbled the ball around a defender, that Bosco first caught sight of his nemesis Angelika seated next to her cousin Thomas on the opposite bleacher. Bosco adjusted his eyes from the still setting sun. He noticed that Black Reginald was seated just two rows in front of Angelika and Thomas. Bosco began to get that funny feeling in his stomach as thoughts of treachery ran through his mind. Bosco nudged Saladin whose mind was elsewhere.

Saladin watched as the Reverend made a rare non-work public appearance to The Rucker with two of his henchmen in tow. Saladin watched as the Reverend led his two associates through the crowd as if he were Moses parting the Red Sea. At the moment Bosco nudged Saladin, the Reverend commandeered three seats right next to Black Reginald. Bosco and Saladin watched together as the friendly conversation then popped up among Angelika, Black Reginald and the Reverend. Neither man could believe their Ray-Bans!

The stunned Saladin and Bosco did not have much time to observe because as soon as the game ended the NYPD began to ticket the many cars that were doubled and tripled parked outside the Rucker on 8th Avenue. A mass exodus ensued which gave cover to Saladin and Bosco's stealthy departure from the Rucker. Neither man spoke on the implications of Angelika's friendly relationship with their sworn enemies. They did speak to the fact of leaving the totally reactionary Tony in the dark until they could figure out what Angelika was putting down. Needless to say Saladin did not get the chance to broach the idea to Bosco about wanting to leave the business. It was better if he kept one step ahead of Angelika and out of the way of the Reverend.

CHAPTER 23

Cool Breeze

Hot, humid and hazy was the best way to describe most days in August in NYC. Although the backroom of Kelly's had the feel of a supermarket meat locker, the temperature amongst the individuals in the room was extremely high.

All were in attendance during the meeting. Saladin took his usual seat on his stool away from the table. He did not want to sit too close to the suspected traitor, Angelika. Tony sat at the head of the table to the left of Bosco, and to the right of Angelika and her cousin Thomas. Thomas' presence at the meeting upset both Bosco and Saladin because each man knew that he had to be aware of the double-dealings done by Angelika. However, his proximity would make it easy for either man to reach out and touch the cousins if the need arises. Bosco did his best to hold his tongue as long as money was on the table. The very moment the last of the bagmen exited the backroom Bosco started in on Angelika in typical Bosco fashion.

He spent the entire meeting in search of the one thing about Angelika or Thomas that he could use to pick a fight with either person, and after careful analysis he found what he was searching for. On one of the hottest days of the year Angelika chose to wear a pair of new leather pants. A smile came across his face as a nasty thought came to his twisted mind.

"I wonder how many cows had to die in order for you to get your fat ass in them thar' pants?"

Bosco said in a voice that imitated a bad western movie. His comment brought a hush to the conversation Angelika was having with Tony, and much to his delight Bosco got a rise out of Thomas.

At the completion of Bosco's comment Thomas pushed his chair back from the table as a prelude to his attack. Angelika who stood directly behind her angry cousin placed her hand on Thomas' broad shoulder, a signal for him to remain seated and calm.

"Don't fret none cuz I gots this here!"

Angelika said as she gently patted Thomas on the shoulder, which kept him seated. Angelika had waited patiently for the opportunity to set the arrogant man in his place. There was no time like the present for Angelika.

The woman turned to Bosco who waited with baited breath for her response to his dis. Angelika wasted little time in getting at Bosco.

"Cousin, Thaddeus is not worth the energy."

Angelika spoke with such emotion that her words hurt Saladin, and Tony, as well as Bosco. The only sound in the room was the hum of the troublesome fluorescent light, which hung over the table. Bosco threw the bag of chips he was eating onto the table as if it were a gauntlet used for a challenge to a duel in 18th century Europe. Bosco did not call for pistols at twenty paces; he instead chose to reciprocate the hate towards Angelika.

"It's a shame that jealously drove you to meddle in other people's business Angelika!"

"You should have thought twice about two timing on her Thaddeus, and then I would have had nothing to tell!"

"Now ain't that a case of the pot callin' the kettle black Angelika."

"What's that supposed to mean Bosco? Don't speak in riddles."

"You know exactly what the hell I'm talking about!"

Bosco purposely left the woman with a question to which there were three possible answers. Bosco waited to allow Angelika to ponder if he would divulge the dark secret in her past. Bosco let several seconds go by before he answered his own question.

"What's the deal with Cash and the Rev, Angelika? Inquiring minds want to know!"

The question had been asked and the question was met with guilty quiet from Angelika and Thomas.

"Don't be quiet. You had a whole lot to say to Black Reginald and Cash at the Rucker!"

Saladin said as he entered the conversation hell bent on hearing the answer to the question. Saladin looked over towards Bosco to see that Bosco had placed a gun on the table ready to do what he thought should be done. Saladin then looked over towards Tony who had a concerned look on his face. He turned his attention towards Angelika and the answer to his unanswered question.

"You come here pretending to be partners with *us* and all the while you are holding court with the enemy."

Saladin paused as he looked directly at Thomas, who looked as if he had lost his swagger. The sight of Thomas convinced Saladin that Angelika had been double-dealing.

Bosco cocked his pistol and placed it onto the table once again.

"Aren't you gonna' answer the man's question. He wants to know if you're sleeping with the enemy."

Bosco was at the point that he did not need much of a reason to smoke either Angelika or Thomas. For once Saladin was not going to be the voice of reason. His entire life was held in the balance and he was not going to tip the scales either way by trusting Angelika. If Bosco would kill Angelika and Thomas, he would not put up any resistance. For her part Angelika did not muster any real defense for herself or a frantic Thomas. She knew that Bosco did not care much for her but he would never kill her. The tension increased in the room, as both parties remained eerily silent, for the next spoken word might lead to death. It was in this atmosphere that Tony entered the conversation and put the matter into proper prospective.

"Why don't we call Ace, Bosco, before you make a hasty decision?"

Like that elusive breeze many New Yorkers searched for, Tony's words seemed to cool the tempers in the room. Tony's role reversal made Saladin and Bosco take a step back. Bosco pulled out his cell phone and tossed it at Thomas and demanded a call to Ace be placed.

Saladin and Bosco calmed down the moment they heard Ace explain the game of duplicity Angelika and he were engaged in on both the Rev and Cash. Ace explained that as long as Cash and the Rev thought he might switch sides they would not feel any pressure to attack. Ace's strategy appeared to be working; therefore Saladin, Bosco and Tony took Ace for his word. Ace informed his friends that he would soon make his return to the NYC. Angelika ended the call and did not tell Ace that she was threatened by two of his partners. Bosco reluctantly put away his gun amidst the sneers of those he wanted to kill. Bosco's actions only seemed to make Tony more curious about the beef between Angelika and Bosco. Against his better judgment, he asked the question to which he received blank stares from Angelika and Bosco as they separately exited the room. Saladin was the last to leave the room. He remained in the room to ponder the truthfulness of Ace's admission.

Saladin understood that Ace had placed himself in a win-win situation no matter what game he claimed to play. Saladin also pondered the fact that the reason for the beef between Angelika and Bosco would soon come to light. He hoped that when it did, somehow he could use it to his advantage.

CHAPTER 24

Taste of Honey

Saladin left the backroom of Kelly's exactly one hour after the meeting had concluded. He could not shake the idea that Ace was somehow an unwilling victim in the evil plan of Angelika. The more he pondered, the more Saladin began to feel his feet slip on the side of the fence of his leaving the business. Once more, Saladin was gripped with the feeling of ambiguity. There was no good reason for Ace to lie; however, he had fabricated a lie of his own the moment he said yes to the idea of hooking up with his three compadres.

"Why was Ace any different from me?"

He asked himself aloud.

Saladin knew it did not matter if Ace alone, or with the help of Angelika was behind the double-dealing. It only mattered that neither Cash nor the Reverend was ready to make their final push to run them out of business. Ace had placed himself in a win-win situation. Since Saladin knew Ace very well, he could count on Ace to choose the side he thought would win the battle. Saladin puffed a half a pack of cigarettes as he worked over various scenarios that would have him and his friends on top at the end of the day. Saladin puffed the rest of the pack as he pondered on how the feud between Bosco and Angelika was much deeper than either party portrayed. Saladin was less certain about Tony's newfound maturity that appeared to be as fleeting as a teenage fad.

Saladin emerged from backroom of Kelly's and his tired but lustful eyes fell upon the luscious gluteus maximus of Shanita. The petite, but shapely female had her back to Saladin, but her first clue to his presence was his strong hand palming her round ass. Shanita turned to Saladin, saw that he had a surprised look upon his face, and a devious but sexy smile appeared on her own as she addressed Saladin's surprise.

"I have no underwear on Saladin, which is just the way you like it!"

Shanita whispered into his ear as not to alert the lone customer to the nature of their conversation.

Shanita then turned to deal with the customer who asked her for a pack of cigarettes. As Shanita went about her job Saladin could not take his eyes off her ass. The moment the customer exited the store Saladin made the young vixen an offer she did not want to refuse.

"I want you to meet me outside after you get off work."

Saladin's proposed.

Shanita did not respond she only needed to smile to affirm her answer.

"Damn, what's taking that chick! I can't wait to get in her pants!"

Saladin moaned.

He had waited patiently in his car doubled parked in front of Kelly's for Shanita to sit her sexy ass in the passenger's seat of his car. The wait quickly made him very anxious. He turned his attention to anything that would take his mind off having sex with Shanita.

Saladin noticed of a group of New Jacks who congregated near the corner of 135th Street. Several of the young men blasted the latest Hip-Hop tunes from their very expensive sound systems of their ultra-luxurious cars blocking the intersection of 135th Street.

"Dumb ass kids gonna' bring The Reverend or Detectives Brown and Johnson down on their asses."

Saladin wondered how long it would take for these ignorant folk to be running from The Reverend and or Detectives Brown and Johnson. All thoughts of business fled from his mind the moment Shanita walked out of Kelly's towards his car.

Saladin reached over to open the passenger's door for his seductress, as he did so he checked the air vents on the passenger's side. He made sure that the cold air from the vents pointed directly on the passenger's seat. Saladin opened the door and Shanita hopped right into the soft leather seat as if it were made just for her. Saladin was captivated by her Nia Long short hairstyle, which for him highlighted her round eyes. His eyes then fell upon her full lips which alerted Saladin to her devious smile. Shanita unhooked the automatic seatbelt, and turned in time to caught the look of lust on his face. She understood that she was Saladin's Lady Du jour; however she planned on being around for longer than a day.

Saladin represented the finest catch for any young girl in the Ghetto. He was rich, nice looking, rich again and had strong, pectoral muscles. Any girl in the hood would do 'whatever' to sit in the seat she occupied. Shanita knew full well that Saladin could step out on her the moment she gave him some sex. Shanita also held no illusions that he would leave his family for her. She was a true gambler who would do whatever it took to prolong any relationship she would have with Saladin.

Shanita looked over to Saladin who had not taken his wanting eyes off her face since she sat in his car. She gave the excited man her sexiest smile then placed her arm on Saladin's shoulder as she stroked the back of his head. Shanita watched as Saladin's eyes roved down her body which pointed the way to his seedy thoughts. She took her hand away from the back of Saladin's head and shut off the air-condition much to the chagrin of Saladin. She positioned her body in a way that allowed her to rest her back against the car door. Shanita was better able to look Saladin in the eyes as she attempted to deflate his feelings of avarice through idle conversation.

The two had spoken before but for the first time the conversation revolved around their individual "Needs" and "Wants." Shanita tried her best to play the role of "money means nothing to me," however, a few well-placed questions on the part of a sly Saladin caused the young lady to come clean and speak the truth.

"I like the things you could give me as well as the places we can go together."

Shanita said as she looked down at her breasts. Her nipples were hardened due to Saladin's readjustment of the passenger's side air vent and they made a vivid impression through her white 'Wife Beater' Shanita quickly folded her arms which enabled her to cover the embarrassing event as she continued to express herself to Saladin.

"I may be a young girl, but I know there are many chicken-heads in Harlem who would love to be in my shoes, but if nothing would happen between us I won't trip!"

Shanita made her point by the tone of voice she used.

She spoke with a voice that made her appear to be older. Saladin listened to every word without comment. He wanted to assess whether Shanita was right for the role of his 'Chick on the Side.' Shanita continued to speak her mind in spite of the fact that she was in the middle of an audition.

"I ain't a freak Saladin. There are many things I will neva' do to you."

Shanita said in a strong voice.

She watched the blank expression on Saladin's face go unchanged and it unnerved the young woman. Shanita was in fear that she had somehow blown her one chance of getting close to the fantabulous looking moneybag named Saladin. Rather than continue on in a one-way conversation Shanita wisely sought to engage Saladin in conversation before it was too late. Looking him in the eye, she posed a question to him.

"What do you think of me?"

Her question brought no immediate response from Saladin. He remained quiet in an effort to figure out Shanita's intentions. Once she posed her question Saladin was willing to set the record straight.

"I think you are smart enough to know that I will never leave my wife."

Saladin bluntly stated. He paused as he noticed a fight that broke out among several of the New Jacks on the corner of 135th Street. He turned the key to his ignition stepped on the gas pedal and the engine roared to life. Saladin looked over to Shanita who had the looked as if she were about to be ejected from the car.

"My dick is hard and I know your coochie is wet. Let's go to my crib downtown and fuck. That is the only offer on the table!"

Saladin said, as he wanted to get to the point and get in some ass.

Shanita sat correctly in her seat and reattached her seat belt in preparation for the ride downtown. Saladin was satisfied that Shanita would work out just fine. He pulled his car out from the curb, and made a broken U-turn as he made his way towards his house to swing an episode with Shanita. Saladin chose to depart just in time as several police cars arrived to investigate the fight. Saladin quietly wondered if his dick had led him astray once again.

CHAPTER 25

Home Comes First

Saladin tried his best to steady his eyes and focus on the dark city road ahead; however the abundant amount of alcohol he had consumed earlier made that task difficult. Saladin remained awake and alert as the adrenaline raced through his body, for his soul was captured by fear. The fear of all the negative possibilities he would face him once he had arrived at his destination.

One half hour had past since his sex session with Shanita was interrupted by the last of several 911 pages from Sunshine. Saladin ignored the first pages from Sunshine, and when he finally answered her pages Saladin received the news that their son Charles was missing. Needless to say he jumped off Shanita and into his car making his way to the Bronx to meet Sunshine.

In spite of his erratic driving, Saladin managed to arrive in front of the 49th Precinct without incident. He located a parking spot close to the entrance of the precinct and haphazardly parked his car between two RMP's. He sat in his car for a moment as he tried to steady himself before he exited his ride. Saladin exited the car and was struck by the eerie silence of the neighborhood surrounding the Precinct. The inebriated man slowly made his way to the front door of the precinct and paused at the entrance as he wondered if he should proceed further on his quest. Saladin quickly rid his self of hesitation and continued on, as he knew he should.

He entered the building and staggered over to the desk where the midnight tour Desk Sergeant waited for him with folded arms. The tall heavy set white man had a look of disbelief on his face which Saladin could only interpret was directed at him. Saladin did not back away; he steadied his body and his mind before he spoke to the obviously annoyed officer.

"I'm looking for Sunshine Moreno, our son Charles is missing!"

Saladin could not recognize his own voice because his speech was slurred.

As he waited for a response, Saladin had to squint his bloodshot eyes to get a good look at the Sergeant and the man's response to his question. The bright light of the precinct nearly blurred his vision because his drunken state dominated his every breath. The Desk Sergeant stuck out his arm and pointed over Saladin's shoulder towards a back area of the precinct.

"Through that doorway sir, she's in the room straight ahead!"

The man spoke to Saladin in such a manner that he should have been offended, but Saladin could not comprehend the tone of voice used on him. As Saladin staggered 180 degrees and moved to the room he was directed to, he heard the Desk Sergeant speak some words of wisdom for his benefit.

"Get your mind right sir, or you will stay the night in jail!"

It took several seconds and a few feet traveled for him to process the comment, but there was no mistaking the sincerity in his voice.

Saladin made his way through a dark corridor towards the room located directly in front of him. As soon as he passed through the doorway he immediately caught sight of Sunshine. She stood on the other side at a window of an enclosed office. Sunshine had her back to the door therefore she did not see Saladin staggering towards the door. Saladin was about to open the door and proceed into the room when the words of the Desk Sergeant finally registered in his twisted mind. He immediately began to spruce up his haggard appearance. Saladin buttoned his shirt then tucked it in his pants but not before he removed his ten thousand dollar Rolex watch from his wrist. He completed his task, looked up and came eye to eye with a visibly disturbed Sunshine. Saladin could also feel his heart sink for he hoped that she would not notice that he was drunk.

In the time it would take a Corvette to go from zero to sixty miles per hour Saladin watched as Sunshine's facial expression change from disturbed to down right angry. In spite of his state of mind Saladin knew that Sunshine was angered by his drunkenness. Saladin felt his heart slip down to his stomach as he turned the doorknob and entered the room. He made his way to Sunshine and attempted to smooth things over with a kiss.

"Hey baby!"

Saladin said as he walked over to his woman to give her a kiss of the cheek. He felt Sunshine pull back from his kiss. The woman did not like the smell of alcohol therefore she held her nose as to not inhale his toxic breath. Saladin quickly recovered from the dis and instantly sought the answer to his darkest thought.

"What happened to Charles? Was he kidnapped?"

Saladin said as he ended his attempt to kiss Sunshine and realized that he was not alone in the room with Sunshine. Saladin became red faced as a complete stranger witnessed his brush off from Sunshine. He was not yet over the embarrassment of the brush off from Sunshine when the stranger, a Police Administrative Assistant addressed his presence in the room.

"Are you Charles's father?"

The older black woman asked in an emotionless tone of voice. The rather slender, brown-complexioned, middle-aged woman's tone of voice stuck Saladin as very confrontational. In his mind the question was evasive, and did not need to be answered. He took an instant dislike to the woman therefore he chose to ignore her question as he waited for Sunshine's answer to his question. Sunshine thought about telling a lie to Saladin because the truth would make him very upset, but the truth was what she decided to tell her man.

"I told you they changed my shift at the hospital and I had to work tonight. You did not come home in time and I had no choice but to ask my cousin Yolanda to…"

The very mention of Sunshine's alcoholic cousin Yolanda brought down Saladin's high, and increased his anger tenfold. Saladin lost track of where he stood and began a verbal tirade against his girl's poor choice.

"How could you leave our son with that irresponsible drunk? She probably fell asleep and somebody entered her house and snatched our child."

"Charles was not kidnapped *Saladin*."

"Then what happened to him Sunshine? Why are we here?"

"Yolanda said he wanted Burger King to eat instead of McDonalds…"

"What happened to him Sunshine?"

Sunshine did not like the tone of voice Saladin used on her. She became defensive because Saladin's concerns about Yolanda were true. Sunshine reluctantly disclosed to her angry man that Yolanda left Charles in the apartment while she went next door to chat with her neighbor. When she returned Charles was long gone. Sunshine watched Saladin's facial expression change the more she explained the circumstances of Charles' disappearance. He was about to explode, and there was not one thing Sunshine could do to prevent his pending eruption. Saladin's exploded in monumental peroration.

Saladin uttered one profanity laced sentence before he was cut short by the PAA. The woman slowly rose to her feet and made her way to the door as Saladin continued his tirade. The woman opened the door to the office to show Saladin the way out of the office.

"This is my office and I ain't got to put up with your crap like Sunshine thinks she must."

The woman pointed to the door as she directed Saladin towards the door.

"Take your drunk behind out to the bench in front and get your mind right!"

The woman spoke with finality in her voice.

"Every cop in this place gets their paychecks from me."

The woman turned to Sunshine and expressed her feelings as directly as she could.

"One word from you and your baby daddy will spend the night in jail!"

Saladin looked over at Sunshine in anticipation of her response. Sunshine did not respond to the woman's statement. The woman then opened the door a little wider which the belligerent man took as a sign to "Get out of Dodge"

Saladin scrambled out of the office to the sound of the door being slammed behind him. He made his way to the wooded bench that was adjacent to the front desk and plopped down on it with a thud. Saladin's mind continued to be clouded by the affects of drinking with Shanita. It was very difficult for to him to hold his head erect. Saladin rested his head on the cold brick wall next to the bench. This position allowed him to rest his head as he contemplated the many fears that reverberated through his mind. He could not help but wonder if he was right in the deception of his friends. Saladin continued to grapple with the idea of leaving the business even though he had set everything up for him to leave. Saladin soon found that holding his head in his hands was the best way to hold his heavy head erect as he changed his line of thought.

Saladin altered his thoughts to ponder the extent of action he would have to take against either Cash or The Reverend, if one or the others decided to make their move. He felt his window of opportunity to leave the business "Hood Rich" with money, and without a major felony or having his friends out to kill him, was closing fast. Once again his thoughts shifted to another more pressing subject. Saladin's cloudy mind tried to play a mental game of chess as he plotted all the necessary moves it would take for him to keep Shanita around without Sunshine discovering his cheating ways, when his thoughts were interrupted by the angry voice of a detective.

Saladin emerged from his thoughts when he heard a plain-clothes detective demand to know.

"What civilian parked in my spot?"

The questioned was posed to the Desk Sergeant who immediately pointed towards Saladin.

It did not help that Saladin was the only civilian to have entered the precinct house in the past forty-five minutes. The plain clothed detective gave a look of astonishment towards how someone as visibly drunk as Saladin appeared to be, could have operated any vehicle. Saladin witnessed the look of the detective and quickly remembered the lie he reminded himself to recite if questioned.

"I did not drive myself here officer."

Saladin said in a deliberate and slurred tone of voice.

"My friend Johnny drove me here!"

He said as he reached for his pocket several times before his hand found its way into the pocket where his keys were located.

Saladin handed the detective what he thought were his keys only to retrieve his Rolex, which he quickly returned to his pocket before he finally handed the detective the keys to his car. Saladin then returned his head to his hands and his mind to his plan for Shanita, without any thought of whether anyone bought his story.

Saladin awoke from a brief nap by a hard tap on the shoulder. Saladin opened his eyes and immediately caught sight of the pair of Boston Converse worn by the person who rudely tapped him on the shoulder.

"Wake yo' drunk ass up!"

Several seconds elapsed before Saladin was able to remember were he was and who spoke to him in such a condescending manner.

"Your keys are with the Desk Sergeant. You're lucky that I'm not in charge of the station this morning!"

The man said in reference to Saladin not being arrested by the desk Sergeant.

The inebriated man raised his head and adjusted his eyes from the light in the station house to get a look at the detective before the man departed the station house. Saladin returned his head to his hands as he wondered if the Desk Sergeant would be the next person to rudely tap him on the shoulder. The only thing that proved to disturb Saladin's rest was his uncooperative stomach.

Sweat began to drip down Saladin's forehead as his stomach began the first stages of reverse peristalsis. Saladin felt like a seasick passenger on a ship in the middle of a storm.

"Where is da' bathroom?"

Saladin begged the Desk Sergeant as he ran over towards the startled officer.

The Sergeant had barely enough time to point in the direction of the men's room before Saladin darted off to feed the porcelain. Ten minutes on his knees over a filthy toilet was enough to remind Saladin of why he gave up drinking; he could not hold his liquor! Saladin made his way to the sink where he tried his best to wash the bitter taste from his mouth by drinking as much water from the faucet as his stomach could handle. Saladin looked through the cracked mirror mounted on the wall over the sink and he took a good look at himself in the mirror and found nothing disturbing about his appearance. He was not the type of person who searched his soul for deeper meanings to life. Saladin was the type of person who never liked to allow things to bother him.

Saladin washed his face for the second time which he hoped would revive him enough that he could keep his thoughts straight in his mind. As he washed his face Saladin smelled the faint smell of sex on his hands, therefore the fearful man feverously cleaned both of his guilty appendages. As he went about his task Saladin could not clear his mind of the implications of Cash and the Reverend coming after the business he worked hard to create. Saladin continued to ponder implications of the merger even after he was finished and made his way out to the comfort of the bench. The closer Saladin got to the bench, the more his stomach began to turn and twist. At first he thought he was about to hurl once more, but the turning in his stomach was caused by something he could not locate. The more he thought of The Reverend the more his stomach turned. Saladin sat down on the bench before he was summoned to the same office he was tossed out of earlier by the surly PAA.

Saladin slowly made his way towards the office. Halfway down the hall Saladin's heart literally stopped at the sight of his son Charles in the office along side his mother. A stronger feeling of relief came over Saladin for his child was safe and sound. The joy he felt was soon suppressed by the look of anger on Sunshine's face. Sunshine had the same look on her face as she did whenever she was ready to hit Saladin upside the head with the first object she could put her hands on. Saladin rushed through the door of the office to step between mother and son before Sunshine went upside Charles' head.

Saladin would have been dead if looks could kill. The look Sunshine gave her man as he stepped between her and her son would have made the dead afraid. Sunshine wanted Saladin to say something slick out of his mouth, which would have given her a reason to pop off at the mouth with her drunken man. She was very proud to see that Saladin had learned from experience and kept his mouth shut. Sunshine expressed her appreciation to the two officers who found Charles, and the female PAA, and then led her family out of the office in single file.

Sunshine led her family outside the Precinct into the early morning air. The relative silence she experienced helped her to calm her frazzled nerves. The ordeal of losing her son and the arrival of his drunken father brought Sunshine's anger to the brink of eruption that she was determined to keep in check.

Sunshine's discipline lasted as long as it took Charles to cross path of vision. The angry woman hauled off and slapped her son upside his clean-shaven head. Sunshine watched as tears immediately fell from his brown eyes. The show of tears did not move Sunshine, because this time he would pay for his selfish ways.

Sunshine pointed in the direction of her car which was parked halfway down the block and demanded that Charles walk ahead to the car. Charles still felt the sting and embarrassment of being hit by his mother, and he moved slowly about his task. Sunshine took the deliberate and slow nature in which he went about his task as his way of trumping her authority. She reached out with her right hand and cuffed Charles by the back of his head and pushed him forward in the direction of her car. Sunshine's heavy-handed tactic was too much for Saladin to remain silent, especially since they stood in front of a Police Precinct. Saladin spoke up but he should have just kept his mouth closed.

"Sunshine, you don't need to man-handle the boy like that. He's just a kid!"

"You need to keep your fuckin' mouth shut and sober the hell up Saladin"

"You don't hafta' be so rough with him and *you damn well better watch how you speak to me!*"

"I want you to put your hands on me in front of the Five-O Saladin."

"Calm down Sunshine, this ain't the time for your drama Queen routine."

Saladin could feel his stomach throbbing in unison with his head. He forgot Bosco's Grandpa Douglass' favorite saying.

"Never argue with a woman."

Saladin thought that he would put the entire issue to rest, but he soon found that matters only got worse for him. Sunshine was now angry enough to kick his ass and his son's ass at the same time, damn the consequences.

Sunshine turned to Charles to see that the young boy had stopped in his tracks to witness the disagreement between Saladin and her. She removed her belt, took one step in the boy's direction and Charles took off towards the car. Sunshine then turned her anger towards Saladin who objected to his woman brandishing her belt at their son. Sunshine held the belt shoulder high in her hand with the idea of hitting Saladin with the belt. Sunshine paused as she calculated the worth of beating the shit out of the vulnerable drunk in Saladin. During her pause, Sunshine was able to look into the soul of Saladin through the window in his glassy eyes which revealed that the man she loved hid a secret from her.

"I know you ain't been fuckin' that bitch, your other son Saladin Junior's mother!"

She began to raise her voice as the idea that Saladin slept with the mother of his first-born child once again. Saladin was surprised that Sunshine was in the ballpark but glad she had named the wrong bitch.

Sunshine's anger towards Susan, Saladin Junior's mother did not allow Sunshine the luxury of thinking objectively on the matter. Saladin, although he was drunk easily denied the accusation made by Sunshine with a straight face. Sunshine gave up trying to get her man to confess to creeping out on her after several moments of debating with him. She instead warned Saladin of what would happen to him if she ever caught him cheating on her with Susan or any other woman.

"If you every think the grass is greener on the other side you're gonna need a Reverend to pray over your dead body!"

Sunshine announced as she approached Saladin and pressed her index finger into his forehead as a point of emphasis. She turned and walked towards her car in a huff, leaving Saladin alone as he wished that he were not too drunk to put his foot up Sunshine's ass for dissing him.

The drunken man did not want to ride home with Sunshine because he knew that she would bitch with him all the way home. He decided that he was going to drive home in *his own car*. He reached in his pocket for his keys but he fumbled them down to the pavement. Saladin slowly reached down for the keys and from the corner of his eye he caught sight of the desk Sergeant and two female officers and the P.A.A standing in the doorway of the Precinct House. They had patiently waited for Saladin to do anything that would allow them to step in and arrest him. The Desk Sergeant had given him a play for being drunk because his son had been missing. Since the story ended on a good note, the courtesy extended had been recalled.

Saladin was able to retrieve his keys after several attempts and he made his way slowly towards Sunshine, as she was about to drive off towards home. Saladin knocked on the passenger's window and Sunshine rolled the window down slowly.

"Aren't you gonna' let me in the car?"

Saladin asked; as he had to stoop down to speak through the window.

"Get your drunken ass in the back with your dumb ass son!"

Sunshine unlocked the backdoor and Saladin sat next to his son who continued to feel the effect of being hit upside the head. Sunshine looked through the rearview mirror at the two selfish men in her life and muttered to herself.

"Dumb ass niggers."

Charles heard his mother call him and his father the word she forbade him to use and he was going to scold his mother for being a hypocrite. Charles was about to fix his mouth when he relieved another slap on the head, this time by his father.

"You're in enough trouble already."

Saladin said to Charles who began to cry once again. Saladin then put his head back in the seat and fell fast asleep.

Somewhere between his conscious and subconscious, Saladin put together the puzzle that had his stomach turning all night. Saladin had saw the green Boston Converse sneakers worn by the detective once before all the henchmen of the Reverend had worn them. The idea that the Reverend had a cop on the payroll explained why he always managed to stay out of the limelight. He was too tired to dwell on the subject. It would have to wait until the morning when his mind was clear. Saladin fell asleep at the moment of his greatest discovery.

CHAPTER 26

Trouble Comes in Threes

Throughout his childhood Saladin often heard his mother say that: Trouble comes in threes whenever a very bad incident occurred. The meaning of his mother's pronouncement went unknown to Saladin until the morning after Charles' disappearance brought it to light.

Saladin placed his relationship with Sunshine in great jeopardy when he crept out with Shanita. She took Saladin's word that he had been out drinking with Ace, but she was made aware that he put hanging out with his friends over taking care of his home. For years she had carried all the weight of raising their son and taking care of the house. Her son's disappearance caused Sunshine to become more determined to force Saladin to pull his weight around the house.

"Shit would not go on as usual until you pull your weight around the house!" Sunshine told Saladin. Saladin did not take the threat seriously because he had heard it many times in the past.

Saladin had been in Sunshine's doghouse more times than he should have, and each time he managed to get into her good graces in no time. He would use his gift of gab, and if that did not work, he would surprise her with some type of expensive gift. Saladin followed his pattern and was disturbed at the results. Doors continued to be slammed in his face and Saladin continued to spend his nights on the sofa bed in the guest bedroom. After another vicious argument with

Sunshine over his role in the house, Saladin drove down to the city to holler at Bosco about Sunshine, as well as his revelation about the Reverend.

For forty-three minutes Saladin who needed him to be a sounding board in his situation with Sunshine held Bosco hostage. Bosco thought he had been called downstairs from his father Tad's house to get important news from Saladin on the Reverend. Instead he was bombarded with Saladin's bitching about Sunshine.

Bosco quietly listened to his friend go on about Sunshine's demands and how impractical it was for him to do what she wanted. Bosco became impatient but he continued to nod his head at the appropriate time in the conversation, in affirming the weak points mentioned by Saladin. It became apparent to Bosco that Saladin was not going to stop the bitching, therefore the moment Saladin paused in thought Bosco took over the conversation.

"I agree with Sunshine. Most of the problems between you two is your fault." Bosco's honest assessment caused Saladin to stop and listen. Saladin listened quietly as Bosco took the time to warn him about stepping out.

"Sunshine is too smart a woman to be blind to all the women Saladin."

Bosco looked directly at Saladin as he continued to speak.

"I won't wanna be you when she removes the blinders!"

Bosco chuckled as he pictured Saladin's fate at the hands of a vengeful Sunshine. Saladin thought it was funny too but he stopped in mind chuckle when he imagined the damaged Sunshine would do to him if she acknowledged his cheating ways. Saladin did not chuckle as hard as Bosco because the joke was on him. The light moment ended when a female passerby moved past Saladin's car carrying a box with a steaming hot pizza inside. The pizza reminded the two men of their pending business troubles.

Saladin was the first of the two men to break the silence because he had more to lose than Bosco. Saladin followed the young lady with his eyes until she disappeared into the lobby of Tad's building. Not being able to see the young lady brought a troubling situation to mind.

"The Feds have totally shut down the heroin pipeline from Sicily. There ain't that much product to get anymore."

Saladin spoke in a tone of voice that was full of frustration.

It was difficult for Saladin to come to the realization that he was not in control of his environment. Bosco had heard the same bit of news earlier that day, and he too could not believe how clever the Mafia appeared.

"I would have never thought that Pizza shops could be fronts for heroin smuggling."

Bosco had to shake his head in disbelief for he had more dreadful news to add.

"The Feds also put the K-bosh on the flow of cocaine from the Columbians. Ain't shit to sell on the street but weed!"

Saladin was very surprised at the revelation made by Bosco. There had never been a time when there was no product to sell. For once, Saladin did not have a clue to what should be done by the crew. He expressed his lack of an answer to their predicament to Bosco.

"We hafta' call a meeting. You, Tony, me, and that trick Angelika gotta have a sit down on what should be done."

Saladin sounded like a defeated man to Bosco and it started him thinking.

Bosco looked down at his diamond-studded bracelet that adorned his left wrist. The bracelet was the first major purchase Bosco made as he entered the world of big money. Bosco adjusted his prized possession several times before he joked with Saladin.

"We can always quit. All our problems would be solved."

Bosco laughed at his joke but when Saladin did not smile, Bosco realized that he might have touched on a serious topic. Bosco adjusted his bracelet once again before he posed a tough question to Saladin.

"How serious are you about leaving the business Saladin?"

"I'm as serious as a heart attack Bosco!"

"How soon are you talking about leaving Saladin?"

"As soon as I can make sure I have enough money to buy my freedom from the business."

"How much money do you think it will take you?"

Bosco had to wait a moment for his answer; Saladin had to make a quick mental calculation.

"It will take more money that I have Bosco!"

Saladin had salted away millions of dollars over the years. If Saladin did not have enough money to emancipate him, there was very little hope for Bosco. Saladin looked over and caught a glimpse of Bosco doing some calculations of his own.

"You're thinking about leaving the business too?"

Saladin said as he checked his Rolex to read the time. It was 12:13pm.

"Don't be surprised Saladin. You ain't the only mutha fucka looking to the future!"

The two shared another chuckle, and once again the chuckle was short lived.

Saladin informed Bosco of his suspicion about the Reverend having a New York City Police officer on his payroll. Bosco was not the least bit surprised by the information. The suspicion was plausible since it explained why the Reverend had never made any of the NYPD's top ten lists. Just as Saladin was perplexed about what to do with the nugget of information, Bosco also had no clue as to what should be done. What the two men could agree on was that Tony should be enlightened with the new information, while Angelika would be kept in the dark. They also set a date and time for their next meeting. Bosco left Saladin's company around 1:00 o'clock in the morning, but not before he left his good friend with some sound advice.

"You have someone in Sunshine that brothers on the street would die to have. Get your house in order before she leaves your dumb ass!"

Saladin nodded his head at the truthful statement then drove off towards home and another night on the couch.

Bosco was glad to end his long conversation with Saladin. He leapt out of the car and stood on the quiet street to stretch his legs while he watched Saladin's tail lights disappear into the traffic of the night. Bosco quietly wondered how long it would take Sunshine to discard the cheating Saladin who was not about to put an end to his ways. His thoughts turned from Saladin's problems with Sunshine, to Penelope who waited in his bed for his return. Bosco swelled with emotion which served to propel him into the lobby of Tad's building. Bosco pressed for the elevator then looked outside to the street through the dirty lobby window. Several recollections of his conversation with Saladin came to the forefront of his mind, and pushed Penelope to the back burner.

Bosco did not know what to make of Saladin's belief of a cop working for the Reverend, but if anyone could put two and two together it was Tony. The sound of the ping that announced the arrival of the elevator brought Bosco's thoughts to another point. Saladin's admission about "needing more to get out of the business" meant that the man had formulated a plan to get money. Bosco wanted very much to get in on whatever deal his friend put together, for big money would no doubt be made. The elevator door opened and Bosco entered. He stepped over the garbage strewn about the floor of the elevator to press Tad's floor. The moment the door slammed shut his thoughts left business and turned to love.

Bosco entered Tad's apartment ready to do work on Penelope. She had returned home from a three-week family reunion to St. Thomas V.I. and Saladin's call interrupted their exchange of body fluids. Bosco locked the door and began to walk down the hall towards his room and Penelope. As he made his way down the hall he caught sight of his father and Ms. Green seated on the couch. The two carried on as if they were teenagers on a first date. Bosco was not mad at his father for finding a new love; he knew those six years of mourning his mother was more than enough time spent cherishing the dead. Ms. Green was not his mother, but Bosco had nothing but love for the funny spiritual woman. In the middle of his thoughts about his long lost mother Bosco came upon the open door of his younger brother Gregory's room. This night Bosco paid no attention to the sloppy appearance of his brother's room. Neither was Bosco about to make Gregory not sleep on his stomach to end his snoring. Penelope waited just two doors down, and time was of the essence.

Bosco made the sign of the cross as he passed Grandpa Douglass' old room. The thought of both his mother and grandfather together in heaven made losing them easier to bear. Bosco came to his room, and before he entered he waved at his father and Ms. Green, who did not acknowledge him. Tad was too busy feeding his girl grapes to pay the world any attention. Bosco entered the room to find Penelope had fallen asleep as she waited for his return. Bosco thought it best that he washed his ass while Penelope was asleep because one of her pet peeves was Bosco not washing before they made love. Bosco returned to his room from his long relaxing shower, and found Penelope still fast asleep. Bosco toweled down and dressed in the dark so as not to disturb his sleeping beauty.

Bosco slipped into bed onto the satin sheets and pressed up against Penelope who was on her side with her back facing the door. Bosco felt his nature rise as he lay next to his girl foaming at the mouth at the thought of getting what he had missed for three weeks. Penelope also felt her man's resolve stiffen but the long wait had killed the mood for her.

"What took you so long?"

Penelope said as she kept her back to her man.

"Saladin pulled my ear about Sunshine all night."

Bosco hoped that he would still be able to get some; therefore he kept his attitude out of conversation.

"Saladin is going to literally fuck himself out of a good relationship with Sunshine!"

Penelope spoke in a serious voice as if her word was bond. Penelope then reached behind her to adjust his penis which was poking her in her back.

"You better keep "Walt Wiggly" in your pants. I'm too tired!"

She said as she yawed loudly. Bosco was frustrated, but he understood Penelope was tired after the long plane ride home. He inched closer to his love, this time instead of seeking sex he sought comfort in a hug.

Bosco draped his arm around the side of Penelope's body and held her tightly against his body. His neatly manicured hand came to rest upon the bed bedside her lovely head. The instant his hand came to rest she kissed it then gently rested her head upon it as if his hand was a pillow. The show of affection was more than he expected.

As they lay nestled to one another, their bodies close enough together to resemble one entity; Bosco felt his world had begun to change. He pushed his business problems to the outer edges of his mind. The threats of the mothers of his children suing him for child support became as distant as the Milky Way. Bosco was truly in love, and he could never imagine another woman making him feel as Penelope did at that moment. His joy was short-lived when in the middle of his thought he felt a single drop of warm water fall onto the back of his hand. To his shock Bosco realized that Penelope was in tears. The reason for the tears soon followed.

"Every time I feel this way about a man that man leaves me."

She spoke in a garbled voice because she was choked with emotion. She took a second to catch her breath before she continued with her thoughts.

"I got this feeling that you are going to leave me. I wouldn't know what to do if that happened!"

Bosco placed yet another kiss on the back of Penelope's head as he searched for words that would comfort her spirits.

"As long as I am on this earth I will always love you."

Bosco words would prove to be prophetic. Events were unfolding that would challenge his pledge to Penelope.

＊   ＊   ＊   ＊

Although Cash was wide-awake, he kept his eyes closed as he lay floating on his back on his waterbed. Cash took a deep breath and filled his lungs of morning air accented with the smell of bacon and eggs. Once again his new girlfriend Juliana had prepared the only hot breakfast she could prepare. Cash took another long deep breath and the memory of his ex-girlfriend Tracy entered his mind. Instead of pushing the memory of Tracy aside as he often does, he allowed the chain of thought to continue.

He did not want to open his eyes for it might ruin his precious memory of good eating and even better loving. The hungry man took another deep breath as the memory of the good aroma of her cooking faded into the past. His reason for kicking Tracy and their child to the curb was that she had become more like a wife to him than a girlfriend; Cash did not want any woman that comfortable with him! Getting rid of Tracy seemed to be his only option.

Cash finally opened his eyes and was greeted by the bright rays of the sun which showed through the windows. The surprise of the morning sun directly in his eyes forced Cash to close them once again. He was angry that Juliana had again left the shade open to the window which allowed the sun to speed the transition into a conscious state of mind. Cash was just about to turn over and bury his head under the covers to get another 15 minutes of rest when the door to the bedroom suddenly flew open which ended the idea of more rest. He was startled enough that he looked over towards his gun which lay in his holster on the dresser. It was not until the door, almost hitting the paper-thin sheetrock wall, opened wide enough to reveal who the culprit was.

Cash looked over towards the doorway at Juliana who stood in the doorway of his bedroom doing her best impression of an angry black woman. Her chest swelled with each breath she took and her brown eyes were red with rage. Juliana held a cordless phone in her hand and in a huff threw it in Cash's direction as she spat angry words at him.

"It's **that bitch** Tracy on the phone! Tell her not to call here anymore!"

If not for an Ozzie Smith type catch; Cash would have been hit in the coconut with the phone. Cash remained as calm as he possibly could as he answered the phone. He remembered how close he had come to being arrested the last time he put his hands on Juliana and decided that she was not worth the trouble at that moment. Cash had an attitude and answered the phone as if the person on the other line was responsible for his trouble with Juliana.

The voice on the other line belonged to that of Tracy the mother of his daughter and only child. Cash could not understand one word she said because she cried as she spoke. Cash had just spoken to the woman two nights prior and the conversation was about him being more of a father to his daughter, Precious Joy. Cash did not want to hear what she had to say because he had heard the crying and begging to take her back already. Juliana waited for Cash to bless the troublesome Tracy out, as soon as it appeared that he was not going to do just that Juliana stomped out of the room and angrily slammed the door as hard as she could. Needless to say Cash was only half listening to Tracy's ramblings. He quickly sought to get the frantic woman to make sense of her conversation.

"If you don't stop the cryin' I'll hang up on your sorry ass Tracy!"

Cash ordered. In a matter of seconds Tracy heeded the warning and calmed down, in order that she made sense.

"Black Reggie's girlfriend called me early this morning. He did not go home last night."

Tracy's voice was full of tension. She knew Cash well enough to know that he could hang up on her before she could fully explain herself. She only hoped that he would allow her to explain.

Cash could not believe Tracy called him to tell him about Reggie. He believed that the call was yet another game to win him back from Juliana. To Cash, time was precious and he was not about to waste time on Tracy.

"What does that hafta' do wit' me?"

Cash asked. The woman knew that if she did not get straight to the point she would be treated rudely. She took a second to gather her thoughts in a concise manner then fearlessly continued to speak.

"On the news this morning a man was found shot dead in his car in Brooklyn, Cash."

"Tracy, you are about to hear the dial tone."

Cash said, as he was ready to carry out his threat.

"The man wore an Orange flight jacket and drove a periwinkle blue Corvette just like Reggie!" Tracy yelled over the phone. Her last statement caused butterflies in his stomach to take flight. It quickly dawned on him that the early rising Black Reggie had not checked in with him after the previous nights meeting with the Reverand.

"I'll call ya' back later!"

Cash said as he abruptly terminated his conversation with Tracy. Cash needed to quell the butterflies in his stomach.

Cash immediately picked up his mobile phone to dial Black Reggie's second mobile phone. If he was out with some chicken-head he would answer his second phone not his primary. After several rings a strange voice answered Reggie's phone and Cash quickly disconnected the call. He could feel his heart race as he jumped off the bed and ran into the living room where the only television was located. It was twelve O'clock in the afternoon and the midday news was underway. He reached the living room to find Juliana watching a romance movie on a cable station.

"Turn to the fucking news right now!"

Cash demanded of Juliana as he continued into the bathroom to run the shower. He returned a few moments later to find that his girl had ignored his command. Cash found it very difficult to keep his anger in check.

"What did I tell you to do Juliana?"

He yelled as he attempted to take the remote from the protesting woman.

"I want to see the end of the movie Cash!"

She responded as the couple had a tug-o-war for the remote control. The realization that everything in the house was his changed his entire demeanor. Cash reached down, took hold of Juliana's do-bee wrapped hair and pulled tight.

"The next time you call the cops on me I'll leave you dead and stinking. Give me the remote you fuckin' chicken-head!"

Juliana handed over the remote without further protest. Cash quickly turned to the local CBS station and waited for any information on the story Tracy described. Five minutes into the news, Cash's worst fear came to fruition. Two minutes later, his pager blew up with pages from all his associates who must have watched the midday news as well.

Black Reggie, his right hand man was dead. There was no doubting that fact. Cash was in the middle of his thoughts of disbelief when his heard the door to his bedroom slam shut by Juliana which managed to change his thoughts from shock to anger. Cash's blood began to boil as thoughts of revenge took hold of his person. He took a quick shower got dressed and left his apartment without speaking a word to Juliana who had barricaded herself in the bedroom. Cash was headed for the local payphone to make calls to his associates that would be hard to trace by the police if they were listening. Cash left his apartment certain that he knew Black Reggie's killers and more certain to get the revenge that was driving his every breath.

CHAPTER 27

Dreams Come True

Saladin abruptly opened his eyes and he immediately began to survey his very unfamiliar surroundings. His brain was slow to awake, therefore he could not ascertain if he was in his subconscious or awake in his conscious. Like a computer screen which painstakingly revealed a long awaited image to its user, Saladin's brain processed the information which made his state of mind all too clear.

Like the lyrics to the 70's song "It's Cheaper to Keep Her" Saladin found it advantageous to keep Sunshine than allow her to simple walk out of his life. After taking the family on a one-week vacation to the very expensive Disneyland in Florida, Saladin then set his attention on pleasing Sunshine. The money he spent made him wonder if the lyrics to the song were necessarily true. Saladin decided that taking Sunshine on their first trip out of the country to Rio de Janeiro, Brazil, would be an excellent way of smoothing things over with his love. One of the reasons Saladin chose the vacation destination was based on what he saw during a James Bond movie, his other reason was more esoteric.

Rio was a world away from the mean streets of NYC. For the first time in his adult life Saladin did not have to put on airs or look over his shoulders for lurking hit men. Saladin was well out his element which allowed him to bond more securely with Sunshine. Her memories of her irresponsible man were replaced with the possibility of a beautiful life they would spend together. The wonderful thoughts of a long life with Sunshine were dashed as the events of his reoccurring dream rushed to the forefront of his mind once again. Saladin turned to his left to marvel at how beautiful Sunshine looked in her sleep. Her altered state allowed him to ponder the meaning of the dream peacefully.

Saladin closed his eyes and re-entered his dream destined to discover its elusive meaning. Saladin drifted into the fog of his subconscious. Although most of his dream was obscured through the haze, Bosco's words were concisely etched in his conscious mind.

Saladin envisioned Bosco seated at the table at his downtown hideaway as he sipped on a glass of Kool-Aid from his Tiffany Crystal. Bosco waited patiently for him to get dressed after a long shower. Saladin suddenly caught sight of Bosco by the door dressed in a black hat and tails. His patience had apparently worn out.

"Wait for me Bosco all I have to do is put on my shoes!"

Saladin said as he ran down the hallway of his apartment after his friend. Bosco stopped at the open door turned to the pursuing Saladin and said simply,

"I must make this trip on my own!"

Bosco then walked out the door and disappeared into a forest of blue trees. Saladin tried to follow, but his movement towards the door was infinitely slow. He wondered why his friend would leave him.

Saladin surfaced from his dream analysis and looked over to Sunshine whom he believed was still asleep. The man became agitated, as the meaning of the dream remained as empty as the word "Love." He tossed and turned in the bed several times as he tried his best to find a position which would allow him to become comfortable enough to solve the riddle of the dream. His erratic movement in bed caused Sunshine to speak on his restlessness.

"The purpose of a vacation is get rid of your problems, not keep em, and relax with your family, not stress them out more,"

Sunshine spoke while her eyes were shut. The moment she opened them and looked upon Saladin's perplexed facial expression she intuitively knew the root cause for his apparent distress. Sunshine sprung into action to calm her man's fears.

She inched closer to Saladin who lay on his back, his hands clasped behind his head as he looked out of the window at the bright moon lit night for the answer to his problems. Sunshine snuggled up to her man and laid her head upon his strong chest. From this position she could hear and feel his heart beating like a drum. Sunshine tenderly caressed his stomach as she spoke.

"You are trying to stay one step ahead of Cash and the Reverend in case they try to get at you for the death of Black Reggie. Everything always works out fine for you Saladin."

She suggested. Saladin never talked business around Sunshine but she always seemed to have the pulse of the street at her fingertips.

"How did you know about Black Reggie?"

Saladin quizzed Sunshine who answered him in a playful manner.

"Girl's gotta have some secrets."

Sunshine untied the strings to Saladin's pajama bottom and moved closer to Saladin than a second skin. Saladin could see right through his woman's scheme. Saladin knew Sunshine's ultimate goal, and he was not in the mood for any of her shenanigans.

"Is that all I am to you, a sperm donor?"

Saladin removed his hands from the back of his head to retie the strings on his pajamas.

"Making another baby ain't on my agenda at the moment Sunshine."

He said as he finished retying his pajama strings then placed his hands to their prior location. Sunshine quietly watched as her avenue of pursuit was closed. The resourceful woman did not give up, she simply took a predetermined detour.

Sunshine had been with Saladin through good times and bad, and the one thing she knew about her man was that he did not like to leave much to chance. He always wanted to be one or more moves in front of his competition. This quality made him a good businessman, but it made him a lousy companion during the bad times. Sunshine had studied her man well enough to know what to give him in order for her to get what she wanted.

She praised his choice of her cousin Bones as his second in command. She reminded him that it was Bones who ran the business when they traveled to Tennessee for Thanksgiving. She also reminded him that he had just spoken to Bosco who told Saladin that business was good.

"Bosco felt good enough about business that he even invited your son Charles to the white linen party he and Penelope plan to have."

Sunshine reminded her man. Saladin pictured the sight of sneaker and jean king Ace, dressed in white linen and a smile came across his face. Sunshine saw the same smile and she knew she had succeeded on the first leg of her journey.

"It's hard to believe that Bosco and Penelope are still together. From the first day they met I didn't think they would last!"

Saladin said as he looked over to the clock on the nightstand and discovered it was three in the morning.

"Bosco's dreams have come true. He has a good woman, he finally has some type of relationship with his children and we are making big money."

Saladin finished his comment and looked down on Sunshine whose look on her face disturbed him.

"What did I say?"

He incredulously asked Sunshine. She looked up at Saladin and began to spit fire.

"Make all my dreams come true Saladin. Stop dissin' me wit' those chicken head and make me your wife but most of all I want another baby!"

Sunshine untied Saladin's pajama strings once again this time she pulled his pants down to his ankles.

"After all the shit you have put me through you should want to make my dream of having a child come true!"

Saladin had no defense for not trying to fulfill Sunshine's dreams.

CHAPTER 28

Hell to Pay

Saladin did not have a chance to pull the key out of the door before he was nearly stampeded by his son Charles. The young boy darted up the stairs towards his bedroom and the Sega Genesis game system his "Uncle Bosco" purchased for him. Three weeks away from home gave Charles a case of separation anxiety. The sooner he could get to his beloved game the better he would feel.

"Damn, boy could you let me get the key outta' the door!"

Saladin said as he laughed at how quickly Charles ascended the stairs to his room. Sunshine stood behind Saladin and had dropped several pieces of mail she held on the ground as she helped Saladin to stabilize himself from an impending fall.

"If that boy would show the same enthusiasm for school as he does for the game he would be a genius."

Sunshine said as he knelt down to pick up the pieces of mail she had dropped.

"Amen."

Saladin responded before he struggled through the door with their luggage.

Saladin entered the house and headed straight to the den where he deposited them. He then dashed out of the den towards the kitchen and the bottle of Welch's Grape Juice he craved all the way from Rio. Saladin nearly knocked Sunshine down as she entered the den just as he dashed out.

"You are just as bad as your son!"

She yelled at the offending man. Sunshine placed the large amount of mail that had gone uncollected onto a small table in the room. She then retired upstairs to check on Charles and to change into her comfortable house clothes.

The best part of any vacation for Saladin was the return home. He always enjoyed himself where ever he went, but for Saladin there was no better place to relax than home. He put on his house shorts and Tee shirt, kicked up on the couch to watch a gangster movie on the television. Sunshine soon joined her man on the couch and for Saladin the night was complete. The couples' blissful moment would be short lived. The telephone began to ring the instant the moment was right for romance. Saladin did not want to answer the phone but the continuous rings forced him to answer. Saladin picked up the phone and spoke in a direct manner.

"Speak to me. It's your dime but my time."

Saladin said as he looked over at Sunshine who looked as if she wanted some cuddling time with him. The caller turned out to be Bones, Sunshine's cousin, and Saladin's lieutenant who was more direct than Saladin.

"There is no easy way to tell you but Bosco was murdered last night!"

Saladin became flash frozen as if he were a pack of frozen vegetables. Sunshine saw the shock come over her man's face as the phone slowly fell out of his hands. Sunshine immediately picked up the phone from off the floor to ascertain the reason her man was in total shock. For several minutes many thoughts as well as memories passed through his mind muddling each thought. The meaning of his reoccurring dream had painfully come to light. Saladin then began to feel a sense of guilt, thinking that maybe he caused his dream to come to fruition.

It took several minutes for him to gain enough composure to get back on the phone to learn the circumstances of Bosco's murder from Bones. Saladin learned that Bosco was killed in his new downtown apartment by a bullet in the face. The police theorized that Bosco must have struggled at the door with the killer before he was shot. No valuables appeared to be taken by the killer. There were no clues to who might have killed Bosco. However, the deceased Bosco did something strange that baffled even veteran police officers.

Bosco crawled from the door leaving a minuscule amount of blood on his beige carpet to his bedroom. He made his way to the closet where he smeared blood on the sleeve of the white linen suit Bosco bought for Charles to wear to the party then fell dead. There was no rhyme or reason for this to happen but since he was a drug dealer the investigation was a cursory one. Very little thought was put into the case once the police found 250,000 dollars in cash in a suit case in the same closet.

Saladin was no detective, but he knew that Cash had to be behind the murder. He soon found him self on the phone with a frantic Tony who was ready to go to war with anyone who might have had a hand in the murder. Saladin did not argue with Tony, he too was ready to go to war but he first had to talk to his and Cash's supplier, Don Giovanni before he would move on Cash. Saladin quickly left his house to rush to the side of Bosco's devastated father, Tad. The man was inconsolable, as was Bosco's younger brother Gregory. Tad had lost another son to the streets and Gregory had lost his last fascination for life on the streets. Saladin promised death to the person who took Bosco away. Tad convinced him to hold off the talk of revenge until Bosco was in the ground.

Saladin did not sleep comfortably in the days leading up to the funeral. In the back of his mind he believed that he or Tony might be the next person to die in a street war. He also knew that sooner or later Don Giovanni would call on him for a sit-down with Cash, since the mafia kingpin would not want his two best workers going to war against one another. The call for a meeting with Don Giovanni came on the eve of Bosco's funeral. He was to bring Tony and Angelika to the famous Rao's on 113th Street forthwith.

CHAPTER 29

The Sit Down

The irony of the meeting-taking place at Rao's was not lost on anyone at the meeting. Rao's was one of the favorite eateries of mobster "Crazy Joe Gallo." Crazy Joe lost his life outside of Rao's partly because he brought blacks drug dealers into the fold like Nicky Bonds which the other mobsters of the day objected. Saladin was a bit leery of attending the meeting because the restaurant was a favorite location for the feds to stake out. When Saladin arrived in Tony's car they were glad to realize that Ben Franklin High Basketball Team led by Walter Berry and Ritchie the Animal Adams were holding their awards dinner at the restaurant. Any black person entering the establishment would be associated with the basketball team.

Tony and Saladin made their way past the Ben Franklin Basketball Team to a back area of the restaurant and a large table. Both men were not surprised to find Angelika seated at the table. She sat with her back to the door and did not see Tony and Saladin arrive. Saladin noticed the only two seats left unoccupied were next to Angelika, also with the back to the door. Saladin did not like the idea of his back was at the door. He also did not like the fact that the Reverend was present and his supplier was absent.

"Where is your father? I thought he would be here?"

Saladin posed his question to Don Giovanni's son Handsome Paul.

Handsome Paul received his nickname not because he was a good-looking fellow. He was a cross between his short stout Italian father and his pale red head

Irish mother. The reason for the nickname was that before he gave the order to whack someone he would always comb his hair.

"I speak for my father Saladin. My words are his words."

Handsome Paul answered Saladin as if the question annoyed him. Tony and Saladin sat down knowing that the outcome of the meeting would favor Cash. Handsome Paul's actions only proved their worst fears.

Saladin and Cash each denied committing the murders of Black Reggie and Bosco respectively. Each man blamed the nasty deed on outside forces neither had control over.

"It sounds rather cliché but I had noting to do with Black Reggie' death."

Saladin confessed. He looked into the eye of Handsome Paul and The Reverend for acknowledgement of his statement. Saladin did not like the look either man gave at his statement. The look on Handsome Paul's face paled to the words that came out of his mouth.

"I am not here for that; I could care less who killed Black Reggie or Bosco! I am here to protect my father's interests."

Handsome Paul calmly stated. Paul thought of himself as a throw back gangster. He lived for the stories his father told about the "Good Ole Days." He longed to walk in the footsteps of those Mafia men who made their wealth and fortune through traditional ways like gambling, prostitution, extortion and racketeering. He likened his work, close work with niggers and Spics to going to a proctologist. For that matter Handsome Paul made up his mind on all compensation before he sat down at the meeting. Handsome Paul peered over to Angelika and gave the woman such a dirty look that she was frightened into silence. Handsome Paul wasted no time in getting down to business.

He dispatched an nervous waiter who attempted to recite the menu for the day. He made sure the man had disappeared before he would discuss business matters. Handsome Paul pulled a long black Ace comb from his suit pocket and placed it on the table next to the dining fork. Needless to say everyone waited for him to comb his hair!

"There ain't gonna' be no war between your camps understand."

Handsome Paul's words were more of a statement than a question. Everyone at the table understood that Paul's word was his bond. He sipped on the glass of red wine he nursed the entire night. Placed the half full glass onto the table and continued to issue his proclamation.

"The first order of business is that there is a limited amount of new product set to arrive any day. Cash will get all he can afford."

Handsome Paul looked across the table directly into the red eyes of the hot-headed Tony as he continued to pontificate.

"Cash will get a part of Bosco's territory as compensation for losing his best earner end of story!"

"What about the loss of our best earner Paul. What kind of compensation do we receive?"

Saladin politely quizzed.

"You and your crew get to live another day Saladin. How is that for compensation?"

Handsome was finished with his business and motioned for the eager waiter to approach the table, however before the waiter moved within earshot of the table he issued a warning to everyone at the table.

"If anyone gets outta' line the Reverend will have my total approval to do as he sees fit with any rule breakers!"

Handsome Paul took a long cigar from his suit pocket and placed it onto the table next to his glass of vino. The Reverend instantly motioned for one of his henchmen who sat at a nearby table to come forward to light the cigar. The mobster immediately motioned for The Reverend's henchmen to stay seated. He then ordered food from the menu for Cash and the Reverend purposely excluding Saladin Tony and Angelika.

Angelika slowly made her way out of Rao's as the result of the outcome weighed heavily on her mind. She made her way through the reminisce of the Basketball Party, and exited the Rao's where she found Tony and Saladin standing and smoking cigarette on the steps of the restaurant. Angelika approached both men who initially did not notice her because their backs were to her. Tony turned around, took one quick look at Angelika, tossed his cigarette down in disgust and walked away. Saladin did the same when he realized that Angelika was behind him, but before he walked away he made sure to flick his cigarette butt in her direction. Angelika did not allow the obvious disrespect shown to her by her colleagues or the cool fall air to deter her from her mission. Angelika draped her fashionably short sweater around her bare shoulders and proceeded to follow Tony and Saladin.

The walk towards Tony's car parked on 116th Street and Second Avenue was a silent one for all involved. The occasional passing car that raced down the nearly deserted avenue occasionally broke the silence of the night. Angelika continued to trail the two chain smoking men up the darkened streets of Spanish Harlem. By the time the trio reached their destination Tony and Saladin had smoked three cigarettes each. The stress to the evening's proceedings had both men vexed as they quietly pondered how they would be able to navigate through the mine-field laid down by Handsome Paul. Tony had wanted to reach across the table to strangle Cash, but with his increased age came a modicum of wisdom. His restraint lasted until he realized Angelika played his shadow to the night. Tony did nothing to dispel Sigmund Freud's theory of displacement when he verbally attacked Angelika.

"What the fuck is you doing here with _us_?"

Tony pointed his finger at Saladin then at himself as if Angelika did not know the *"Us"* he had referred.

Tony who had opened his car door slammed it shut then walked around the rear of his car to confront Angelika. He stopped within inches of Angelika as he pointed his stubby fingers in the woman's face.

"Take your fat ass back to Cash and The Reverend before I forget I treat you like the trick you are!"

Tony was full of rage at this point.

He spat his words out as if he had rid himself of unwanted sunflower seeds into Angelika's face. Angelika stood her ground. She did not back down to Ace, and she was, as she thought in her mind not going to back down to Tony. When the angry man paused for air she decided to defend herself.

"Ace will be in town tomorrow for the funeral. You can take up your beef with him!"

Angelika calmly stated as she removed Tony's finger from her face.

Experience had taught Angelika how to deal with an angry man. She spoke to Tony in a calm but firm voice.

"If I sold you out to Cash and The Reverend you two would have stepped to Ace and me already."

Angelika continued to speak without emotion in her voice.

Her tone of voice seemed to make the air outside colder than it appeared. Sal-adin who was about to enter Tony's car at the time Tony went after Angelika, made his way between the two combatants. Deep down inside his soul Saladin could not bring himself to believe that Ace sold them out to the enemy, therefore he wanted to give her one last chance to explain which side of the fence she and Ace stood.

"Why should we believe you are on *our* side? Everything you have done bene-fits you not us Angelika. Convince us that you have not turned coats!"

Saladin demanded. Angelika was one who believed that actions spoke louder than words, thus she pulled her hand out of her purse and with it came her thirty-two-caliber automatic.

"If I was, if Ace and me worked for the enemy you two would be dead!"

Angelika announced as she put the safety on the pistol and neatly placed it back into her purse. Saladin and Tony were stunned. They let their guard down which could have been fatal. Tony was not deterred the least bit by Angelika's gunplay.

Tony was not accustomed to backing down either. He was not going to be punked by Angelika.

"For all we know that could be the gun that killed Bosco!"

He yelled. Angelika was furious at Tony; however she maintained her poker face for she had to complete her mission. She curtailed her emotions long enough to try to set the record straight on her relationship with Bosco.

"Its about time I set the record straight."

Angelika stated. She did not hesitate in her response.

"Bosco caught me cheatin' on Ace. In turn I told Bosco's girl, the one who ran away with the mailman he cheated on her."

Her blasé attitude caused a response by Saladin who until her comment was silent.

"Bosco ain't here to defend himself, but you are Angelika. You'd betta' start to defend yourself!"

Saladin demanded of Angelika as he leaned against the rear panel of Tony's Mercedes Benz as he waited for a response from the accused. Saladin's strong demands facilitated an even stronger response from Angelika. The calculated woman lost her cool and the ghetto in her oozed to the surface.

"The only thing I betta' do is stay black, die and pay taxes. I don't hafta' defend nothing I do!"

Angelika informed Saladin who did not have the chance to answer because Tony had to reciprocate Angelika's remarks.

"You're high yellow; you don't pay taxes—the last one I can help you with anytime!"

Angelika ignored Tony's remarks and continued on with her mission.

"There is too much at stake for either of you to act on pure emotion. Bosco meant a lot to all of us, but finding his killer is secondary to dealing with Cash and The Reverend!"

Angelika paused as she waited in silence for a response from either man that was not forthcoming. She took the silence as a way to continue.

"We don't have the luxury of time. If we don't do something soon we will all be out of business!" Her pronouncement had a ring of truth. They rode on an emotional conundrum; which clouded their judgment. Clear thinking is one of the attributes that separated the average from the above average in the business.

"We gotta find a way to deal with The Reverend before we can deal with Cash."

Tony asked as he leaned against his car along side Saladin. Tony went into his pocket to retrieve a blunt he prepared earlier that evening. He lit the blunt, took two puffs and passed it to Saladin who continued the C-cipher. Angelika refused to get high and passed the blunt back to Tony. As he got high Saladin began to contemplate the future.

Once again Saladin had reached the proverbial fork in the road. Each time he chose to remain in the business at this juncture he was not sure of the path he would take. Which of the paths he chose to take is sojourn? Saladin would have to use extreme measures to arrive at his destination. He was not sure of what path he would ultimately take but Saladin was sure that things would work out fine. Saladin returned from his thoughts in time to receive half a blunt from Tony. Saladin continued the C-cipher, however instead of handing it back to Tony Saladin tossed the blunt onto the ground. His actions caused Tony and Angelika to take notice of Saladin who did not realize what he has done.

He exhaled the last of the marijuana from his lungs slowly then spoke with a newfound calmness.

"Once we get started there will be a heavy price for all of us to pay."

Saladin finally realized that he threw the blunt on the ground. He walked a few steps to pick the blunt off the ground and walked back to Tony and Angelika. He offered the blunt to Tony who immediately refused to puff anymore. Saladin then threw the blunt back to the ground and continued to share his thoughts.

"If we win, we still may lose. There are no guarantees."

Saladin concluded.

"There ain't no betta' way to go out than in a blaze of glory!" Angelika said as she checked the time on her watch once again. Tony offered his own opinion on the matter.

"Tell us somin' we don't know Saladin. This is war but wars take money. The last time I checked we did not have any product to sell!"

Tony said as he rummaged through his jacket pocket for his last cigarette. He found a broken one and tossed it to the ground.

"All we need is a plan and the rest will follow!"

Tony said as he used a piece of stale gum as a substitute for a cigarette. Angelika looked over to Saladin to see the wheels in his mind were spinning hard. She

knew Saladin had worked something in his mind and it was time to share his plan
with his colleagues.

"Saladin, please let us know what you've been working out in your mind."

Angelika said as she readjusted her sweater to prevent the cold from penetrating her chest. Then she attempted to coax the answer from Saladin by handing
him a tasty morsel of information.

"I learned where Cash has his largest stash house. How does that figure into
your plan you're cooking up Saladin?"

Angelika asked Saladin. The news could not have been any better for them all.
Saladin was not about to go into the details of his plan in public but he assured
them that they would have the money to go to war with Cash and The Reverend
very quickly. Saladin did not feel comfortable talking business before Bosco was
laid to rest. Angelika was glad to hear that she was not going to be held up any
longer because she was already late for an important meeting. She looked out to
the street at an empty cab that stopped for a red light.

"I would like to chat with you fellas longer but I am late for a date. I have to
speak to a man about a bone."

Angelika abruptly stepped out into the street and hopped into the passenger's
seat of the cab. Tony and Saladin stood silent for a brief instant because they
could not believe how blatant she was about cheating on Ace. Once the cab with
Angelika pulled off, Tony turned to Saladin to discuss an unaddressed issue that
haunted each of their minds. Tony kept his eyes on the cab as it moved down
Second Avenue and he spoke to Saladin.

"I don't believe anything that chick said. I know our boy thought about the
gains he would have made if he sold us out."

Tony turned to Saladin and recognized a strange look in his face.

"You didn't fall for her bullshit?"

Tony quizzed his friend.

Saladin took his time with his response for he had to recall him by his 7th
grade teacher Ms. Cuthbertson.

"Nothing is impossible only improbable."

Tony did not understand the riddle Saladin had just presented him and asked
for the meaning of his statement.

"It's very possible that Ace was on the verge of selling us out but it's improbable that Cash killed Bosco."

He informed Tony. Saladin looked at his watch to reveal that the witching
hour had past some forty-five minutes ago.

"Drive me to my downtown apartment, we have to bury a friend tomorrow Tony!"

Saladin and Tony quickly hopped in the ride and sped off towards downtown and the dread of the morning procession.

CHAPTER 30

Who's on First?

Funerals are often solemn occasions where the close friends and the loved ones of the deceased express their grief in a private manner. Family and friends often have time to deal with their relationship with the deceased in their own time and way. It is rare thing to experience a funeral of a non-Celebrity that garners the curiosity of strangers. Bosco's funeral fit the mold of spectacle.

United Funeral Chapel was packed with throngs of people who wished to see Bosco for the last time. Tad was surprised, but happy to see that a great many people held his son in the same high regard as he had done. The crowd inside the chapel was large enough that the service took place outside on the avenue via loud speakers. The mass of people who were unable to enter the chapel, gathered outside, only served as a magnet to attract even more people to mill about the chapel.

Spectators stopped to see the person worthy enough to have five hearses filled with flowers as well as the money to be buried in a supposed gold-plated casket! The crowds outside the chapel blocked traffic along the major avenue to the point where the police had to be called to control the traffic. The masses of people outside the service were unable to hear the moving sermon.

Reverend Dorothy Hicks had prepared a generic eulogy for Bosco. She did not know the young man, and it was obvious from his manner of death, his profession as a hated drug dealer. When Reverend Hicks stepped out to the pulpit she could see many young people lined up out to the lobby of the chapel. She looked down to her left and saw the contrast of strength in the faces of the adults in Bosco's family, and pain in the faces of the younger members of the family. Revered Hicks scrapped the generic eulogy for one more appropriate.

Reverend Hicks highlighted the apparent love many felt for Bosco, while glossing over his sins in life. The focus of the eulogy was choices one has made and will make in life. All during the eulogy Saladin felt that Reverend Hicks had somehow read his mind. In the middle of the eulogy Saladin looked around the funeral chapel and noted the people who were conspicuously absent. When the Reverend read from Proverbs 7-verses 5 through 7, Saladin literally felt Armageddon being fought in his mind for his soul. Saladin reached over to hold Sunshine's hand for support as he opened his heart to the words he believed were directed at him.

The end of the ceremony saw Bosco take his last ride to Woodlawn Cemetery in the Bronx. (Woodlawn is the final resting place for numerous celebrities like Malik El Hajj El Shabazz, and Duke Ellington.) After Bosco was laid to rest a small number of people were invited to dinner at Tad's house. There was a considerable drop off in the turnout at the interment and Tad made sure that only a limited amount of people were invited back to his apartment for dinner.

Saladin arrived with Sunshine to Tad's apartment with mix feelings. A strange feeling came over him as he greeted several of Bosco's distance relatives at the door. Saladin continued to recant the Reverend Hicks' phrase.

"When one door closes, another opens."

Saladin made his way down the long hall of the apartment unsure of how he would get along without Bosco. Saladin held Sunshine's hand tightly to support his wavering emotions as he progressed deeper into the abyss of the unknown.

As he moved past Tad's room, Saladin noticed the door to the room was slightly ajar. He recognized the figure of Tad and his girlfriend in the room. The sight of the tough man seated on his bed crying inconsolably struck Saladin. Tad buried his head into Ms. Green's stomach as she rubbed his head in an attempt to comfort her man. Sunshine also witnessed the entire scene, and as a gesture to preserve their privacy she closed the door to the room and continued up the hall towards the living room where the sound of familiar voices could be heard.

Saladin arrived at the doorway to the living room and paused before he entered. Sunshine did not stop at the doorway because she saw Penelope serving food in the kitchen. She jettisoned Saladin's hand as she went to assist Penelope in the kitchen. Saladin watched, as Sunshine wasted no time in donning an apron and getting to work to service the nearly fifty people who crowded into the apartment. From his position in the doorway he scanned the crowded room and noticed that Tony was engaged in a conversation with a man. Tony stood directly in front of the man who held the hand of a girl who looked as if she had just graduated from high school. Her hairstyle and dress all looked like that of a teen-ager while her body was that of a healthy woman. The young girl saw Saladin's intense stare and leaned over to tell the man who held her hand. When the man leaned over to receive information in his ear Saladin could see that that man in question was Ace!

He looked same as he did before his motorcycle accident; however he had put on more weight, which showed, on his round chunky face.

"Yo' Saladin why you lookin' at my girl like you is?"

Ace yelled loud enough for everyone in the room to hear. Saladin moved through the crowd until he was close to greeting his friend. He watched as Ace struggled to his feet with the assistance of a cane for his "Homeboy" handshake with Saladin. The embrace was as warm as it had ever been. The absence of Ange-lika at the funeral and interment was explained by the presence of the young girl Ace failed to introduce to Saladin. There was plenty of small talk between Ace, Saladin and Tony, that was until they found themselves in Bosco's room with several of Bosco's key associates.

The food served at Tad's house was not as spicy as the conversation that took place in Bosco's old room. Saladin, Ace and Tony slid into Bosco's room for a private conversation only to be later joined by B-Nice and Terrance Whittle, two of Bosco's closest associates.

When the two men entered the room the topic of conversation centered on who could have killed Bosco? Theories of who could have killed Bosco were tossed around the room like a pair of dirty socks. The conversation took on an entirely different level when someone asked a pressing question:

"Who is gonna take over Bosco's bizness?"

The question had been hanging over the room like a dark curtain. Saladin was not surprised that Terrance was the first to pose the question being that he was the most aggressive of Bosco's associates. Saladin looked towards Ace, who was seated on top of Bosco's dresser looking over old photos. Ace was not about to answer. Saladin then looked over to the window where Tony stood. The fading sun cast shadow over Tony's face but Saladin knew that Tony was not about to answer either. Saladin was about to speak on the issue when Ace jumped in first.

"You mother fuckers are fighting over a dead man's business. Let him be good and buried first before you three start fighting over money!"

Ace said as he flipped through a series of photos of Bosco with his family at his elementary school graduation. Ace's words caused Saladin to realize that one of Bosco's associates had been missing from the interment and the gathering.

"Where the fuck is Albino Charles? He ain't here and he did not go to Wood-lawn! Where is he?"

Saladin demanded.

"He said his mother had a heart scare right after the service. He went to the hospital to see her!"

B-Nice answered.

"Let's get back to the question at hand, which one of us is gonna take Bosco's seat at the table?"

B-Nice continued as if nothing else in the world mattered. Tony took offense to the lack of respect he believed Bosco's memory deserved and he spoke out on the issue.

Tony turned his attention from the sights out the window towards B-Nice and Thomas with fire in his eyes. Ace had not been around Tony in sometime but he knew that Tony losing his infamous temper. Tony made his way over to the bed where both men sat. It did not take long for the two men to feel the brunt of Tony's anger.

"If I had my way, all three of you would never sit at the table with any of us!"

Tony spoke with enough force that there was no response from either B-Nice or Terrance.

"Hold on Dick"

Ace said as he motioned for Tony to slow down.

"Don't get your blood pressure up. Terrance and B-Nice have no clue that they are fighting over scraps."

Saladin said in an annoyed voice. Saladin was looking directly at Sounds like Terrance and B-Nice when he said this. Saladin's statement produced a puzzled look on each man's face. They had no idea what Saladin and Ace spoke about.

"What kind of Game is you three tryin' to run on us?"

B-Nice demanded. Tony was very obliged to fill the clueless men in on their situation.

The intense young man did not pull any punches when he explained the situation to B-Nice and Terrance.

"There ain't a bizness to fight over 'cause there ain't no product to sell!"

Tony spoke with such conviction that there should not have been any reasonable doubt, but when money is involved, reason sometimes gets lost. B-Nice and Terrance continued to insist that Bosco's business was fine and that one of the two should be named the head of it in order to head off bloodshed. It was obvious to Saladin that both B-Nice and Terrance were stuck on stupid. If they wanted Bosco's business they were going to have it lock, stock and barrel!

"We are gonna give the two of you everything you deserve, B-Nice and Terrance. Even Albino Charles will be a full partner!"

Saladin's announcement made both men happy because each believed that in the end they would absorb the other pieces of Bosco's business in a short time. What the men failed to do was read the fine print.

"Everything Bosco had now belongs to his three closest associates. *Bon appetite* gentlemen!"

Tony declared in a poor French accent.

"Mangi Bene!"

Saladin added in a proper Italian accent.

"Bueno Diaz!"

Ace responded with his Spanish accent.

The laughter that ensued between the three began to dissipate when Penelope barged into the room. Penelope was on a mission to find some answers.

Penelope pushed open the door to the room and nearly knocked down Saladin whose back rested against the door. Sunshine, Tony's girl Dujour, Ace's young stuff and Ms. Green followed Penelope into the room. The women had an idea that some shenanigans were taking place out of their sight. The intrusion ended the talk about business which was exactly the reason for the intrusion. Saladin was then volunteered to venture off to the liquor store for more booze. On his way out of the apartment Saladin stopped into Tad's room to console the distraught man. Saladin knew he could not say a thing that would brighten Tad's spirits, but the one thing he did do was listen.

The more Tad spoke, the more Saladin began to realize how ghetto the older man had been back in his day. There was no way to tell by his cool demeanor how violent and quick-tempered he had been as a youth. Like the classic story he gave up the street life for the Army, and the discipline he needed to find and keep a good job after his tour of duty had expired. He did all that for the love of Bosco's mother.

"Karma came back to me Saladin. Get out before all your deeds come back to you."

Tad's warning did not fall on deaf ears. Saladin checked his watch and realized he had spent twenty minutes talking to Tad. The young man excused himself and left for the liquor store.

Just like every other project building, the elevator took a long time to arrive. As Saladin waited, he had enough time to ponder the advice of Tad about leaving the business. He also had enough time to dwell on the conversation he had with Bosco's brother Gregory outside the funeral chapel about revenge. Gregory was young enough and angry enough to ruin his life with a careless act of vengeance. Saladin believed that he had talked sense into the young man, but he knew nothing is impossible only improbable.

"Your father has already lost his wife to sickness, two sons to the street *and* a father. No matter how you feel, make your father proud, live righteously Gregory."

Saladin replayed those words and more that he issued to the young man to keep him from doing the wrong thing. The elevator finally arrived and he squeezed in the already crowded sweatbox.

As the door closed he again began to feel empty as if part of him had been left behind. Saladin contributed the feeling to the loss of Bosco but he would quickly find out that the feeling had to do with Bosco but not in the most obvious way.

CHAPTER 31

Just One for the Road

Alcoholics and Ex-Lovers had at least one thing in common, they both believe in having one for the road. Regardless of the cost, they are willing to step up to the plate one more time as if the last drink or the last episode swung would be better than any other time. One could have subscribed Saladin to that school of thought. Not long after Bosco was laid to rest, he called a meeting at Kelly's that only Tony and Ace would attend.

Tony arrived at the meeting energized. He was happy the meeting was called at Kelly's because every time they sat around that table he would make huge amounts of money. He entered the back room to find that Saladin and Ace were already present and seated around the table. Tony was also glad the annoying hum produced by the fluorescent light which hung over the table was no more. Tony took a seat at the head of the table to the right of Saladin and to the left of Ace.

"What's up?"

Tony said as he plopped down onto the new leather chair. Tony sat and eagerly awaited the answer to his question. Saladin wasted no time in getting down to business.

Saladin called the meeting to first tell his partners that he no longer wanted to be in the business. Tony took the news hard. He thought that Saladin called the meeting because there was new product on the street, or there was word on who killed Bosco. Ace was not surprised at Saladin's announcement. He gathered from the information Angelika gave him while he was recovering from his injuries, that either Saladin had sold them out to Cash, or he was about to leave the business. Ace was glad that Saladin had chosen the latter, but that relief brought about a tough question he had to pose to Saladin. Ace sat forward on the chair, placed his clasped hands on the table and kindly asked his question.

"This ain't no freaking' movie Saladin. No mafia guy is gonna let millions of dollars walk out on them. How are you gonna get out from under Don Giovanni?"

Ace then sat back in his chair and waited for his answer.

"I have saved my pennies quite nicely thank you."

Saladin joked as he spoke in his Harvard ESE voice. Ace had to laugh at Saladin's mocking the rich in America. Tony did not find anything funny. He had been thrown for a loop and his two partners were finding the moment humorous. It was his idea to bring everyone together, and because of their association Tony had been elevated to a higher status in the business. He had no contacts with any of the major suppliers of coke or heroin. Bosco's death ended his coke supply and Saladin's departure would put an end to his heroin pipeline. Tony was not the least bit amused at having to start over from the beginning. Tony unzipped his jacket top in frustration. Ace saw the show of frustration and addressed the matter.

"Tony Dick he has to do what is best for him. You and I will survive his leaving. You're a big boy!"

Tony grew even more frustrated at the idea of being lectured by Ace.

"I ain't mad at him for doing him, but he could have given me a heads up. You know what I'm saying?"

Tony exclaimed.

Saladin did not like the fact that Tony and Ace talked about him as if he were not in the room. His mother used to do the same thing to him when he was a tyke and it used to drive him crazy.

"Tony, I am right here in the room. If you have anything to say either of you can address me!"

Saladin spoke to his partners in a aggressive but considerate voice. Tony looked directly at Saladin, this time he directed his question to Saladin. Tony did not have to wait for his answer.

"I can't leave either of you two hanging."

Saladin said as he pulled a pack of Double Mint gum from his jacket pocket. He offered a stick of gum to Ace then to Tony, both of whom declined. Saladin crammed a stick of gum into his mouth and chewed as if it was a steak dinner. He continued to speak only after his taste buds were satiated.

"There is a Columbian guy who has a stash of Heroin he needs to unload in a hurry. We have a chance to make a killing one last time as a unit!"

Saladin then unwrapped two more sticks of gum and stuffed them into his mouth. He did not realize what he had done until he saw the strange look Ace and Tony gave him.

"You must have given up smoking, Saladin?"

Tony quipped. Saladin removed a wad of gum and chucked it into a nearby garbage can. Tony could not laugh he could only manage to shake his head. Ace could not pass an opportunity to joke on Saladin.

"You are like that guy in the movie Airplane Saladin; He picked the wrong week to give up smoking!"

The room erupted in laughter. The joy of laughter was abbreviated by a thought that rushed through Saladin's mind. The absence of Bosco's loud laugh brought the question to light.

Saladin halted his laugh first as the thought of Bosco raced through his mind. Ace saw the change of his friend's facial expression and immediately knew the reason for the change.

"When are we going to step to Cash, Saladin?"

"The Reverend is easier to get to, Ace."

"How's that Saladin. He has mob protection"

"We can bring him down with just a well placed phone call, Ace."

"Make it happen, trooper."

Ace reached over the table and slapped Saladin high-five as a way of sealing the deal. Tony sat idle during the exchange. He did not like when people took his complacency for granted as Ace and Saladin had done. Tony tapped on the table to gain the attention of the two men before he spoke.

"Don't speak for me. You forgetting what Handsome Paul said; "If anything happens to Cash or the Reverend he will come after us!"

"Nothing worthwhile is gained without the threat of danger Tony."

Ace responded to Tony with quickness. Tony was not finished. He looked over to Saladin and posed yet another tough fact.

"It's easy for you to say Saladin. You are leaving the business, and all the problems that will be caused when you move on Cash and The Reverend."

There was no easy answer for Saladin. He simply stated the truth. Saladin stood up to pull mail out of his mailbox because the leather seats made his behind sweat.

"I ain't crazy Tony. No matter where I go Handsome Paul can still reach out and touch me."

Saladin said as he sat back in his seat satisfied that his underwear had been removed from between his cheeks.

"My word is my bond. I'm down until the end!"

Saladin started to reach for his pack of gum again but he decided against falling into his addiction. Saladin walked over to Tony and extended his hand. Tony took his hand without hesitation. Ace made his way over to add his hand on top of his friends.

"It's do or die time!"

The three men cheered in unison. Saladin, Ace and Tony were locked, loaded and ready for war!

CHAPTER 32

Damn the Torpedoes...

"Your story would make a great work of fiction but it is not the type of story this paper would peruse!"

Saladin heard that same phrase with each call he placed to the local newspapers with the tales of The Reverend. He found irony in the fact that his true story was found too unbelievable for even the notoriously free press of New York City. Since crossing Handsome Paul overtly it was decided that guerilla warfare was the best way to justify the means of destroying both Cash and The Reverend. Saladin was left to deal with the distasteful task of dropping dime to the police. He chose Detectives Johnson and Brown for the recipients of his good news.

"How much of that bullshit are you gonna' believe Johnson? We know everything going on uptown and we ain't never heard of no extortion of drug dealers or no dirty cop."

Officer Brown immediately said the instant his partner Johnson ended his phone with a confidential informant. The expression on Johnson's face led Brown to change his question to a statement.

"We are the streets! In the last five years shit ain't go down without our having knowledge before hand."

Brown had to lower his voice because his statement could be misconstrued by many of their colleagues who wanted to see the dynamic cocky duo take a hard fall. Johnson sat hands folded behind his head. The greasy feel of his S-Curl deter him from clasping both hands behind his head as he teetered in his chair as if he was member of a circus high wire act. As Johnson responded to Brown's statement he continued to further challenge the laws of gravity.

"Back in the days I had a girlfriend who had this saying "Nothing is impossible only improbable.""

"What's that supposed to mean Johnson?"

"What it means is that this mysterious Reverend could explain several unsolved murders and why many high level drug dealers fear showing their wealth. Let's investigate to see how solid the lead is before we take the tip to the FBI!"

The two detectives investigation was made very easy for the information Saladin provided was extremely useful.

The first person to fall into the hands of the law was the dirty cop. Faced with the prospect of life without parole he turned states evidence. He gave up details of The Reverend 's business as well as the location of the remains of 10 murder victims. Like dominoes one after another The Reverend's associates turned on him. They hoped that if The Reverend were behind bars he would not be able to sever the link to him by killing them! The news that the Reverend would be behind bars for the rest of his life pleased Saladin, however he did not like the method used. He had to convince himself that "The end justifies the means!" One was down and with Cash to go Saladin knew he would have to step out of the shadows and get it popping!

"I'll bet you Cash will survive the winter!"

Ace said as he placed a piece of packing tape on a box labeled "Saladin's Music."

Tony immediately challenged Ace's bet.

"Ace, I'll bet you Fifteen Hundred Dollars that he won't make it past Christmas!"

Tony said as he pulled that same amount of money from his pocket and placed it onto the box labeled "Saladin's movies."

At that point of the conversation Saladin emerged from the kitchen with kitchen utensils in hand. He tossed them into a box filled with other kitchen goods.

"Don't count people like Cash out. They tend to survive shit that would destroy most mortals!"

Saladin said as he wrote the words 'Saladin Army' on the box and then sealed it tight.

Ace motioned for Tony to help him move the box with all of Saladin's music over to the door where the rest of the boxes awaited the arrival of the moving company the next morning.

"I can't see how he can last long? We burned down the building that held his money and drug stash. He ain't got no product to sell 'cause the streets are bare!"

Ace said as he and Tony returned to the living room where they found Saladin lighting a rare cigarette.

"What ya gotta' be stressed about Saladin? The body of the dude we dropped off the roof has not been found yet?"

Tony said as he walked over to Saladin and gave him a slap on the back.

"There would not have been a body to find if you did not drop him Tony Dick!"

Ace interjected in a matter of fact tone.

"It was cold and I lost grip of his ankles Ace!"

Saladin shook his head in disbelief. Picking on Tony did not stop with the death of Bosco, which helped to add some levity to the serious situation. He took several long puffs on the cigarette before his nerves were calm enough for him to speak.

"He won't step to us!"

Tony and Ace said in unison.

"You are probably right. Cash will think Buck 50 had something to do with the situation."

Saladin looked for a placed to drop the ash from his cigarette but he threw out all the ashtrays he owned. He instead placed the ash in the palm of his hand. Tony saw Saladin place the ash in his hand and handed him the can of soda he had just finished drinking. Tony then mentioned to Saladin and Ace that Buck 50 was crazy enough to go after Cash. Tony then looked around at the empty apartment and wondered why Saladin had to vacate the premises.

"Why do you have to leave this apartment Saladin? This is the bomb!"

He questioned his friend as he looked around the empty living room.

"In order to start over again I must start with a clean slate. I don't want to have any guilt about my choice."

Saladin said as he dropped the ash into the empty soda can. Thought of guilt brought Saladin back to mind a story told to him by Penelope. Saladin could not shake the statement the Penelope made to him about Albino Charles.

"Every time I see him he gives me money. Albino Charles acts like he is trying to make up for Bosco's death."

Albino Charles' conspicuous absence from the dinner after Bosco's burial seemed more than just a coincidence. Coupled with his eager attitude towards stepping into Bosco's shoes raised concerns with Saladin. He chose to keep his suspicions from Ace and Tony because he knew that each man would shoot first and never ask questions later. Often he wondered why Bosco touched his son's white suit, but he was almost sure his friend had left a clue from before the grave! Saladin smoked several blunts with his friends all the while he continued to verify in his mind his suspicions of who killed Bosco? As the trio locked the door to Saladin's defunct den of sin Ace asked for a meeting the next day.

"I have somin' to show you dogs!"

Ace said to Saladin as the exited the building. Saladin agreed to the meeting but he continued to search for the elusive Albino Charles. Since Bosco's funeral it was rare that anyone laid eyes on him.

Saladin met up with Ace on 151st and Riverside Drive on a cold winter evening. They had been in search of the elusive Albino Charles for three long months. In spite of the bounty on his head the man could not be found. It was the last night before Saladin was set to meet with Don Giovanni and two nights before he would embark on his trip to Italy. The meeting place at 151st and Riverside Drive was important to Ace because it was where he lived for the first 14 years of his life. It was the place where he last lived without looking over his shoulders. Saladin pulled up on the park side just after 4:00 PM. The sun had already set for the night. From his car Saladin could see Ace as he stood staring over the stone ledge that ran one half mile along the park side overlooking the famed Hudson River and New Jersey. The moment he opened the door to his car he was struck by a blast of strong cold air that made him feel like a fool for leaving the warmth of his car. Saladin knew Ace had called him out in the dead of winter for a reason that could not be discovered from the inside of his car.

Saladin bundled up and made his way over to Ace whose eyes were fixated on the lights of New Jersey.

"Tell me sumin' good. I left my warm bed and a warm body to be out here with you Ace?"

Saladin's teeth chattered uncontrollably as from the cold.

As soon as he was close enough to Ace not to shout.

"It depends on what you call good news Saladin!"

Ace shot back. The man then pointed down over the stone ledge at the over grown grass below.

"If you can listen hard enough you can hear him scream."

"What the fuck are you talking 'bout Ace. It's too cold to speak in riddles Ace."

"Albino Charles, Saladin. He is down there."

"There ain't uttin' down there but rats Ace! I don't hafta' look down there to know that!"

Saladin looked in the direction in which Ace pointed. Saladin did not see anything out of the ordinary. He looked back to Ace who encouraged Saladin to look once more. Upon his second more intense look Saladin could make out the outline of a white tee shirt. Saladin looked over for Ace, but he had moved to take a seat on one the benches which lined the area. Saladin noticed that Ace no longer walked with any discernable limp which made the use of a cane obsolete. Saladin quickly made his way to sit beside Ace on the bench. The night did not seem that cold to Saladin at the moment.

"Is he dead Ace?"

Saladin asked as he pulled out a cigarette from the pack of cigarettes from his coat pocket.

"I thought you gave that shit up Saladin."

Ace said as he pulled a solid gold lighter from his coat pocket and lit Saladin's cigarette for him. Saladin did not respond to Ace's observation because the taste of his first cigarette in three months was pleasurable.

"I did not kill him Saladin. I was so full of anger that I had one of my boys tie him up, cut him up real good and toss him down there for the rats to nibble on."

Ace took a joint from his pocket and lit it with his lighter then took long drags on the joint as a means to ease his mind.

"I wanted him to die slowly. To think about what got him in that situation!"

Ace said between puffs on his joint. Saladin began to feel a chill but it was not from the weather it was from the way Ace spoke.

"How long has he been down there?"

Saladin asked as he pulled long on his stale cigarette. Saladin tossed the cigarette to the ground and reached for the joint Ace smoked. He needed something to take his mind to a place where he could understand Ace.

There was a lull in the conversation because Ace was not sure if the answer to Saladin's question was the sane thing to say.

"He's been down there three days! I wonder what he looks like."

Ace wondered aloud.

"Don't go there Ace this shit is fuckin' weird already."

Saladin said as he inhaled the last of the joint and tossed the roach to the ground. The two men continued to engage in small talk until Tony arrived twenty minutes later. When Tony heard the reason for the meeting he opened the forty ounces in celebration. Saladin was happy but the misery Albino Charles must have felt while being eaten alive stayed on Saladin's mind. He no longer had the stomach for the business, but there was one last piece of business he had to conduct before he retired.

Just before the three men parted ways Saladin asked Ace a question that was bothering him.

"Why did he kill Bosco?"

Saladin turned to Ace with a pained look on his face.

"He killed Bosco because he felt dissed at being passed over for a promotion!"

In the end jealously and greed was the reason why Bosco was killed.

CHAPTER 33

Box or Throw Rocks

The morning did not come fast enough for Saladin. It was his moment of truth and he had no choice but to follow through with his decision to leave the business. He left his house earlier than usual for his meeting with Don Giovanni not sure how the old man would take his desire to walk away from the business. Saladin hoped that he could make the old man an offer he could not refuse.

The chosen location for the meeting was the promenade just under the Verrazano-Narrows Bridge in Brooklyn. Their prior meeting spot along the banks of the Gowanus Canal was changed because the Environmental Protection Agency was conducting yet another study of the polluted canal. Saladin wondered why in the last two days he had been called to meetings that took place in the elements. He was glad that the temperature was a balmy 46 degrees; he was able to view the beautiful scenery as he waited for the arrival of Don Giovanni.

As Saladin gazed up at the towering structure he was removed from his thoughts as he could not help but feel small standing under the massive Verrazano-Narrows Bridge. Saladin likened standing under the bridge to the time his mother and Stepfather took him and his siblings to Saint Patrick Cathedral for their first and only Mass. Just as he had done then Saladin stood and wondered all things metaphysical. Saladin was not alone in his thoughts; he was surprised at the amount of people who used the thin band of concrete that ran between the entrance to New York Harbor and the Belt Parkway. The sight of many wintertime joggers, walkers and fishermen made Saladin marvel at the determination of the people who did what they wanted to do despite their sur-roundings. As Saladin followed the path of one particularly beautiful brunette jogger he noticed Don Giovanni fishing just a stones through away. Saladin felt his heart race as he made his way over to the fisherman.

Saladin walked over to where the Don put his pole into the Atlantic Ocean. He stood very close to the man and remained silent. Saladin took the silent time to take stock of the last major roadblock to his emancipation. Saladin tried his best to remember how the Don looked twenty years earlier but all he could see was the person that stood before him.

Don Giovanni was fifty years of age but he looked much older. A beating with a baseball bat on his knees took much of the mobility. His weight ballooned as the result of his lack of mobility. His steel white hair added to the Don's older appearance. Saladin continued in vain to picture the younger more vibrant Don Giovanni but his thoughts were interrupted when the voice of the present don addressed him.

"When were you going to tell me about our planned trip to Sicily Saladin?"

Don Giovanni said as he cast his line into the water. Saladin was not sure how he should answer the question.

Saladin looked behind him to see the Don's right hand man Benny was seated on a nearby bench who was noticeably shivering from the cold. Saladin then turned his attention back to the Don and the question at hand.

"I tried to get word to you but evidently…."

The Don silenced Saladin when he motioned for him to be quiet. Excuses drove the man crazy. To lie to him was a worse offense. Whenever someone dear to Don Giovanni made excuses he often changed the subject to allow the offender ample time to correct their error. He gave Saladin the same opportunity when he asked about his family.

"How's your half Pisano brother and sister Saladin?"

The older man asked Saladin.

"They are fine. My brother is a district manager with K-Mart in Virginia and my sister enlisted in the Navy."

Saladin responded as he watched as the Don teased his fishing line.

"What happened to that beautiful mother of yours? Did she ever marry again?"

The Don asked as he teased the line once again. In a sudden fit of rage he tossed the entire fishing pole into the Atlantic Ocean.

"I ain't got time for this convert bullshit! Dam Feds got everybody nervous!"

The man uncharacteristically muttered under his breath. Saladin heard the faux pas and needed no explanation.

"My mother is doing fine. She just took husband number three."

Saladin answered the Don's innocuous question but he knew he had better get to the point of the meeting.

The Feds, FBI, DEA, and the ATF continued to breathe down the neck of the mob on the heels of the Pizza shop drug case. Also, the first hints of the mob's involvement in the overpricing of replacement windows in many NYC Housing Projects put everyone in the mob under the spotlight. The Don had lived through the worst of times by his cautious nature. He never took anything for granted which is why he chose the unusual outdoor meeting with Saladin. The noise produced by the traffic from the Verranzano-Narrows Bridge above, a highway to their backs and the Atlantic Ocean at their fronts made it difficult for the FEDS to eavesdrop on their conversation. Saladin knew that the Don would only give him a moment to explain therefore; instead of beating around the bush he got right to the point.

Saladin looked out over the Ocean at a large container ship that was set to navigate its way under the huge bridge and wondered if that was the means to how illegal drugs could be imported in the country. The sight of the ship and the idea brought the main reason for the meeting.

"I want out of the business."

Saladin bluntly stated. He reached into his pocket with his gloved hand, retrieved a locker key and presented it to Don Giovanni.

"This key is to a locker which holds 250K dollars. It is yours!"

Saladin said as he returned the key to his pocket. The Don did not waste anytime in his response.

"Cash had a little problem with fire and robbery. You wouldn't know anything about that would you Saladin?"

To be honest at the juncture would be to invite more drama.

Saladin looked the Don directly in the face and said,

"I want to get out of the business. Going after Cash would only keep me in the business or make me dead."

Saladin paused for a moment and got right back on the topic of getting out of the business. The Don listened to Saladin as he said all the right things about family and his desire to leave. The wise man allowed Saladin to shoot his load and then countered with talk of money.

"Why would I let a million dollar customer leave for a mere 250k? Don't insult me Saladin that would not be a *wise* thing for you!"

The Don said as he pulled the straps on his coat tighter together as if he were ready to depart. Saladin was on the clock and there was no time to play coy. He had to keep the old man stationary.

"The 250K is a down payment. When I get back from Italy there will be a second key and safe deposit box with two million dollars. When I get back safely from Italy you will get the key."

Saladin spoke with a little more urgency in his voice. He looked at the Don who wore a mean poker face. There was no way Saladin could tell what the man thought which was exactly what the Don wanted.

The Don waited until a rare jogger moved by before he continued to speak.

"Money is hard to come by these days. Many people I know would be glad with just 250K but I am not those people. When things get back to normal I can make much more than what you offer!"

The Don turned towards Benny who had begun to hustle his heavy frame off the bench and to his feet. Saladin did not want the Don to leave but he was not about to kiss the man's ass. He was going to leave the business with or without his blessing.

"There has not been two million in product on the street in months. This is money you do not have to work for."

Saladin paused then spoke in the direct manner that made the Don take notice.

"The money, all of it is yours but I am getting out! I left you two good people to take my place that should be enough!"

Saladin fixed his skully cap on his head and was set to leave when he saw the Don mention for Benny to sit back down.

"I am glad that you did not use the fact that your stepfather and I were buddies. I would think less of you!"

The Don said as he pulled his hat down on his head to prevent it from blowing off his head in the strong breeze that blew up.

"Your stepfather would have never lied to me about anything Cash."

Don Giovanni said as another wind gust surfaced, this time his fedora flew off his head right into the Atlantic Ocean. Benny again was sent to leap to his feet but the Don seated his with a simple hand motion.

"You remind me of your mother. No matter how much help I tried to give her she always took just enough to feed you and your siblings!"

The Don then pulled up the collar on his jacket to protect his ears from the biting cold.

"I want 3 million, not 2.5 million and I will not deal with that hot head bastard Tony! I will only deal with Ace."

The Don said as he looked directly in the face of Saladin for the first time. Saladin did exactly what his stepfather taught him to do.

Saladin looked the Don directly in his eyes, as the eyes are the gateway to a man's soul. Saladin detected a new emotion from the Don, one that he never expected to see, envy!

"When are you going to retire? Your son Paul looked to be taking on more responsibility."

Saladin quizzed.

"Don't worry about **my** family business and I won't catch you in a bold face lie."

The Don motioned for a hesitant Benny to get up off the bench.

"Get your fat ass up you dumb fuck!"

The Don ordered and Benny leapt out of his seat and rushed over to Saladin.

"Word of advice Saladin, keep looking over your shoulders. The shit you did while in the business always has a way of catching up to you."

Don Giovanni then took a cane Benny had concealed under his coat and pointed directly behind Saladin. The young man immediately turned around to see whom the Don had pointed out, he saw an old lady with a dog and a middle aged man doing karate. The sight of the two people did not ring alarm bells with the cautious man.

Saladin's path home led directly past the two individuals in question. He pulled his skully cap further down on his head until part of his vision became obscured by the hat and made a mad dash for his car. With great trepidation, Saladin quickly made his way past the two people. There was no incident, but Don Giovanni's point had been taken.

"One day he would have to face his past head on!"

CHAPTER 34

Prestidigitation

Saladin awoke from his four-hour sleep feeling less rested than when he fell asleep two hours into his flight to Italy. He was ready to start a new life devoid the stress and constant danger of the illegal drug trade. The drone of the engines served as a backdrop for Saladin to paint his thoughts.

He adjusted his seat in a way to make sure his back could rest against the window. He caught sight of a woman seated in the adjacent row who wore a white suit that reminded him of the type of suit Sunshine wore as she saw him off on his voyage to a new world. Saladin closed his eyes as he reminisced about the warm kiss she shared with him at the terminal gate. He could once again smell the sweet fragrance she wore and the look of joy she bestowed upon him when he informed her of his plan to finally leave the business. Saladin's moment was interrupted by a gentle nudge from the stewardess.

"We are about to land. Please adjust your seat for landing."

Saladin opened his eyes and was met by the lovely face of a dark-haired, olive-complexion young woman.

Saladin did as he was instructed but the face the young girl reminded him of Shanita. He remembered how well the young woman took the news of his desire to leave the business, but the same could not be said for the news of their relationship.

Saladin recalled the tears that fell from her pretty face as he told her that their relationship had to be put on hold while he smoothed things over with Sunshine.

Saladin felt his eyes well up with tears of his own as he recalled Shanita's pledge to him.

"I will always love you!"

Shanita told him.

There was no denying that her love for him was genuine, however he did not know exactly what to do with her love. As the plane began its final descent, Saladin had to force his thoughts from pleasure to business.

Saladin was more than happy to finally plant his feet firmly on the ground in Sicily. Saladin could not imagine flying on a small plane, but the flight from Rome to Palermo was on a small plane. He exited the small plane, much to his delight and followed the two dozen people on the plane with him to a building leading to the terminal. Once inside the terminal his lawyer Michelangelo Esposito greeted Saladin.

Michelangelo had made the journey to Palermo two weeks before Saladin as his point man. He set up several meetings with key Black Hand members that would expedite Saladin's departure from their business. As his lawyer approached, Saladin noticed two fierce looking men at the man's shoulder.

"What's with all the muscle?"

Saladin said while the two men embraced in a handshake.

"This is Palermo Saladin. Life is cheap around here!"

Michelangelo responded.

"Get your bags and let's get out of the public eye!"

Michelangelo said as he instructed one of the two hired men to take possession of both of Saladin's bags.

Saladin was immediately out of the terminal into a waiting car. Saladin did not know that he had left the frying pan in New York City and leapt into the fire in Palermo.

The city of Palermo served as a contradiction in almost every way imaginable. The ancient city, with its picturesque view of the Mediterranean and warm friendly people was the hellish center of an all out mob war waged by the mafia Dons for the control of the business. Saladin did not have to speak the language fluently to know that fear gripped many of the cities inhabitants. Armed soldiers patrolled the streets and the bodies of vendetta victims turned up on a continuous basis. These occurrences were enough to make anyone nervous, let alone a mafia Don. Saladin was only scheduled to stay in Palermo for one week, however nearly two weeks had passed without the meeting with his supplier-taking place.

"Don Pelosi is a cautious man. He wants to make sure its safe to surface."

Michelangelo assured Saladin.

Saladin understood the situation but he did not like to wait.

"Don't forget I'm paying a local Capo Per Diem for the use of three of his soldiers and protection."

Saladin reminded Michelangelo as the two sipped on Cappuccino during lunch.

"By the time I return state side I would have spent most of my money!"

Saladin continued. He planned to leave the business with most of his massed fortune of nine million dollars but with three million pledged to Don Giovanni in New York, and two million pledged to his supplier Don Pelosi, the longer he remained on the island the less money he wanted to pay for protection. Saladin did manage to get out of the villa on a few occasions making his way to a local market. A black man in Sicily should have drawn suspicion from the authorities (The Mafia) but Saladin had a disguise that allowed him to blend into the population.

Saladin carried a basketball with him everywhere he traveled. He made sure to dress in a sweat suit each day, appearing to the locals as just another American basketball player venturing down from the mainland to see the sights of the island. A Black American basketball player did not represent a tempting target for a money conscious Mafia man. With the exception of Michael Ray Richardson and Joe Bryant, if they were good they would not be in Italy. Although Saladin was able to move around fairly easily, he never relaxed due to his New York paranoia. Someone might try him before he had the chance to meet with Don Pelosi. The important meeting took almost three weeks before taking place.

The meeting between the Don Pelosi, Michelangelo, and Saladin occurred at the Don's palatial villa just on the outskirts of the city. The forty-something year old Don did not speak any English therefore Saladin had to trust Michelangelo to translate for him. The meeting moved in such a fast paced manner that Saladin was left with the impression that the meeting interrupted a more important matter. To further that theory the Don did not seek any more than the two million he had been promised. At the conclusion of the meeting, Saladin felt as if the Don had treated him like a "quickie". It did not matter that much to Saladin because he had made his last deal in the drug business, or so he thought.

CHAPTER 35

When all Else Fails…

Not one week after Saladin ventured to Italy, the tenuous business relationship between Ace and Tony came to an abrupt end. The business relationship was terminated because in part Ace would not speak to Don Giovanni on Tony's behalf and secondly Tony's associates botched the deal that Saladin hooked up with the Cuban.

Tony and Ace nearly came to blows over the lack of respect Tony believed his partner showed when he did not speak to the Don about his inclusions as a partner.

"If the man ain't willin' to deal with you then maybe you need to find another supplier of your own!"

It was Ace's way to find the solution to their deal. Ace would not deal with Tony because of how Tony handled the deal Saladin had set up.

The Cuban was too leery to make one big drop because the flood of product on the barren streets would draw major attention. He thought it best to make four equal transactions. The first transaction went off smoothly because Saladin sent Bones to make the drop. On the second drop of $100,000, two eagled eyed uniformed police who rightfully deemed the pair suspicious stopped two of Tony's boys in a taxicab.

Tony's boys carried the money in a large brown paper bag, which they placed, under the seat of the cab. The police searched the cab and found the bag with the money. The cab driver pleaded ignorant to seeing the men carry the brown paper bag in his cab, so it was up to the two men to seal their own fate. Had the two men accepted ownership of the money, that would mean prison! The two men denied the bag and the police were shocked when they realized the contents of the bag. The police had no choice but to take the names of the two men and send them on their way without the money. Needless to say all dealings with the Cuban were dead! With the deal dead and Ace unwilling to cut him in on any heroin deals, Tony was left with his dick swinging in the breeze. Tony's bad luck did not stop business, with his dirty deeds, his personal life finally caught up to him. Tony needed to think and he thought he had found the perfect plan.

Tony entered the door of the Manhattan Lounge alone. He sent his two trusted associates home, determined to drown the sorrow of his latest drama over a bottle of Heineken Beer solo. His brother's girlfriend Deandra was three months pregnant and he might be the father! The news of becoming a father together with his business woes caused anger to ferment in him like yeast in the beer he drank. Tony wanted to take his frustrations out on someone deserving enough to warrant a true Bronx beat down. Tony found his victim via a familiar laugh.

As Tony tossed down Heinekens at the bar he heard the familiar laugh of a long time nemesis. Tony slid off the bar stool and followed the laugher until its source was verified by his eyes. The laughter belonged to Jeffery Halsey, the man who welched on a $10,000 dollar bet three years earlier. Jeffery lost the bet and skipped out of town without payment. Tony vowed that if he ever met the cheater he would give him one chance to pay before he would kill the offending man. Jeffery sat at a booth with three fine women drinking and having a good time. The sight of Tony before him brought with it a sense of urgency from Jeffery.

Tony did not mince his words when he addressed Jeffery.

"I'm going to go to the bar and finish my drink. When I come back if you don't have my money Jeffery I'm gonna kill you!"

Jeffery knew Tony said what he meant. When Tony turned to walk back to the bar Jeffery jumped up from the booth, pulled his 357 Magnum from his belt and fired two shots into the back of Tony's head. Tony was dead before he hit the floor. Jeffery then ran out of the lounge and into the night. The bar quickly emptied of patrons before the arrival of the police and Tony's murder went head first into the Cold Case File of local Precinct. The Chinese proverb came true for Tony. He wanted very much to be feared and it was the fear that he would carry out his threat that led Jeffery to extinguish his life.

CHAPTER 36

One Foot Out of the Grave

On the morning of his scheduled departure from Palermo, Saladin sat and waited anxiously for his lawyer Michelangelo to call. The call meant that his bodyguards were ready to escort Saladin to the airport and an indirect flight to the United States. Saladin's anxiousness stemmed from his long absence from his love Sunshine and his son, making getting home very important. His bags were packed at dawn and he was ready to leave when he received the call from Michelangelo. The call was not what he expected.

By early afternoon Saladin was in the back seat of a Fiat heading for the town of Corleone instead of a jumbo jet heading for the Big Apple. Michelangelo relayed the message that Don Pelosi sought an urgent meeting with Saladin. There was an instant where he thought about skipping the meeting instead and catching the plane to New York. Saladin changed his mind when his lawyer reminded him how long a reach Don Pelosi owned. Therefore Saladin nibbled on fresh calzones and sipped on espresso supplied by his two bodyguards instead of munching on salted peanuts and sipping on a soda supplied by a fine stewardess.

The ride to Corleone provided him with a snapshot of people and land his stepfather recanted in many stories. Saladin continued to take in the scenery until his car pulled up just outside a run-down villa just on the outskirts of Corleone. The driver of the car turned around and motioned for Saladin to exit the car and he did as directed. Saladin made sure he did not forget the bag of basketballs he brought with him. He walked through a dilapidated gate and directly towards the villa.

Saladin made his way through the door of the villa and into a large room. The floor of the room was covered with dirt and with the exception of a few chairs the room appeared to be bare. He called out in English and his limited Italian for someone to greet him. Saladin could hear rumblings from a large door that was just a few feet from were he stood. Saladin was not alone very long; three men emerged from behind the large door. Two of the men were armed, one with a rifle the other with a doubled barreled shotgun, the third man held no weapon. The man with the rifle took two chairs face-to-face and motioned for Saladin to take a seat in one of the chairs.

The man then stood directly behind Saladin while the man without the weapon sat in the chair across from him. The third man stood over the shoulder of the man without the weapon. The face on the third man was much more relaxed than the others. Saladin mentally sized up the three men in hopes of figuring out circumstances of his visit.

"Where is Don Pelosi? I was supposed to meet with him!"

Saladin said as he looked over his shoulder at the man who stood behind him then he turned his attention back to the man seated in front of him. Saladin waited patiently for the reply. Several long seconds passed before he received any response.

"What business do you have with Don Pelosi?"

The man seated in the chair said in broken English. It was hard for Saladin to understand what the man said but he was able to quickly decipher the man's sentence. There was not hesitation in his response to the question.

"My business is with The Don."

"I speak for the Don. What is your business with him American?"

"If you spoke for him **my man,** you would know my business with him. Is that not true?"

Saladin quickly shot back. Saladin's answer only seemed to bring the tone in his inquisitor's voice up a notch. The man behaved as if time was of the essence, Saladin gathered by the man's tone of voice, and the way the man holding the shotgun looked at him. Saladin was in the middle of contemplating how much to tell these strange men when his inquisitor gave him a clue to the information he sought.

"Why did you give Don Pelosi one million American dollars?"

The man asked Saladin in a clearer tone of voice than he previously used. The question put Saladin on the defensive.

He gave the Don two million but these men only knew of one. He wondered if the truth would set him free or damn him to hell. Saladin quickly determined that the truth would put in on better standing with the men.

"I gave him two million dollars, not one million."

Saladin corrected and then continued his statement.

"I gave him the money to get out of the business, to buy my freedom!"

Saladin bluntly stated. The man seated across from him motioned for the man who stood behind Saladin to come to him. The man did as directed. His inquisitor whispered into the man's ear then the man disappeared behind the large doors.

"You came all the way to Italy just to give the Don money to get your freedom?"

Saladin's inquisitor questioned. Saladin looked the man in the face to answer the question.

"Yes! I don't want any problems with The Don, you or your boss. All I want is to be left alone."

He responded. Saladin's response was the last word between the two men for a loud crash took his inquisitor's attention away from him.

The crash sounded to Saladin much like pots falling from a high shelf. The room suggested to him that the villa was not domiciled, but it was probably a safe house. He watched as his inquisitor spoke to the shotgun toting man then he also disappeared behind the large door just as the man with the rifle had done. Saladin did not what to make of the situation but his New York street sense signaled him that there was much more going on than he could see.

Saladin sat in the room for what seemed like an eternity with the quiet man, as he waited for his inquisitor to return to the room. While in the room Saladin began to hear the infectious tune his stepfather would sing whenever he returned home in a good mood. Soon Saladin was humming the tune aloud as he patted his hands to the rhythm. Saladin did not know the words to the song but singing them made him remember his Stepfather. His humming did not go unnoticed by the man with the shotgun. The look in the man's face was one of wonder.

From his stepfather Saladin heard stories of life in Sicily and how the Vendetta was a part of life for them. It was a vendetta against him by a local family that brought him to America. Money was a good way to soften a man's resolve, but money was also a good way to get a man killed. He also knew that to understand bits of the culture was a way for a stranger to open doors that are normally closed.

Saladin hummed the tune in remembrance of his stepfather, but also a way to break the ice with the man he had pegged as the true leader. The man with the shotgun took the vacated seat then looked Saladin straight in the eye as he spoke.

"Are you making fun of my culture?"

The man spoke in an English accent but one could still hear his Italian roots in his voice. Saladin opened a door for him to say enough to be able to walk out of it in the end.

Saladin sat with the man and told some of the stories his stepfather told to him about the people and the events he experienced while he lived in the old country. Saladin was not sure if the man was feeling his stories but as long as the man listened there was a chance that he could remain alive. In the middle of one story the inquisitor returned to the room. He had a surprised look on his face to see that the charade was over. The two men had a brief conversation; the inquisitor disappeared behind the doors once more.

"You did tell the truth about the money."

The man said then propped the shotgun up against his chair.

"It was a good thing you did."

The two did not exchange another word until the inquisitor returned to the room.

The inquisitor returned to the room with a handkerchief in hand. He walked over to the individual who was seated across from Saladin and opened the handkerchief in front of his face. The man examined the contents then the two men exchanged words in Italian.

"It will cost you three million American for your freedom. There would be no negotiations."

The man simply stated.

Saladin had the money and he knew there was no bargaining with the men. He had survived to that point, why push his luck just to keep one million dollars. Saladin reached down to retrieve the bag of basketballs he had carried with him in the room and tossed it towards his inquisitor.

"There is one million exactly in those basketballs. That is all the money I have."

Saladin concluded.

He looked closely at the handkerchief the man seated across from him held and noticed that the white cloth had turned pink in spots. The man holding the handkerchief noticed the puzzled look on Saladin's face and answered the look in kind.

The man maneuvered the handkerchief down in order for Saladin to see its contents.

"The Don worked for my boss. He thought he had balls big enough to steal from my boss, now Toto has the Don's balls!"

The man proudly exclaimed.

Saladin tried his best not to throw up at the sight of a man's bloody severed testicles being held in a handkerchief. He knew the mafia was a brutal organization. In Saladin's mind castration raised the bar to a new level.

"Now get the fuck out of here before I have your bloody tongue to go with the Don's bloody balls!"

The man commanded. Saladin did not rush out of the room he slowly got up off the chair and backed his way out of the villa.

When he reached the car he immediately plopped down in the backseat. He pick up his last pack of cigarettes lit what he thought was one and began to puff. His bodyguards were miffed at what would make Saladin smoke three cigarettes at one time, so they questioned him.

"What had happened inside the villa?"

Saladin took several drags of the cigarettes and answered.

"Toto Reali!"

The mention of the most powerful and most vicious mobster on the Island made his bodyguards cross themselves. The driver turned on the ignition and zoomed away from the Villa. Saladin had dogged a bullet, but an even bigger bullet to dodge awaited him in New York.

CHAPTER 37

Daylight and Darkness

The first moment Saladin felt he could relax was when his plane touched down in the early morning hours at John F. Kennedy in his hometown. The flight back to the city was just as precarious as his escape from Italy, with three million dollars left of his original nine million dollar fortune. He paid a huge price to get out but if he had to pay one million more he would have done it in a heartbeat. The dark, stressful life as a big time drug dealer was behind him. Saladin could look forward to sunny days ahead with Sunshine and his son Charles. Nothing on earth could have killed his joy.

Saladin ran through the doors of his upstate home eager to hug his son and lay his lips on Sunshine. He was a bit surprised to find that the house was empty; his family was not at home.

"My flight was delayed one day, maybe they had something important to do?"

He theorized about his family's absence from home and from the airport. Saladin found light in the gloomy situation. He would be able to rest in peace and quiet, for he felt the affects of jet lag begin to creep up on him.

The bed would wait until he checked the answering machine; maybe Sunshine left a clue to her whereabouts. Sunshine did leave a message and the dinner she planned at their favorite restaurant on City Island. The answering machine also held the message from Ace concerning Tony.

Saladin understood that sleep would have to wait for he had to handle some important business before he could meet with Sunshine later that day. Even though he was no longer in the business the rapid pace of his life did not slow down.

Saladin took an expensive cab ride to the city. The ride time was almost doubled for a serious accident backed up traffic for miles. He used the increased travel time to get some much-needed rest and to plan his route that would ultimately lead to City Island and dinner with Sunshine. He called Sunshine's cell phone as well as her mother's house but there was no answer. Saladin was not alarmed for Sunshine might be at work or at her aunt's house in New Jersey. He decided to contact her after he made his first stop.

The first stop was to hook up with Ace at Ace's mother's house in the Bronx. Saladin had to do some calling around before he located Ace at Angelika's mother's house. Saladin walked through the door and was surprised to see Angelika and Ace all lovey-dovey. Saladin did not let the unusual sight faze him because he came to find out the circumstances of Tony's death.

Saladin quietly listened to the story of how Tony was killed from Ace, who sipped on a glass of Kool-Aid Angelika eagerly poured for him. At the end of the story Saladin asked the obvious question of Ace.

"What are we gonna do about Tony's murder Ace?"

There was a long bit of silence before Ace uttered a single word response.

"Fuck!"

Ace's response was not what Saladin expected. When pressed further by Saladin, Ace elaborated on his response.

"Tony wanted to play tough guy, and he got killed. Let his flunkies avenge their boss's murder."

Ace stated. The cold nature of his words gave Saladin a sick feeling in his stomach. Ace sounded more like Cash the longer he spoke.

Prior to his trip to Italy, Ace, Bones, Tony and Saladin were set to kill Cash at Cash's house in New Jersey. The killing had been aborted because there was too much activity in the normally quiet neighborhood. Ace's tone of voice reminded Saladin of a piece of unfinished business they had to deal with. Saladin asked about Cash.

"Is the move on Cash still on?"

Ace then hit Saladin in the head with a bit of juicy information.

It was a good thing that the four men did not go through with the hit because the FBI arrested Cash in the early morning hours. Wiretaps and informants pinned the title of Kingpin on his shoulders. Saladin was not amused the least when he learned that Cash skipped out on the highest bail ever set by the Federal Courts.

"There is no business left for you in the business Saladin."

Ace stated. Saladin listen to Ace but his eyes were drawn to the smirk on Angelika's face. She knew something about Saladin but it gave her more pleasure to keep the information to herself.

After one hour of talk Saladin gladly left Ace and Angelika's company. His business relationship and friendship with Ace was over and Saladin was not willing to deal with the weird couple any longer. As he stood outside and waited for the cab to arrive, Saladin called Sunshine's cell phone once more to which there was no answer. He then in turn called Bones' Sunshine's cousin.

"Sunshine's cell phone is broken and dinner is still on at 10:00PM."

Bones said. Saladin was satisfied with the answer he received from his trusted friend and changed his thoughts to his drop-off he planned with Don Giovanni. As Saladin entered the cab he happened to look back at the living room window to see Angelika. The smirk was still present on her face. Angelika's smirk made Saladin wonder what troubles faced him over the horizon.

The money drop with Don Giovanni went flawlessly. Saladin met with the Don and his unhappy son Handsome Paul near the Gowanus Canal at a run-down diner. Saladin ordered a greasy hamburger as he placed the key to the safe box on the counter next to a grumpy Handsome Paul. Saladin sat quietly and ate his burger as he thought if he should ask the Don the question of who killed his stepfather. The finality of the situation must have made the question apparent to the Don who again offered another tidbit of advice for Saladin.

"Digging up the dirt of the past has a way of mudding up one's future."

The Don paused, as he did not want to choke on his salad.

"You may not want to hear the answer to that question and to the question of who killed your good friend J.T."

Don added as he pushed away the health salad and made way for the greasy burger the waitress brought to the counter.

Saladin did not question the Don any further on the matter.

"Good bye!"

Saladin said as he removed himself from the counter and exited the diner. His senses were immediately assaulted by the stench of the canal as well as the response to his question. Saladin learned from the first piece of advice he received from the Don but he was not going to rest until his question about his stepfather and J.T. were answered. Saladin looked at his watch and understood that he had five hours to meet Sunshine on City Island. He had just one more stop before he saw his baby.

If one would take the length of the rail used on the New York City subway system and stretched it out it would stretch nearly 300 miles away to Chicago. Saladin felt he traveled that distance as he traveled from Red Hook Brooklyn to Sky View on the Hudson co-op in Riverdale in the Bronx. Three trains and a bus placed him at the doorstep of Tony's bereaved mother. The woman did not want to allow Saladin into her home but the pregnant Deandra insisted that he was allowed in the apartment.

Saladin was sad to her that the immediate family only attended Tony's funeral. His mother did not want any of the people she blamed for his life style to attend. The more Saladin talked to the woman the more he could see that she would kill him if the law would permit such things. She was in denial of the type of man her baby grew up to become. He could not tell her the amount of people that her darling son had made others feel just as she felt. Saladin offered money but she refused his "Blood Money." On his way out of the door he gave several hundred dollars to Deandra and extended an offer to help to her. When Deandra closed the door on Saladin he knew that the young girl would take him up on his offer for help.

Saladin made his way to the nearby bus stop, having less than twenty dollars in his pocket he had to take the bus. All the banks were closed and he could not get any money until the morning. He waited in line with little old white ladies for the bus to arrive. As he stood waiting Saladin blocked out the ignorance he heard from the church going mother of Tony. She had lost a child to the streets and yet she still denied that she was part of the problem. Saladin did not have time to worry about her he was on the way to City Island and dinner with Sunshine. There was nothing more important to him.

CHAPTER 38

Never Shit Where You Eat!

The lone bus ride across the Bronx was a pleasurable experience for a person who had forgotten what many of the neighborhoods he traveled through looked like. Saladin smiled as he remembered how as a youth he would jump on a train or bus to explore the city. His mother would worry about his traveling long hours alone, but Saladin would assure his mother that he could take care of himself. He had to chuckle aloud much to the wonderment of the person seated next to him on the bus because he received the same response to his mother upon mention of her fears for his trip to Sicily. Saladin would have done better to remember his days as an explorer because he was on the wrong bus.

Saladin was not totally lost, he took the BX12 bus to the Orchard Beach instead of the BX23 to City Island. The two places were near one another but they stood on the opposite end of the same small Island that jets out into the Long Island Sound. With nightfall fast approaching and his adventurous spirit rekindled Saladin thought it best to walk to City Island instead of waiting forty-five minutes for the bus. Saladin was pointed in the correct direction by the bus driver and off he went to find Sunshine.

Somewhere in the middle of his walk Saladin thought that he had bitten off more than he could chew but he pressed on until he stood in front of Tony's Sea House the last restaurant on the long strip of restaurants that lined the lone main street of City Island. It was Sunshine's favorite because one could eat with the views of bridges and homes located on the other side of the Long Island Sound. The food was also to die for! He walked through the doors of the crowded restaurant as it often was at night in search of Sunshine. He stood and carefully scanned the room until he caught sight of Sunshine who sat in a booth not far from the door. Her seat faced the door and Saladin could see that she was involved in a conversation with someone. Saladin brushed off his dusty shoes and rushed for Sunshine and the worm greeting he was destined to receive.

As Saladin approached Sunshine it became obvious to him the she was involved in a conversation with a woman. A few steps closer Saladin began to get a funny feeling in his gut. A few more steps further revealed his worse fear. Saladin had been set up! Sunshine was in a conversation with Shanita his side chick!

Sunshine had not laid eyes on him as yet and his human instinct of flight took over. The problem was that for some reason his legs would not turn around. He continued on until he ended up right in front of the table with the two women of his life. There was no denial good enough to extract him from the mess his libido placed him. The player had been played!

The conversation inside was relatively calm between the three. Saladin wanted to run and hide in the lobster tank but he sat and took the medicine for the pain he had caused the two women. He flashed back to the many times Sunshine caught him in compromising situations with ladies and he was able to get back into her good graces after a lengthy cool down period. The look in Sunshine's eyes or the tone of her voice did not give Saladin a clue to what Sunshine thought. As he sat he prayed to God harder than ever to get him out of the mess he created through his own deeds. God listened and granted Saladin's prayers.

The night could not end fast enough for Saladin. He did not eat a bit of his food as he wondered what would happen when Sunshine and he were alone. Their moment along occurred after Sunshine placed a grateful Shanita home via cab. Shanita, who did not speak directly to Saladin the entire evening, paid him no attention as the cab pulled off bound for Harlem. Sunshine walked ahead of Saladin towards the parking lot and her car that was in the back of the lot. By the time Sunshine reached her car her anger was no longer controllable. She turned around and immediately punched Saladin in the face. The blow caused Saladin to stumble backward but he was determined to take whatever she dished out in order to get back in her good graces. Saladin's goal proved fruitless.

Sunshine withdrew her fist from Saladin's face only to return to his face with a pimp slap to the other side of Saladin's face.

"I put up with your shit for too long Saladin."

Sunshine wept.

"I know I messed up Sunshine. I..."

Sunshine cut Saladin off before he could start to say all the right things that made her a fool in the past. She did not plan to be a fool any longer.

"I turned my back when I caught you fucking wit' that chicken-head in the Bronx. I even accepted that fact when that *Bitch* Carolyn bore you your first child."

Sunshine's voice began to fill with enough anger that Saladin decided it was best for him to take several steps backwards.

He had never seen Sunshine as angry as she was but he only had to wait a few minutes more to change his opinion.

Sunshine continued to mumble the word fool over, and over again to herself. Saladin was not sure whom she referred to and he was not the one to find out.

"I could always deny them other women because I did not see it but this shit I cannot deny!"

Sunshine concluded. She took several deep breathes then continued her catharsis.

"I had to talk that young girl into an abortion in order to keep her from going to the courts and child support. How do you think that makes me feel Saladin?"

Sunshine's question went unanswered by the wise Saladin. His lack of response caused Sunshine to quip.

"This ain't the first time I had to save your ass!"

Sunshine said as she once again opened her car door and prepared to leave.

Her comment brought about a response from Saladin. He never asked Sunshine for her help and he could not understand why she would say such a thing.

In a rare show of emotion Saladin challenged Sunshine.

"What da fuck you talking bout Sunshine? I don't remember askin' you for help!"

Saladin said with a self-assured voice.

His statement immediately put a halt to Sunshine's tears for the man had just stepped onto a land mine she was more than happy to explode.

"I saved your ass when I got your good friend J.T. killed!"

Sunshine's statement was met with disbelief by Saladin.

"Killing somebody ain't your thing Sunshine."

Saladin said with a laugh.

Sunshine was afraid of bugs and there was one way she could have done that which she had professed. To humor himself Saladin continued on with his line of questioning.

"What could he have done that would want you to see him dead?"
Saladin said with a chuckle.

"Your good friend planned to kill you!"

Her answer was not the least bit funny.

Sunshine took several minutes to draw Saladin a road map that led to that fact that his one time good friend wanted to have him murdered. Saladin's next question was the obvious one.

"How did you know?"

Saladin asked reluctantly. Sunshine's answer was just as obvious to anyone who paid attention.

"I was in his bed when he made the call to have you killed!"

Saladin was devastated. What he thought he knew about two of the people closest to him was a lie.

Sunshine relished the devastated look that came over his face as Saladin realized that he was not the only person in the relationship to have stepped out. She went one up on him because she messed with his best friend. Sunshine allowed Saladin to absorb the severity of it all before she concluded her story.

"I think he wanted you dead because of me and because you were a threat to his business. In any event I told Bones and he took care of JT for me and for you."

Sunshine got in her car and slammed the door on the shocked Saladin.

She started the ignition and rolled down the window to give her parting shot.

"I don't want your money and I don't want you near our children. You have done enough hurt to last me a lifetime."

Sunshine position the car in reverse then said in a strong voice.

"I hope our child; the one I am carrying will make it onto this earth. God might take it from me just like I took Shanita's from her. Don't call us, we will never call you."

Sunshine said as she backed out of the space and narrowly missed running over Saladin's foot. She could have run over his foot and he would have never known. He was numb from the pain of the loss of everything he thought he had wanted.

Saladin was literally left in the parking lot with nothing. He had no family, no money in his pockets, no job and most of all no clue as to how he was supposed to live. In his moment of reflection a couple emerged from a nearby car. They were in the middle of their own fight and overheard most of the argument between Saladin and Sunshine. Saladin watched as the man approached him with a bottle of wine in his hand.

"My brother, I think you need this more than I do!"

Saladin took the bottle of wine and a closed fisted five from the man who then walked away arm in arm with the woman he loved.

Saladin tucked the bottle under his arm and made his way for the bus that did not start running again until the morning.

CHAPTER 39

Adjured

Days past before Saladin found the courage to venture out of his empty Westchester home. It took two weeks for him to go as far as Central Park. In that time Saladin did not attempt to contact Sunshine he knew her well enough to leave that situation alone. Within months decided to sell his house upstate and move back to a small apartment in the city. He wanted to get rid of anything that reminded him of the business and have the family he lost. Saladin moved quickly on that matter. The last item he had to deal with was what to do with Kelly's Variety Store. He could not decide that until he sold the number running business.

Saladin made his way to Kelly's on a sunny Sunday afternoon. He had made his decision to give the number business run out of Kelly's to a local numbers runner and sell the store to a young man who wanted to open a real candy store. Saladin made his way into the store and ran straight into Shanita who was busy cleaning up the store in preparation for the change of ownership. The first look Saladin received was an angry look from Shanita. Her facial expression changed when he emerged from the backroom two hours later.

The moment Saladin emerged the backroom and caught sight of the tight jeans Shanita wore his heart began to flutter. He had lost the first true love of his life became of his dealings with Shanita therefore if the young girl wanted to be with him he was down for whatever. Saladin walked up behind Shanita and touched her on the hip.

"You know were that got us the last time Saladin."

Shanita said while she continued to wipe down the counter. Saladin moved even closer to Shanita pressing his lips against her neck.

"Baby please don't, I can't finish anything you start right now."

She half-heartily begged. Saladin did not heed the girl's pleads for he knew she wanted him as badly as he wanted her.

"I want another baby Saladin. That is all I need from you!"

Shanita said as she turned around to reciprocate Saladin's kiss.

"A baby is all I can give you at the moment."

He said before he plunged his tongue deep in her mouth. The lovers broke off the kiss and were amazed to find two men in their presence. Saladin immediately recognized the two men as Detectives Johnson and Brown but the detectives did not immediately recognize him.

"Very good show you two. A very good show *indeed!*"

Detective Brown said in an excellent Cary Grant imitation.

"Bogart and Bacall could not have done it any better."

Brown said as he clapped his hands two times as to mock a standing ovation.

"Why they gotta be white people. Black people can be in love too like Ozzie Davis and Ruby Dee."

Johnson joked. Saladin did not like the joke on him therefore he had a joke for the two men.

"Whenever you two are finished playing Amos and Andy you can tell me who you are and what the hell you want!"

Saladin reference to the "Uncle Tom" like characters of the 1930's shut down all jokes for the remainder of their conversation.

Johnson removed his lollipop from his mouth ala Kojak and pointed it at Saladin as if it were a weapon.

"Fuck around little boy and your ass will be in jail within the hour!"

Johnson yelled as he pulled out his badge to identify himself and his partner.

"We are looking for Saladin Martin. Would you know where he is smart ass?"

Johnson finished his sentence and placed the lollipop back into his mouth. Shanita heard Saladin's name and nervously glanced up at the barrier of the name in question. Detective Brown who was in the process of matching Saladin's face with a location needed only Shanita's stare to confirm his suspicion about Saladin.

"He is Saladin. Don't you remember we stopped him on the highway sometime ago?"

He reminded his partner. Saladin did not have time to play around he wanted them to get back to the point and 'Get the fuck out!' before he said something he might regret.

Saladin motioned for Shanita to leave him and the police alone. Once Shanita left their presence Saladin moved to get them to the point of their call.

"You know who I am. What do you want from me?"

Saladin asked. Johnson still hurt by the Amos and Andy joke went straight for the jugular.

"We are investigating the murder of Thaddeus Taylor. The number to this store appeared on his phone. What business did you have with the deceased?"

Saladin did not hesitate with his answer.

"We knew each other from back in the days. I am the only store that carriers his favorite candy."

Saladin reached over to the candy jar and pulled out a handful of Sugar Daddies and tossed them onto the counter.

"Ain't too many places that still carry that candy is there?"

Saladin boasted.

"The candy *is* hard to find but you can cut the bullshit. We know what type of business you're are in and we know you, he did not call you ten times in one week for candy!"

Brown stated as he tossed his stale gum form his mouth and tossed it to the floor of the store.

"You were a big player when we stopped you on the highway then and we all know a leopard can't change its spots."

Brown said as he plopped one of the caramel covered candy into his mouth.

"The more we dig Brown the deeper his grave will be!"

Johnson said as he tossed his lollipop into the garbage can next to Saladin as if he were a basketball player attempting a three point shot.

"People like you always make mistakes. As soon as the Feds disband the task force we'll be back for your black ass!"

Brown stated. The two men were not finished they decided to play the role of angel and devil. The detectives' game was for the benefit of Shanita whom they knew was listening to every word.

"When we come back for you I bet your girl will stick by you."

Johnson's voice was full of sarcasm when he spoke.

"I wonder if she would stick by him if his wife and kid came back home Johnson."

"How true, how true Brown, but he loves her."

"Men like him rarely stay with a woman too long. Don't you think Johnson?"

"You're quite right Brown. He'll get her pregnant and kick her to the curb post haste."

"But they are in love!"

The two men spoke in unison then finished with a feminine laugh. Saladin understood that Brown and Johnson were mocking the two gophers from the Looney Tunes, which he found **very droll**. After their brief chuckle Johnson got right back to business.

He asked Saladin once more about his relationship with Bosco.

"Will you stick to your "Candy story" Saladin?"

Saladin nodded his head in affirmation. Johnson was delighted with Saladin's response.

"When we come back for you there will be no deals for you. Peace out homey!"

Johnson said, as he was the first to exit the store. Brown walked up to the counter after his partner exited the store to speak to a visible shaken Saladin.

"Your girlfriend Sunshine did not want to give you up. After all the shit you put her through I'd bet she'd be willing to go to the mat for you if the need ever arised."

Brown removed the Sugar Daddy from his mouth and tossed it into the garbage next to Saladin and gave sound effects as if he were Marv Albert calling a basketball game.

"We don't know a whole lot about you but if you were dumb enough to leave Sunshine for that *sexy, chocolate, immature* chick in the back you're dumb enough to make the mistake that will take you down!"

Brown turned and walked out of the store satisfied that he shook Saladin to the core.

Saladin composed himself and called out for Shanita who came running.

"Get your bags packed! We'll be out of the country for at least one month!"

Saladin was not one to run and hide but he knew enough to know that it was time for him to get the fuck outta' Dodge! He got out of the business at the right time and he hoped he would not have to pay for anything he had done in the past in the near future.

CHAPTER 40

Broken Bones Heal

There was nothing better to heal broken bones than time and immobility. Set the broken bone; apply a cast if possible and if lucky nature would take its course. There is no such remedy for the fragile human mind. Sometimes time and Mother Nature can make matters much worse. Saladin found this out the hard way.

After his visit from the Police, Saladin took Shanita on a month long trip to the Caribbean. The young girl had never been out of the Empire State and the trip pleased her greatly. She was good for him but Saladin knew that the thing that brought them together would one day tear them apart. When the day came for her to leave he was not sad, but relieved. Shanita knew that he could never love her as much as he loved Sunshine, and she held out against hope as long as she could. After four years together and a daughter named Anita, they parted ways.

Saladin was relieved that the end of his relationship with Shanita came because his life was very unstable at the time of her departure. Saladin first moved Shanita to Atlanta, Georgia where he hoped to begin a successful clothing line with a partner. Saladin promptly plopped down $1 million on the table to start the business only to have the partner sell the designs to another firm for two million dollars. Saladin did not let that one setback stop him. He promptly moved Shanita and their child to live near his mother in Tennessee. It was Tennessee that Shanita decided to take their child and move with her parents in Maryland. His stay in

Tennessee was sort lived because his mother divorced her husband and felt the call of New York once again. Saladin was sad that his mother could not find happiness but he was glad that she wanted to give up the expensive house in Tennessee and move back North.

The sale of his mother's house in Tennessee enabled him to purchase her a home in Westchester County and buy him a Co-op in Brooklyn. All the moving had siphoned away a huge portion of the millions he had left. Saladin having no income and no prospect of money coming his way he grew desperate. As in most people his desperation sparked a flash of brilliance. Saladin decided that he would open a chartered bus company, not one that would rival Greyhound but one that would provide a need for the community.

The bus service would allow people from the city to travel sometimes many hours to the prisons were their loved ones were held. It allowed families to be dropped off at the prison not some bus station many miles from the prison. In no time Saladin was a legitimate businessman. He did not stop there. He also had the foresight to purchase several Brownstones in Harlem and in Bed-Stuy, Brooklyn before gentrification saw the prices of such homes skyrocket! Saladin was on a roll, however something was missing in his life. He had to find closure.

Saladin often drove through Harlem just to get a view of the old life, but he never got out of his car. He did not want to catch a flashback of the money and power he once commanded. Saladin was content to be a voyeur rather than a participant in the life. During one such drive Saladin happened upon Morningside Park, the place where he learned how to do everything from shot hoops to feeling on girls. As he waited for the light to change he heard his name screamed out by someone who passed his car. It was his long forgotten friend Todd. The two talked as if they had last seen each other yesterday. Todd was sure not to mention Sunshine but he did tell Saladin about the annual Father and Son Day for old time businessmen.

"You need to come through Saladin. People would be very happy to see you!" Todd said as the two men shook hands and parted ways.

Saladin told Todd that he would attend but deep down he was not sure that he would.

Saladin made his way to upstate FDR Park, the place where the father/son picnic was held. He could not stay long due to a prior commitment, but the moment he saw familiar faces he was glad he did attend. Saladin sat at the table with people who were in business around the same time he was in business. He sat with people like Lavender Troy, Todd and Cheese! Lavender Troy was once a mid-level drug dealer and fierce street fighter who liked to knock people out for fun. Saladin was surprised to hear that Troy worked as the head chef at a popular restaurant in Brooklyn. Saladin was equally surprised to learn that Todd and his long time girlfriend Lartesha had married and divorced. Cheese had not changed. He was as blunt as anyone. Saladin listened and had not said much about anyone in his past. Cheese wanted to know about Saladin and what he was up to.

"What happened to all of your hair Saladin? Your girl Sunshine?" Cheese asked.

"Gone!"

His answer to both questions was short and direct. Then in a stunning twist Saladin opened up to ask about the whereabouts of Cash and Ace. Those questions had dogged Saladin for years.

Todd was able to give Saladin the answer to the question about Cash since he had major dealings with Cash and needed to know if the former Kingpin of Harlem would one-day step to him.

"Cash is like Elvis. Everyone sees him but no one has proof."

Todd paused as he too had a question from the past.

"Did Cash really kill Bosco?"

Lavender Troy and Cheese looked down Saladin's throat as he gave his answer.

"Nope, the answer to that question has been long since buried."

Saladin answered. Saladin was finally able to speak about Bosco without shedding a tear.

The conversation between the four men surfaced around Bosco and his five children all of whom had managed to that point not follow in their father's footsteps. The mention of Bosco caused the curiosity in Cheese to surface once again. He went about finding an answer by making a statement.

"Ace can't come around us anymore. He is the undisputed kingpin in all of New York."

Cheese paused then added.

"He and Angelika are still together and they still cheat on one another like clock work!"

Saladin knew where Cheese comment was supposed to end and for years Saladin did not speak on the topic, but now was the time to end all the speculation about the nature of the feud between Bosco and Angelika. Saladin had all at his table waiting for his word.

"The beef between the two started when Bosco saw Angelika on tape at the Rooftop having Cash pee all over her!"

The eruption of disbelief at the table was so loud that Pee Wee Willie and a few others pulled out their guns in preparation for war!

Saladin left late that evening happy that he finally attended. Although he could not bring his upper middle-classed son Saladin Junior to a function surrounded by major felons, Saladin was finally able to begin to close the book on one more chapter of his past. He however was not able to close the chapter on the feud between Angelika and Bosco. Saladin could not tell the entire story. Even as he sat in his car heading towards his namesake's football game on long Island he could not figure out how Bosco found out that Bones and he ran a train on Angelika. Bosco never blamed Saladin or Bones he blamed Angelika.

Saladin arrived at New York City Long Island all Star challenge held at Hofstra University just in time to see his son being slammed to the turf by a New York City opponent. Throughout the game the same New York City player stuck to Saladin Jr. as if he were glue. Saladin Junior, the same New York City cornerback shut down a legitimate blue chip receiver. In the end, the Long Island All-Star won the game over New York City Going away. After the game Saladin, his son, his son's mother Carolyn, his son's stepfather and younger sibling all went to dinner. His son made the choice of restaurant and Saladin was surprised that the upscale boy chose dinner on City Island.

Saladin dined in a restaurant a few hundred feet from where Sunshine walked out of his life. There was no mistaking the eerie feeling Saladin had about being on City Island once again. Saladin's eerie feeling also surfaced because of the company at his table. Throughout the dinner Carolyn complained that the restaurant was not up to her standards. Her husband, the commodities trader spent the entire meal with his cell phone stuck to his ear or typing on his Blackberry. The little girl spent all her time whining for her pet dog Waldo. The conversation at the table brought everyone together when Saladin junior announced what college he would attend in the fall.

He announced that he would like to attend the University of Miami on a Football Scholarship. Saladin and the Stepfather were happy about the choice, but Carolyn had other ideas. She wanted her son to attend Stanford University or Notre Dame. She figured that once exposed to the rigors of academics at those institutions her son would have to make a choice between sports or the books.

"I don't know why you are happy Saladin our child support agreement states that you have to pay for any college he attends."

Carolyn's husband pulled the phone form his ear for just a second as a sign of displeasure with his wife's airing private matters in public. Carolyn looked at her husband and dismissed him with the ghetto, read the hand, gesture. Saladin did not make any comments to Carolyn. She was a hard person to get along with and since he was a legal businessman dealing with her had gotten much harder.

The night ended with Saladin giving his namesake the keys to his car in order for his son to have an excuse to come back to New York City to spend time with a chick he had met at 125th Street. Saladin did mind being without his car, because his adventurous spirit kicked in once again. He would once again ride the Bx23 Bus to the Bx12 to the A train. Saladin stood at the bus stop and waited patiently for the bus to arrive. It was a warm clear night and the lights from the homes across the sound shimmered over the water. Saladin stood with his mind open to what he had missed in his life and where he was headed. The good thing about being legal Saladin thought was that he no longer had to constantly look over his shoulder. The bad part was that Shanita and Carolyn took turns taking him to court for child support. The feeling he was being watched disrupted his moment of reflection.

Saladin turned around to see that a young man stood directly behind him. The young man stood almost two inches taller than Saladin and outweighed him by 130 pounds, but that did not frighten Saladin. The young man proudly wore the football jersey of the New York City football player who successfully shut down Saladin junior.

"That was a good game son. You shut my son down real good!"

Saladin extended his hand to shake it with the young boy.

"We have time for that later. Look over there in the restaurant window."

The boy demanded. He looked through the window as the young man had asked. Saladin first caught sight of a pretty young girl about ten years old eating dinner with a very beautiful woman. The woman had a familiar face. Saladin looked back at the young man in disbelief.

"She didn't see you pop. You two cost me 10 years of heartache. Whether you two get back together is another thing."

Then Charles extended his hand and gave his father a piece of paper with his phone number.

"I can only guess what happened between you two then but I'll leave it to you to call me and explain."

Charles became choked with emotion.

"I don't know if I or my mom would hug you or punch you in the face!"

Charles said as he quickly turned and walked into the restaurant before he carried out the latter thought in place of his mother. Saladin was left with his mouth open and shocked at how he was reacquainted with his long lost child. Instinctively Saladin began a frantic search for his cigarettes. In the midst of his search a broad smile came across his face for he realized Saladin no longer puffed on cancer sticks. He gazed up at the stars that were hidden behind the occasional cloud. The sight of the distance ball of fire brought him back to the words of his stepfather.

"You see the stars where they were not where you see them."

He would remind him each time he wished upon the stars at night. Saladin was not where he used to be either. He no longer lived the stressful lifestyle of a drug dealer. He was older and he hoped much more wiser than he was a decade earlier. At that moment Saladin's thoughts was interrupted by the roar of the engine of the BX 12 that approached his position. Saladin did not have time to debate with himself a choice had to be made very soon. Saladin saw a nice looking young lady exit the restaurant. The caramel coloured skinned young woman brandished a pack of cigarettes in her hand.

"Can I trouble you for a cigarette?"

Saladin asked the twenty something year old. The woman flashed a smile at Saladin and passed him the pack. He could not take his eyes off the young lady for her smile seemed to light up the night. Saladin returned the pack of cigarette back just as her boyfriend exited the restaurant. The young man took immediate offense to some old man talking to his female. The young man pulled his drooping pants up to fit upon his waist for a millisecond before they returned to the position of just below his buttocks.

"I don't want you talking to nobody Ebony. Get your fucking ass to the car!"

The young man then flashed his gold fronts at Saladin as he walked behind Ebony in a show of force to the man who he felt invaded his relationship. Saladin shook his head for he did not believe that the young man could have been him ten years earlier. As the young couple argued on the way to their car Saladin realized he did not have a match to light the cigarette. He looked to his left to see that the bus pulled up in front of the restaurant and several souls unlucky enough not to own a car boarded the bus. Saladin took a deep breath and was overpowered by the scent of saltwater. He understood that to enter the restaurant would be the start of a very uncomfortable situation. To leave would close the door on his son. Neither option was palatable.

Saladin tossed the cigarette he borrowed to the ground and against his better judgment he entered the restaurant to the embarrassing confrontation he knew would take place. He had spent most of his life chasing money and all the things it could buy. Saladin had to face up to the priceless experience of being a responsible adult. This time he did not pray to God to get him out of his troubles. Saladin instead prayed that he made the right decision.

978-0-595-38443-3
0-595-38443-9

Made in the USA